Sandor Dyle had come to the planet on vacation, not to get involved with the search for a serial killer. But he had a special talent that was not available on that world, and he finds himself teamed with a local police official who may just have been set up to fail, with his inestimable assistance.

He couldn't have that.

Managansett Press

Don D'Ammassa is the author of:

Horror
Blood Beast
Servant of Chaos*
Caverns of Chaos*
Wings over Manhattan
The Gargoyle
That Way Madness Lies*
Little Evils*
Passing Death*
Date with the Dark*
The Devil Is in the Details

Science Fiction
Scarab
Haven
Narcissus
Translation Station
The Sinking Island*

Mysteries
Murder in Silverplate
Dead of Winter*
Death at the Art Gallery*

Fantasy
The Kaleidoscope*
Elaborate Lies*

Nonfiction
The Encyclopedia of Science Fiction
The Encyclopedia of Fantasy and Horror
The Encyclopedia of Adventure Fiction
Masters of Detection Vol I*
Masters of Detection Vol II*

*published by Managansett Press

SCARAB

Don D'Ammassa

SCARAB

Chapter One

The morning upon which Mikki discovered the dead man was an unseasonably pleasant one.

It was midway through the Secant of the Scarab and while the weather had been considerably drier than normal, the night temperature routinely dropped low enough that condensation froze during the long hours of darkness, leaving glistening treacherous patches scattered through those portions of the city where the pavement was unheated, or where no pavement existed. Since Mikki rarely left the poorer sections of Soshambe and earned what passed for a living largely in the public traverseways, the conditions underfoot were of no small concern. Sometime during this particular night, however, the oppressive cloud cover had parted and the bright morning sun was warm on his shoulders and unprotected head. Sprays of mist drifted through the streets and gardens of Soshambe like lost souls, and the more superstitious citizens would give them a wide berth until they were gone. Mikki could not afford to wait for a more propitious time and told himself in any case that it was foolish to fear the dead when the living were so much more dangerous.

This late in the year, the planet Tashista had receded far enough from its primary that one and sometimes two moons were visible during the daylight, hovering surreptitiously above the horizon, competing for control of the tides. Among the less educated, sight of the larger moon Lucora's brooding visage in the daytime sky was openly discussed as a bad omen. More erudite citizens joked about the lingering influence of superstition while secretly purchasing wards and charms to be worn concealed under the voluminous clothing that was currently in vogue. The peculiar nature of Tashistan social change encouraged the appearance of sophistication without demanding any concrete evidence of enlightenment. Heavy precipitation fell primarily as sleet at this time of year, sometimes carrying over into the Secant of the Rapier. On most days, the sky was filled with brooding galleons of cloud, but the recent preponderance of unusually heavy winds at high altitude conspired to keep the skies above Soshambe clear and sharp on this particular morning.

The wealthier Sham gazed at the firmament and shook their heads, muttering to one another about the problems this contrary weather would bring when the growing seasons arrived, the effect on the water table, the likelihood that the farmers of the Beatic Valley would use the threat of drought or stunted crops to raise the price they sought for pina fruit, suratic grain, doldren bread, and the delicate kurilic pastries that were currently a mandatory staple at every social occasion of the fashionable Hierata. The effect would pyramid as well. Tavarian herders were dependent upon the Beatics to feed their animals during the declining secants; any increase in their costs would be passed on to the Hierata with as much exaggeration as they believed might go unchallenged, and the Hierata were, for the most part, indisposed to haggle over price. Mercantile concerns were for the lower-class Moshamadur. The Hierata would simply pay the inflated prices and raise the social taxes, government fees, and employ other, less formal methods to recoup their losses at the expense of the lower classes.

Formal class designations were, of course, banned by the Accord of Alyshambo, and the Hierata, literally "those set free of place," now publicly referred to themselves somewhat more tactfully as Kishamkur, "those who have brought luck and hard work together." Nevertheless, in the lowest-class Nashamata neighborhoods, where the streets were unheated, the power grid didn't always work even if your credit balance was violet, where the buildings might be structurally sound within the definition of the municipal authorities but did little to keep out the insidious nasura pollen during the growing season or the damp and decay of the rainy season, details of the weather carried a significantly different meaning.

Mikki found the body quite by accident, as it had been concealed so efficiently that, under normal circumstances, local carrion eaters would have disposed of the flesh long before the smell of decay might have alerted another passerby to its presence. Indeed, had Mikki ventured to examine the remains more closely, and had he possessed the necessary knowledge to draw the proper conclusion, he would have noted that the body, while cool to the touch, was still noticeably warmer than its surroundings, evidence of the freshness of the kill. The blood, and there was a good deal of it, had thoroughly congealed, the stains dark enough that initially, in the dim light, he had misidentified them as the inroads of oxidation, but it had not completely dried. Rust and tarnish would not be allowed to mar even the most insignificant installation in Kishamkur, where the Hierata might bruise their eyes by gazing upon such blatant evidence of decay and imperfection, but here in Nashamata Park, neglect was the order of the day. After all, in the view of the orthodox Sham, anyone unfortunate enough to dwell in Nashamata was either spending every free moment seeking to earn his or her way into Moshamadur, the great median between the rich and poor sections of the city, or was so hopelessly recalcitrant that no person of substance should feel compelled to waste time or credit on their behalf. Certainly the physical appearance of an unused maintenance shed in the wilder portion of Nashamata's park was a matter beneath consideration.

Mikki would not have argued the last point. The disorder of the place, though inconvenient in purely physical terms and aesthetically displeasing, was actually helpful to his present endeavor. The lawns had gone wild before he was born, and the flourishing shrubbery, no longer trimmed and contained, had run rampant, climbing up into the lower branches of the chukhara trees, shading out less hardy growth, forming impenetrable walls and opaque canopies. Nasura seeds had taken root here and there, shooting up toward the sunlight in those few areas where they were able to penetrate the layers of chukhara. In its wild state, with the fresh buds free to develop rather than being harvested and fed to Tavarian livestock or milled down into flour for doldren bread and other comestibles, the summit of each woody stalk exploded outward as the internal pressure grew too strong, sending streamers almost as far as a man could throw a fist-sized stone, anchoring to whatever accessible surface these might strike, and from these outshoots, fresh buds arose, seething upward toward the light. The geneticists who developed the plant had intended to produce a fecund and rapidly developing food source, but their success had wildly exceeded expectations.

Mikki had made his way through the leafy warren to this spot, hoping to find a better condata, or secret place, in which to conceal the small horde of hard credit he had accumulated. In

Nashamata, theft was not viewed in quite the same fashion as elsewhere in the civilized worlds; after all, it took wealth to move to a better part of Soshambe, which everyone knew to be the primary goal of any sane citizen, and if one should prove resourceful enough to accelerate the accumulation of credit through the acquisition of that possessed by a less foresighted rival, then it was against the natural order to punish such initiative. Of course, if one plundered among the Moshamadur, that was another matter, one requiring the immediate response of the Prefecture. And theft from the Kishamkur was a concept few had the temerity to mention publicly, even in jest.

It had been a slow week and his earnings were not as high as he had hoped. Mikki earned most of his credit carrying parcels from one place to another, running errands into Tashamir for the upper crust of Nashamata, because even within the lowest strata of society, there are still smaller stratifications, subdivisions, levels of prestige and material well being. The small minority of Nashamata who hovered on the brink of elevation sought to practice the more relaxed lifestyle to which they expected to ascend and were occasionally willing to expend credit to avoid onerous trips to Tashamir. There were even some who possessed the wherewithal to seek immediate displacement to Moshamadur, but who chose rather to remain where they were, either because of its greater familiarity, or because they found themselves content with their status within the more circumscribed quarter. Business connections sometimes transcended class and it was in fact true that the highest of the Nashamata lived a more luxurious life than the lowest of the Moshamadur. A very few individuals, it was rumored, had found means to function within all three levels of Sham society from their base within Nashamata, but these were of the criminal class, and respectable Sham had no converse with such. At least such was the public attitude. If the same sentiments had been shared in private, there would have been no criminals and no need for the Prefecture.

Most of Mikki's earnings went to support himself and his sister, but when he had a particularly busy week or was commissioned for more arduous work, he sometimes had a few coins left after meeting expenses. He set some hard credit aside in a small woven bag, carefully concealed from everyone, even those few he called friends. Nor did he know where any of his friends kept their own savings; the subject had become so personal that references to individual condatas had become vernacularly obscene. While Mikki was still a child in his parents' home, they had been burglarized so frequently that he grew up knowing better than to conceal coins or any other portable object worth keeping within his dwelling while he himself was absent. The ideal solution would have been conversion from hard to soft credit, establishment of an account with the secure municipal databank, but Mikki was still short of the minimal balance that would be required to avoid service charges that would rapidly erode his savings. So he sought a physical location to serve in its place.

The abandoned storage hut had seemed ideal for this purpose when he had stumbled across it a few days earlier, while trying to hide from a gang of miscreants who had spotted his courier's pouch and chased him from the traverseways to the park before he had finally lost them by crawling through a hedge and lying still in a small hollow until the sounds of their indignant wrath had grown distant. Mikki's stash was currently hidden in a power junction box near the outer city wall, but he was not comfortable with the possibility that a maintenance crew might decide to break the monotony of their own indolence by making a routine visit that could prove very non-routine if they searched under the flooring, in the hollow area that was designed to provide insulation from ground water. Today's excursion was to determine whether or not this was a viable condata; if it proved to be such, he would transfer his savings at the earliest opportunity.

The door to the hut was metal, streaked with dark brown stains which he inaccurately interpreted as rust, and secured with an old fashioned card lock, one which he was quite certain he could circumvent with his illegal pocket discharger and/or judicious application of brute force. Both proved unnecessary, however, for when he gave the handle a tentative jiggle, the door shifted invitingly in its frame. With a quick glance around to make absolutely certain he was unobserved, Mikki lifted the handle and pulled the door open.

It was dark within the narrow cubicle, but not murky enough to conceal the humped shape, or rather shapes, which had been placed inside earlier that same day. Not a great deal earlier either, as the Prefect's office would ascertain later when its technicians examined the scene. Mikki was unable at first to mentally reassemble the fragments into a recognizable form, even after he had realized that he was looking at flesh and blood and bone. It was the tatters of clothing that led his eye to trace the line of a thigh, the crook of an elbow, the shattered remnants of a human chin. He had seen some brutal and unpleasant things in his short life, had twice witnessed violent death. On one occasion a cargo carrier had lost its load on the overway, dropping several tons of offworld trade items into the traverseways of Nashamata, most of which were spirited away so quickly that the recovery crew initially believed it had been sent to the wrong location. But the falling load had crushed two pedestrians almost within arm's reach of Mikki, who had been working at the time as a courier for the Carminati, one of the established gangs of the underways, physically carrying information that they didn't wish to expose to the monitoring facilities of the datanet. And again, less than two secants later, old Mosha Tappur had gone out of his mind with pain from suratic cancer and had attacked an itinerant medicator with a pruning blade before being subdued. The medicator had succumbed to stab wounds within reach of the cart of remedies which might have saved him, had anyone nearby possessed the knowledge and the inclination to intervene on his behalf. As it happened, the cart had been subsequently stripped bare and was already being disassembled for its electronic and mechanical parts when the last spurt of its former owner's blood sprayed across the pavement. Mosha Tappur had died as well, due to the excessive zeal of those restraining him. On both occasions, death had been bloody and violent as well as unexpected, but neither incident was at all alien to the Nashamata, where the decline in city services and the frantic struggle to succeed at the expense of everyone else had necessarily generated a callous indifference to misfortune, so long as it was someone else's misfortune. A lifeless body concealed in an abandoned outbuilding was an entirely different order of business, particularly a body mutilated in such an insanely dehumanizing fashion.

Mikki turned away from the sight and vomited noisily into the bushes.

* * * * *

Tantra Brach spotted Mikki running along the traverseway between the decaying fortress building that now housed the Lucharist Society and the esplanade where those who could spare the time came to play ultima, blookis, or one of the less popular board games like kubits, kibitzed by onlookers whose expertise was never quite up to making a match of their own. The game players were islands of stillness, interspersed among a stream of variegated peddlers, usually amateur artisans hawking their own wood carvings, weavings, string tie sculptures, and similar items from their makeshift carts. Others offered foodstuffs of varying qualities, loaves of doldren bread, pastries which claimed to be every bit as good as the kurilic delicacies enjoyed by the upper classes, and skewers of roasted meat whose origin was not always discernible. Technically speaking, all forms of commerce were restricted to the Tashamir market district and street peddling was forbidden, but this stricture was only enforced in Moshamadur, dwelling place of those very merchants. The Prefect's enforcers were too tactful to notice any violations in Kishamkur, and couldn't be bothered to pay much attention to whatever might take place in Nashamata. It was not a matter of tolerance so much as disdain.

Ordinarily, the young man's haste would not have been a matter worth noting and Tantra would have proceeded without a second thought. She knew that Mikki's ambition to hoist both himself and his sister out of Nashamata was probably doomed to failure, despite his energetic efforts to accumulate credit. Shayne had contracted a neuroviral infection which attacked the nerves in both of her legs, not severe enough to cause complete paralysis, but sufficient to impair her movement drastically and effectively confine her to their quarters. Occasionally Mikki was able to find employment for Shayne, usually illicit small assembly work she could complete in her room, but for the most part she was a dead weight on his line of credit, unable to support herself. The medical aid available at their income level was not sufficient to provide for physical therapy let alone prosthetic devices, and the cost of nerve replacement surgery was beyond the economic status of even many of the Hierata. Alone, the boy had promise; his tireless enterprise made up in sheer volume what he lacked in formal training or physical ability. He seemed to have an instinctive feel for the pulse of the city, and was often first on the scene when a new opportunity arose. He severed his working relationship with the Trefoils just before their leadership was wiped out in one of the intermittent gang wars that erupted in the underways, and was already working as a courier for the Slagrunners when they assimilated most of the defunct Trefoil territory into their domain. Only a few days before Abi Parva struck it rich with his improved programming design for the datanet communications stack, Mikki had run several small personal errands for the old man without charging him, and when Parva moved up to Moshamadur, he had magnanimously turned over his larger, better maintained apartment to Mikki and his sister without demanding the customary domiciling fee.

But there was something strange about his present haste. Mikki ran with less than his ordinary certainty, as though he had no specific goal in mind, changing direction as he entered the esplanade, angling toward a cluster of people observing a better-than-average ultima game, then shifting away, parallel to the waist-high wall that was the demarcation between the esplanade and the lower traverseway. Tantra was out on business of her own, had only come this way because it was the shortest route between her home and that of a fellow artisan whom she hoped would be willing to loan her a tube of Lachrymonian Azure until she had a chance to replenish her own stores once a fresh supply was received in the artists' quarter. The friend would extract a steep price, of course; Tantra accepted that fact without a second thought. She'd have done the same if their roles were reversed. Matters of credit were supraordinate to simple friendship.

One quick glimpse of Mikki's distraught expression was enough to communicate to her the magnitude of his distress, and *anything* which evoked that sharp a reaction was implicitly exploitable. Unconsciously, Tantra reached into her pocket and rubbed the hard credit that rested there, moving the face of one piece over that of another. She altered her route to intercept her young friend.

"Mikki!" she called in a modulated tone, then with more force when he failed to respond. "Mikki Seurat! Wait a moment."

His steps faltered and he stopped, turning uncertainly toward her. Tantra flinched as their eyes met; there was definitely something wrong here. Mikki's gaze was slightly unfocused, as though he were staring through her transparent substance into some other reality, where lay something disturbing. It appeared to take a few seconds before he could even recognize her, despite their longstanding acquaintance and occasional business relationship. On several occasions, she had used both Mikki and his sister as models for portraits; the girl in particular had a fragile attractiveness that translated well to canvas, so long as the too-thin legs were masked or counterfeited. Distracted as he obviously was at present, Mikki stood irresolutely in place until she reached his side. Tantra found herself torn between the desire to know what had evoked such odd behavior and the feeling that perhaps it would be better just to turn and walk away and pretend the encounter had never taken place. There was something in the boy's face, in his eyes, that frightened her.

"Mikki, what's the matter? Has something happened to Shayne? You look terrible."

For a split second, she thought she would have to repeat herself. The absent look had not left Mikki's face, and he paused longer than seemed proper before answering. "Shayne?" He blinked, then gave an almost imperceptible shake of the head, partially answering her question and regaining some semblance of equanimity, although his features became more animated than usual. "No, listen Tantra, could I borrow some hard credit?" He drew a deep breath, regaining control of himself. "Just enough for a datanet call?"

Tantra stepped back, dismayed at this breach of social etiquette. One did not borrow or loan hard credit in such an informal fashion; there were prescriptions for such an exchange: guarantees, registration of the transaction to protect the lender, interest terms to be arranged in advance, payment schedules. It was an unprecedented social lapse for Mikki to have suggested a loan without first laying the groundwork for formal negotiation.

Mikki seemed to have realized his *faux pas* immediately, but he rushed on. "I'll pay you back, I promise, but I have to report a . . . a crime to the Prefect. Before anyone else discovers it and claims the witness fee. I'll share it with you, honestly." He plunged both hands into his pockets, withdrew them immediately with a gesture of helplessness. "Do you have stylus and paper with you? I'll sign an agreement right now, one quarter of the fee for your trouble."

Tantra never went out without her sketch pad and stylus, which she produced slowly, her mind processing this input as rapidly as possible, searching for leverage. "Plus the replacement of the credit for the call?"

"Yes, certainly. But let's hurry. I don't think anyone will find it soon, but there's always the chance." Without telling her where he had discovered the body, he described his grisly experience in crisp, uncompromising terms.

A few moments later, Tantra stood beside Mikki at a public datanet terminal, listening to him describe what he'd found in Nashamata Park. By the time he was finished speaking and had severed the connection, she had withdrawn into her own thoughts, wondering if even her share of the reward was worth becoming involved, however peripherally, in business such as this. Although she considered herself an educated person, a freethinker, she could not entirely escape the underlying fabric of superstition which crossed class lines, the intricate web of luck and unluck, wards and curses, omens and charms that existed beneath one corner of the blanket of culture that embraced all of Soshambe.

Violent death, even murder, was a fact of life in Nashamata, although largely confined to the rivalries of the underway gangs. The anarchy that prevailed beneath the visible surface of the quarter overflowed onto the traverseways and public places from time to time, but the Prefecture reacted strongly to such incursions. Tantra had lived through her childhood and half her adult life in this environment, and she was no stranger to violent death, felt the tug of fascination which it held for most people. It was something she accepted in her surroundings, as did her peers, and murder in itself carried no extra freight of supernatural significance.

But the particulars of this crime were a different matter. It was definitely considered bad luck to be involved in any way with Scarab, and this sounded very much like his work. The Prefect was under great pressure to bring his periodic reigns of terror to an end, and the interrogations of both suspects and witnesses had grown increasingly brutal in recent days. Of course, she wasn't really a witness herself and had nothing to tell them, but she still regretted having become involved. At best, her identification would be cross-referenced to a violent crime. Artists like herself often cultivated controversy in order to build a mystique that would raise the value of their work, but contrary to the common wisdom, not all publicity was beneficial. She could only hope that Mikki would not find it necessary to mention her name to the Prefect.

* * * * *

Marym Dunnis sat in her office, reflecting upon the incongruity of the single window that broke the unadorned surface of the wall behind her desk, a wall never meant to contain a window in an office she had never meant to occupy. A child prodigy, born to a wealthy family in Kishamkur who had provided her with unlimited access to the datanet educational services, she had spent her early years absorbing as much information as she could coax out of what she now recognized as a data system that was seriously antiquated by interstellar standards, although the official line was that it was reliable, known technology which should not be replaced simply because another system was fashionable elsewhere. Tashista was one of the oldest settled worlds in the region, but the peculiarities surrounding its founding had set it on an isolated and self-indulgent course. A nearly universal drive for material advancement at any cost clashed with the official sentiment that Tashistan society was superior to that of the rest of sentient civilization because its culture had been designed scientifically rather than arising from the random evolution of varied genotypes.

During the early days of the first generation, the colony had been managed in every detail, even to the construction of an artificial language that had supplanted the varied linguistic backgrounds of its diverse populace, drawn from a segment of the self-styled intellectual communities of a score of older worlds. Tashistans of the current generation scorned and remained aloof from the accomplishments of other worlds, and there was a systemic reluctance to import concepts or technology from these "inferior" cultures, many of which had long since eclipsed Tashista in every conceivable fashion. Exotic foods, gemstones, rare elements, literature, music, and a few other items were imported on an ongoing basis, but the lack of viable exports would have kept such trade at very low levels even if Tashistans had been more interested in trading with other worlds. Fortunately the planet was fertile and one of the most amenable to human occupation; the colony had become completely self-supporting within three generations. This effectively insulated Tashista from the mainstream of human civilization and had turned what might have been one of the leading worlds of the Concourse into an insignificant backwater.

Tashista's social structure was supposed to be ideal and therefore stable, but every living culture evolves and grand designs oft go awry. Class distinctions had been intended as no more than functional labels, without any implication of a hierarchical structure. Serge Luchar and his followers had envisioned a civilization in which prestige and self-satisfaction were derived from able performance of one's function and in which the accomplishments of each individual were recognized and applauded without leading to the disparities in distribution of wealth common almost everywhere else. They were proponents of an obscure philosophical system known as relationism, which defined every individual person, concept, and object in terms of its impact on other persons, concepts, and objects.

Unfortunately, whatever the validity of their philosophy, the society they created had already experienced radical change during Luchar's life span and he spent his declining years living alone in an automated laboratory in a remote part of the So Mountains, bitter and disillusioned. The first generation of Tashistans born on the planet displayed an infuriating unwillingness to find satisfaction in living his vision rather than their own. They turned Luchar's own words against him, insisting that personal satisfaction could only be achieved by judging one's material wealth *in relation* to that of others. There began to develop a system of symbolic rewards, by which one could measure progression through the structure of society, which led in due course to the physical separation of the highly successful from those less fortunate. This lower class had schismed again under the pressure of the fierce competition to gain access to the higher class, and there were additional fracture lines within each of the three major divisions. In all three, status was marked by formal and informal awards and symbols. One such symbol was the office window.

Marym rose and turned away from her desk, walked the three short steps that allowed her to touch the sensor which opened the window. The unfiltered air rushed in, driven by a rising midday wind, chill, moist, tangy with the odor of Tashamir's markets. She drew the air deep into her lungs, enjoying the sharp bite within her chest, then exhaled. Her lungs purged, she closed the window with another touch, but remained standing there, staring down into the Soshambe Maintenance Yard. Only the oldest, least dependable equipment was stored here; the small collection of advanced equipment within the city was reserved for use in Kishamkur, of course, and the generally functional if somewhat antiquated collection below was used primarily in Tashamir and Moshamadur. Nashamata's upkeep was not considered a priority within the city and what little was performed was almost invariably accomplished by manual labor. After all, if the living conditions in the poor quarter of Soshambe were less than desirable, it provided an added incentive for its residents to seek more gainful employment, make a greater contribution to society, and fulfill their assumed inner drives for self-actualization. Why expend limited resources providing disincentives for progress? Only the minimum effort needed to maintain basic hygiene and easy passage through the traverseways could be justified.

Marym was a product of her society, and she shared much of this attitude herself, although she was intelligent enough to recognize that it was a rationalization designed to protect the perquisites of the Hierata. Her transfer to the Nashamata Prefecture was technically a promotion in recognition of her demonstrated abilities and potential, but she had hoped to replace the aging Prefect of Tashamir. He had stubbornly refused to die or retire, however, and this posting had opened unexpectedly when her predecessor had been diagnosed as having terminal suratic nerve disease. As recompense for accepting this less than desirable position, her superiors in the Tashistan Prefecture at the capital city of Samarka had arranged for this window to be installed in her office, an honor she would not normally have received until she had been confirmed in her appointment after a suitable period of evaluation. She only wished that the view had been better. Even a panoramic overview of Nashamata Park, unkempt and unstructured though it might be, would have been preferable to the unrelenting ugliness of maintenance robots, automated cleaning vehicles, underway scrubbers, and less identifiable equipment, much of it inoperable, subsiding slowly into piles of electronic and mechanical junk.

Her desk clamored for attention.

"Yes, what is it, Tani?" She remained by the window.

Her receptionist's voice sounded as though she were within the room, although it was actually being transmitted from the outer office. "We apparently have another Scarab murder, Prefect. Just called in from a datanet terminal. The body was found in a remote section of Tamil park."

"Wonderful." She sighed, turned to face her desk. "Whose team is on it?"

"Tiko's. And I sent along Vernan from biologics."

Marym nodded to herself. Tiko was the best investigator she had, although she was honest enough to admit that wasn't saying much. Promising minds rarely languished long in Nashamata's Prefecture; despite public opinion to the contrary, there was enough crime in the more affluent quarters to require every bit of talent available, a fact which was not admitted openly. Most of the present generation of Hierata had been born into that class rather than having earned their way in, and the younger generation had lost the sense of honor and purpose of their ancestors. Tiko was reasonably conscientious and intelligent, but he was subject to wild mood swings, alternating between plodding dullness and hyperactive but essentially unproductive histrionics.

"Witnesses?" The question was a matter of form rather than serious inquiry. During the past three years, a series of brutal mutilation killings had been committed during each Secant of the Scarab, eleven the first year, ten the second, and already five this time around. Six if this latest proved to be the Scarab's work. In only one instance had there been witnesses.

"None," Tani replied. "An unemployed man rummaging around in the park stumbled on the body. Called it in for the finder's fee."

Marym nodded to herself. "How about a replay?"

"It's on standby."

She crossed to the desk, stood beside it, moved a pile of duty rosters to one side, revealing the inset screen of her datanet access. A blinking cursor in the lower lefthand corner indicated a data queue awaiting display, and she touched the icon to release it.

The face that appeared as the connection cleared was young, male, and clearly struggling to find a compromise between excitement and revulsion. Marym touched pause, froze the picture before a word was spoken, her eyes scanning the display from top to bottom. The witness was thin, long-haired, clean shaven and well washed, slightly younger than herself. His eyes had a wary look, even more pronounced than was common among those struggling to survive in the Nashamata. His clothing was inexpensive but in good repair. Tani had indicated he was unemployed, but he clearly wasn't a street beggar, so he earned a living either by performing transient labor or as a hireling of one of the underway gangs. He might be a professional criminal himself, but she doubted it; he lacked the hard, aggressively self-assured look that gang members used to mask their inability to compete for legitimate positions. His mouth was open, the tip of his tongue just visible. She advanced the replay a few frames, watched him moisten his lips before speaking, paused it again.

"Tani, who's the second face?"

Just past the left shoulder of the witness, a considerably older woman stood half turned away, affecting a lack of interest, but with one eye slanted toward the back of the younger man's head.

"Identibase says she's Tantra Brach, a moderately successful artist, specializing in abstract portraits, although she earns more credit doing commercial illustration. Does well enough to maintain a soft credit account with a pretty good balance. She'll make her way into Moshamadur in another couple of years at her current growth rate, although her earnings will have to go up some if she plans to stay there as anything other than a marginal resident."

"Any connection with the witness?"

"Nothing of substance. She has transferred some small credit to him periodically in the past, for services rendered."

Marym nodded to herself, a habit of which she was unaware. She released the replay and listened while the story unfolded: terse sentences, obvious strain and excitement mixed in the voice. The witness, one Mikki Seurat, claimed to have been wandering around the park with nothing to do when he noticed a maintenance hut standing open. Curious, he looked inside and discovered a human body, as yet unidentified, mutilated in a fashion that indicated it could be the latest Scarab murder. In accordance with the law, he was reporting the incident and requesting the twenty-credit finder's fee awarded for capital crimes.

Marym stopped the display at the disconnect a moment later. "Tani, do we have anything on Seurat, the witness?"

The reply was instantaneous; Tani was good, too good to be wasted in this assignment, Marym thought. If she eventually escaped into a better posting elsewhere, she would have to find a way to take Tani with her. And she was determined to escape the trap that was Nashamata.

"Two complaints of minor vandalism several years ago, no charges ever placed. No arrest record. I netted the Brach woman as well. Her father was involved in the protests that led to the Accord of Alyshambo and was arrested several times, but she's clean."

"I'll want a complete datadump on them both, but I don't suppose we'll find anything."

"I scanned the highlights. Nothing suspicious except . . ." Tani paused.

"You don't believe he was idly wandering around the park either, do you?"

Tani laughed through the netlink. "He's never held a steady job for any period of time; no formal training to speak of, and he's not built right for manual labor. But he dresses well enough, supports a younger sister who's a semi-invalid. Definitely a hustler, and a fairly successful one to have survived under those circumstances. He's not the type to waste time on recreation. I'd wager he was looking for something to steal, maybe hoping he'd find some abandoned tools or some scrap metal he could exchange for hard credit."

"Sounds about right." She sighed. "Let me know as soon as Tiko reports in."

Marym sat down slowly, staring into space for a few seconds while she reordered her thoughts. With the fingers of her right hand, she reached out and pressed a series of icons. As she did so, five small blips turned blue on her desktop, each indicating a case file held in virtual memory. The Scarab murders presented a risk and an opportunity. Her predecessor had been unable to make any headway in solving the case, hampered as he was by the inadequacy and inferiority of both staff and equipment, as well as the reluctance of the city government and the other Prefects to expend any great effort solving a crime in Nashamata, no matter how heinous or spectacular it might be.

If only Scarab would strike once outside of the district, she thought. If one mutilated body were to be found in Tashamir or Moshamadur, or even lofty Kishamkur itself, there would be no rest until the culprit, or culprits, was found and brought to justice. In that situation, she knew, the city would be forced to provide the resources necessary for a thorough investigation. But then she realized the obverse of that coin; a murder in another quarter of the city would be outside of her jurisdiction, and there would still be no way she could further her career by its resolution. If Scarab was to be the agent of her escape, she'd have to apprehend him with the limited resources available to her.

Which might not be enough.

Chapter Two

Sandor Dyle wondered, not for the first time, what perverse impulse had lured him into taking the long way home in order to escape the tedium of Ventana. Admittedly, the attractions of that highly touted resort planet had been exaggerated unconscionably by its promoters, and he had exhausted the supposedly infinitely variegated recreational sites much more quickly than was his usual habit. The cliffs at Kandalahar were indeed magnificent, but far less extensive than he had been led to believe, requiring only a single day's visit, and the cave paintings in Umbulapur had archaeological and anthropological implications but no particular artistic value. The Mohar Valley was pleasing to the eye, but no more so than some of the hinterlands of his home world, Hazard, and he'd seen more impressive forests and jungles on several other worlds which did not stake their commercial well being so emphatically on revenue from offworld visitors. There were indeed several dangerous and picturesque native creatures, but their grandeur and menace were both ameliorated by the fact that the survivors of their breed lived in large zoos designed to mimic their normal habitats. If they still existed in their former wild state, their numbers were so small that they remained virtually unknown.

Halfway through his projected stay, bored, angry—although more at himself for having been fooled than at the promoters who had carried off the scam—Sandor had decided to cut his losses and make arrangements for an unusual three-planet hop, skip, and jump back home. Tashista was the skip, and he was partway through the seven-local-day layover when word came that the *Soaring Star*, the luxury liner on which he had booked passage, had muffed its docking with the orbiting habitat above Ramadar and would be delayed for an uncertain period of time while repairs were being completed. Tashista's comparative isolation from the Concourse at large meant that no other passenger vessel was due to arrive for an even longer period of time, and he might well be trapped here far longer than was palatable.

"Damn this backwater planet and its insular people!" He realized he was being somewhat unfair, but he indulged his tendency toward temper tantrums in private. It made his public behavior that much more thoughtful and restrained, and at his age, he felt he could justify pandering to his occasional less than admirable moments.

He was pacing the length of his room at the Samarka Offworlder, an establishment ostensibly designed specifically to cater to the varied needs and desires of visitors not native to Tashista, including even the occasional non-human sentient, but almost certainly intended also to insulate the populace from the potentially unsettling influence of non-Tashistan ways of thought. Not that this world was particularly repressive; there was no legal restriction preventing Tashistans from interacting with offworlders. There were, however, various subtle but nonetheless effective ways to erect barriers between peoples. While the first generation of colonists was settling in, an artificial language had been created and imposed on the population as part of an experiment in social control. Succeeding generations had reverted to the nearly universal human argot, but some trace of that original, arcane barrier of language remained implicit in the culture of this world. Some words and phrases carried subtle nuances that remained opaque to visitors, and some common subtleties were lost on the resident population. Sandor routinely expended considerable effort researching the current social, political, and cultural climate of any society he intended to visit. It was too easy to run afoul of local custom, even law, and while most worlds made some allowances for the ignorance of tourists, it was possible to get into really serious trouble simply because mores and customs varied so widely among the increasingly varied and fragmented human culture. On those few alien sentient worlds where humans could survive without artificial life support, the chance of an unpleasant contretemps was even greater. Leaving aside such unpleasantries, there was also the simple fact that one could better experience the richness of a new environment if one had some comprehension of the intricacies and peculiarities inherent to its social structure. Unfortunately, Tashistans did not just shelter themselves from gross external cultural contamination. They made it as difficult as possible to gain anything but the most superficial understanding of their cultural norms. Sandor normally associated this with a planetary inferiority complex, but he had modified his opinion in this instance. Tashistans seemed to be genuinely disinterested in what happened outside their atmosphere. Their eyes were almost universally turned inward.

Sandor's insatiable thirst for knowledge and his almost childlike curiosity about the twists and turns exhibited by his fellow sentients was abetted by an amazingly retentive memory, and the training he had undergone to improve his ability to observe, correlate, and draw conclusions from apparently unrelated facts allowed him to adapt to new environments with alacrity. In a civilization which had spread so widely through the universe that no one person or even organization could claim to have a thorough understanding of the overall shape of that expansion, there were very few rivals who approached his breadth of experience.

Frustrated by the news that he might be forced to remain on Tashista far longer than he had expected, longer even than he had projected for the entire circuitous voyage back to Hazard, he moved restlessly around the room. If he were to remain for such an extended visit, he would have to find a way to put the layover to use. He already knew that there were only limited library facilities available; Tashista was not overtly isolationist, but its intercourse with offworlders was diffident, irregular, and terse. Trade was limited as much by choice as by Tashista's lack of any truly exportable products. Scientific and philosophical treatises and the occasional work of overblown fiction were the chief non-native selections in the library at Samarka; the social studies, histories, anthropological, and psychological works which made up the bulk of Sandor's normal pleasure reading were poorly represented, and mostly out of date. Significantly, there had been no serious attempt to study the evolution of Tashistan society, even locally.

There was a low tone from the opposite end of the room and Sandor turned to see a red, telltale blinking on the datanet screen, indicating an incoming message. Welcoming anything that might promise some respite from his present ennui, he crossed the room and accepted the call.

"Ser Dyle?" The face that formed on the screen was that of an older man, hairline receding, the thin strands of gray edging toward white, a broad nose and narrowly set eyes that moved restlessly back and forth. A good mouth, strong full lips, laugh lines at each corner; a small, very neat beard, cut close at the ears, growing longer as it approached the point of the chin.

"Yes, this is Sandor Dyle. And you are?"

"Preston Zaks. I wonder if I might have a moment or two of your time?"

Sandor was intrigued by the possibility of diversion, but too practiced to allow his reaction to manifest itself visibly. "This would be with regard to . . ?"

"A matter of business." Zaks glanced briefly to one side, then back again, but not so quickly that Sandor hadn't observed and concluded that someone else was present, outside the range of the scanner at the other end. "Business," he reminded himself, had a fluid meaning on Tashista. Virtually every human activity was defined in terms of commerce. "I could come up to your room if you'd like, or I would be honored to entertain you in the Spherium." The Spherium, specializing in offworld cuisine, very conveniently adjoined the Offworlder and could be reached without exposing oneself to the elements, which currently consisted of a very cold, insidious rain.

"The Spherium, I think," he replied cautiously. "Will your companion be joining us as well?"

The other man appeared momentarily startled, his forehead creasing; the mildly genial smile stiffened for a split second, then returned. "I did give that away, didn't I? Subterfuge has never been one of my talents. Nevertheless, there will just be the two of us. This is a matter of some delicacy, I'm afraid, the details of which I would prefer to explain in person. It would be inappropriate for my companion to be connected to our discussion, no matter how remotely."

"Very well then. When shall we meet?"

Zaks fidgeted visibly and dropped his eyes. "I have no present commitments, Ser Dyle. Would you be available immediately? I believe this approximates your customary dining hour. I really would appreciate your generous understanding and prompt cooperation in this matter, and I truly believe that you will find our conversation profitable."

Resisting a very human urge to balk at the suggestion that he was being bought, Sandor breathed deeply and agreed, breaking the connection before the other man could do so. After all, he told himself, this might represent just the relief from monotony for which he had been searching.

Besides, he had never had been able to resist a puzzle.

Sandor Dyle was an anachronism. In a society where implanted databanks and nearly universal public datanet systems made vast quantities of information available to all but the very lowest on the economic scale, rigorous formal education was confined almost entirely to rigidly defined specialties. There was clearly too much data for any single human mind to acquire a thorough knowledge of any but the most minutely constricted field. As a consequence, everyone specialized in a particular skill, and the specialists were themselves interchangeable, all having received virtually identical training and each having been indoctrinated with the same precisely defined method of resolving problems. Researchers now spent most of their time designing observational techniques and recording data, which was then correlated through the datanet. If cause and effect or any other relationship existed, it could be described and analyzed mathematically and interpolated to predict future data by sophisticated electronic extrapolative routines. Related research could be called up by the touch of an icon. Results were immediately entered into the datanet and made available to anyone whose interest included the same subject matter. In a society where education was a commodity like any other, Sandor was one of the great consumers, gobbling down information with an insatiable hunger, employing his remarkably retentive memory as the repository for myriad discordant facts. And sometimes, when the right situation arose, Sandor was able to discern a pattern that escaped the perpetual regressive analysis of the datanet, and make the tiny but vast leap from input to output that is called insight, which was still beyond the ability of any non-sentient data handling system.

Sandor paused at the entrance to the Spherium, sparsely occupied this early in the day, wondering if there was any way that he could observe Preston Zaks without being seen first, but before he had the opportunity to do so, a uniformed employee holding a holopak in one hand greeted him by name.

"Ser Dyle, your party is waiting above. May I show you the way?"

The Spherium was an enormous glassine sphere inside of which an intricate web of platforms had been constructed, each holding from one to six tables. The supporting structure of the platforms was articulated, and was slowly but perceptibly moving, shifting each in relation to those adjoining, rising, rotating, dropping, or moving horizontally within the limits of the translucent superstructure. The man waving from a position approximately one-third of the way toward the apex of the sphere was identifiably Preston Zaks. Sighing, reminding himself once more that he needed to exercise more regularly, Sandor waved away the offer of a guide and crossed to the nearest stairway.

Zaks pressed both palms to his chest in greeting when Sandor reached his table. It was a substantial chest, in proportion to the substantial body that adjoined it. Not for the first time, Sandor felt that his attenuated body was grossly out of place here. Although his two meters gave him a height advantage over almost everyone on Tashista, their greater bulk was still intimidating. "I apologize for the necessity that you climb so far, Ser Dyle, but this was the closest table fitted for privacy that was available."

Sandor refrained from breathing heavily despite the fact that the gravity on Tashista was perceptibly higher than that which prevailed on the worlds he preferred to frequent and touched his own chest in acknowledgment as he seated himself. "Discretion is almost always worth the effort, Ser Zaks, but I admit freely I cannot fathom why a city official of Samarka would arrange a marginally clandestine visit with a transient offworld scholar temporarily stranded on his world."

Zaks was in better control this time. "I continue to be impressed with your abilities, Ser Dyle. It's the sash, of course." He indicated the violet swatch of cloth that girded his not inconsiderable waist; threads of iridescent green twisted in unspecific patterns. "Offworlders are not usually so knowledgeable about our customs."

Sandor smiled and sat back in his chair, which shifted slightly to accommodate him. "The purple sash indicates municipal government, the green lines general administration, I believe. And judging by the balance between the two hues, I'd say you held a position of considerable authority."

Smiling broadly, Zaks nodded. "Very good, Ser Dyle. The only error you made is in assuming that I serve here in Samarka. I am in fact the Kudara of Soshambe, which lies a half day's journey from the capital."

"Soshambe, that would be 'the city between the mountains and the valley,' would it not?"

"Actually, it is literally 'the people between the mountains and the valley,' but the artificial language imposed on our ancestors by the Lucharist movement was never very precise and did not long survive their removal from the seat of power. But please, before we discuss business further, let me order you some refreshment."

As a matter of fact, Sandor felt distinctly thirsty, and he leaned forward with alacrity, scanning the menu inset in the table. He ordered an exotic fruit drink by touching the appropriate icon. "Are you not ordering also, Ser Zaks?"

"I did so beforehand, specifying delivery only once you had placed an order of your own. I took the liberty of including a selection of kurilic pastries; they're scandalously expensive here, but of the finest quality."

"I will trust your judgment, Ser Zaks."

Seconds later, Sandor was surprised by the arrival of a human waiter, who delivered two very large drinks and an intricate, twelve segmented serving tray filled with dainty pastries of various sizes and colors. He sipped at the drink, which was deliciously tangy, letting the cool liquid slosh back and forth in his mouth, savoring the flavor, before gulping it down noisily in accordance with local custom. "Very refreshing," he announced, at which point Zaks tasted his own and declared himself equally pleased.

Social proprieties having been satisfied, Sandor became more serious. "Now indulge me, please, Ser Zaks. Flattered as I am by the attention of the chief official of a local municipality, I can't help wondering about the purpose of this meeting. To what do I owe the honor of your attention?"

Zaks blinked and avoided answering the question. "It's not precisely accurate to call me the chief official. As Kudara, I oversee the coordination of activities between the other administrative areas, but each retains primary control of its own specific functions. My department has little actual authority; it's somewhat of an honorary position."

"With all due respect, Ser Zaks, I believe in actual practice the Kudara's wishes carry a great deal of weight."

"It *is* customary to accede to the Kudara's requests," Zaks smiled. "That's why we pay so much for the position. The high annual fee encourages a rapid turnover, discourages the establishment of too static a hand at the top."

"It also prevents able but non-affluent citizens from reaching the highest levels of government, doesn't it?" Sandor raised one hand to stroke the right side of his thick mustache.

"If they have the ability to excel in government, they would have previously demonstrated that talent by succeeding economically. We reward those who embrace both luck and hard work; it takes more than mere desire or ability to make an effective leader."

"Surely, a person's value cannot be judged in purely economic terms."

"What other measurable criteria do we have?"

"The most accurate of measurement fails if you are evaluating the wrong attribute. And it is my understanding that most of your wealthiest class, the Hierata, have actually inherited rather than earned their status."

Zaks was clearly uncomfortable and dismissed the subject with a gesture. "As enjoyable as this conversation may be, there are other, more pressing matters which we need to discuss. I understand that you have acquired an enviable reputation as a problem solver."

"I have been retained in a professional capacity on a few occasions, as a matter of fact, and I believe my performance was deemed adequate on each of those occasions. I am not presently seeking employment, Ser Zaks. My financial situation is quite healthy, even by your standards."

"Heir to the Dyle Dataphile fortune, author of one of the most widely used internal systems analysis programs, and so on. I've accessed your public profile, Ser Dyle. I hope you won't consider me impertinent, but under the circumstances, I had to be certain that I was approaching someone with the capacity to be of assistance."

"Not at all. If I was concerned about the information contained in my profile, I would have taken steps to restrict access. But as I said, I am not currently in need of employment; I'm on vacation, as a matter of fact." He sampled another of the pastries, which were indeed delicious, and nodded his satisfaction to the other man.

"If they traveled well, Tashista might have a more viable export trade." Zaks reached across the table and selected a pastry of his own. He was still clearly reluctant to advance to the purpose of their meeting.

"May I ask what provoked you into accessing my profile in the first place? I'm not so important that my presence on Tashista would arouse any official recognition, let alone a visit from one of its most powerful citizens."

Zaks chuckled around the remnants of his pastry. "Power is a relative term, Ser Dyle, but that's another subject entirely. As a matter of fact, I had never heard of you before today; your name was passed on to me by another."

"Ah, the mysterious absent companion. A member of the Lucharist Society, I imagine, or at least a sympathizer. And a person of some influence here."

Zaks stopped in mid-chew, his eyes widening. "And how did you draw that conclusion, Ser Dyle?"

Sandor leaned forward, pretending exasperation even though, in truth, he was enjoying himself immensely. "Come, come, Ser Zaks. If you're soliciting my help, surely you shouldn't be surprised when I draw logical conclusions from the evidence at hand. If you think about it, you'll see that my observations aren't very mysterious. My profile is a matter of public record, but only a very few people would know that I was here in the first place and have any reason to access it. To recognize the name, my secretive sponsor must be fairly well traveled offworld, which eliminates all but the tiniest fraction of your populace. Oddly enough, the most cosmopolitan of Tashistans are the Lucharists, strong advocates of isolationism, a holdover from the early days of this planet's history. It would be political suicide for a Lucharist to advocate the use of an offworlder to solve a Tashistan problem, so . . ." He let the balance of the sentence fall away.

Zaks sighed theatrically. "All right, Ser Dyle. Your conclusions are accurate, although I'm sure you'll excuse me if I don't provide the actual name. Unless you know that as well?"

Sandor shook his head, although he suspected he would be able to make a good guess after spending a few minutes accessing the profiles of prominent Lucharists. Not that it mattered particularly. "So what specifically is the problem that has caused a Lucharist to compromise his or her own feelings and appeal for help, albeit through an intermediary, from an offworlder like myself?"

"To be fair, it is I and not my associate who is the prime mover in this matter. But she . . . there is a matter of an old debt owed, and my present difficulty is one of great concern to me and to my city."

Zaks was plainly distressed, sincerity and concern altering the tone of his voice as he spoke, his face twitching nervously as he turned to sip at his drink. Sandor waited for him to recover his equanimity.

"Ser Dyle, have you accessed or heard anything during your stay concerning the Scarab murders?"

Sandor frowned. "Scarab? That's your name for the current season, isn't it? No, I've heard nothing about any murders." He made a vague gesture. "Your news media don't seem to dwell on crime the way they do on most other worlds, or perhaps your crime rate is phenomenally low."

Looking vaguely uncomfortable, Zaks mumbled something about differing definitions of criminality, clearly intent upon dropping the subject as quickly as possible. "The Scarab killings are something unprecedented on Tashista. They started three years ago, apparently at random, at least with no discernible pattern, no real clues. They all take place during the Secant of the Scarab and they all involve rather . . . grotesque mutilations. Dismemberment, usually, and sometimes bizarre displays with . . ." he hesitated and licked his lips nervously, ". . . with portions of the victims."

"I take it they have continued this year?"

Zaks nodded. "The sixth known victim was discovered two days ago, stuffed into a storage hut in a public park. The twenty-seventh in all."

Sandor let an indrawn breath whistle through his teeth. "And it took you this long to decide you needed outside help?"

The other man's eyes flashed. "I told you, we have differing standards about crime and how it is treated. You won't appreciate this, Ser Dyle, but in some segments of our society, life is very cheap. Criminal gangs in the poorer quarters are essentially independent of government control; so long as they confine their activities to the less . . . respectable neighborhoods, there is a tacit agreement to accept a certain level of lawlessness. The criminal class provides something of a stabilizing force in some quarters. The Scarab killings have always taken place in Soshambe's Nashamata district, and public outrage has never been a major issue. In point of fact, there has been a rather distressing fascination with the killings in other parts of the city."

"I take it the situation has altered this time. This latest incident took place in a more affluent district, I suppose?"

"No, no. The pattern has held. The park is within Nashamata. Under ordinary circumstances, the report would have been filed as an internal matter for the local Prefect, who would have ordered the usual investigation, doubtless with no better results than previously."

"If it's of so little consequence, then why choose to deal differently with the situation on this occasion? Why bring an offworlder into the investigation?" Dyle made no effort to conceal his distaste.

"You needn't be so censorious, Ser Dyle." Zaks was clearly offended. "Every society has its shortcomings, and we're aware of the interpretation that would be placed on our action, or rather our inaction, elsewhere in the Concourse. I am also aware that we are not the only world whose social customs incorporate a differentiated system of justice."

Sandor could think of several such examples, and nodded, granting the point. "My question remains, however. What sets this present incident apart from the others?"

"The latest victim was not a resident of Nashamata; he was the son of the Kishamkur Prefect, apparently out for a night of adventure in a place where he didn't belong. As you have pointed out, the younger citizens of Kishamkur were born to wealth and security, and many of them are fond of taking unnecessary chances."

Sandor allowed himself to express mild surprise: a lifted eyebrow, a small movement of the head. "This changes the official position, I gather?"

Zaks nodded. "You are an intelligent man, Ser Dyle. You undoubtedly understand us well enough to realize that a certain degree of crime, even violent crime, is considered unavoidable, if not officially tolerated. We cannot turn a blind eye in this case. Even if the latest victim had lacked significant family connections, the fact that he was not of the Nashamata is enough to give the case a new urgency."

"Understandable, if not admirable. But I still fail to see why you have approached me. I would have thought you'd prefer to resolve the situation yourselves."

"We are a quiet world, Ser Dyle, far from the main trade routes, limited in our intercourse with even our closest neighbors, largely through our own choice. But we do make an effort to keep abreast of affairs beyond this system, and your reputation could hardly be considered obscure. The recovery of the stolen artifacts on Zonderzee was widely reported here, as well as your success in identifying the assassin of the Solistician of Mercada. The individual who brought your name to my attention indicated you were also credited with the resolution of the Sulinar Cult murders and the kidnapping of the daughter of a prominent political figure on Zere."

With a disparaging gesture, Sandor dismissed the charge. "Grossly exaggerated. I was only one of several consulted in each case. The Zerean kidnappers had made so many mistakes, the local authorities would have captured them soon even without my assistance. The solution to the Mercadan assassination was staring the authorities in the face, but they had been blessed with so many years since their last capital crime that they suffered from institutional paralysis. You could easily have determined the guilty party yourself, given the facts that were available."

"Your modesty is becoming but unconvincing."

"Modesty is not numbered among my virtues, Ser Zaks. The mastermind behind the Cult murders was a genetically enhanced genius who would have continued his reign of terror indefinitely had I not detected a pattern in his actions of which he himself was unaware. The Zonderzee affair was even more challenging, since the thieves had used an intricate scheme involving random choices to arrange the concealment of the stolen goods. The local regulation against artificial intelligence systems hampered the authorities. Had I not noticed a correlation between the increase in freight charge backs and the average datanet access time . . . but that's neither here nor there. May I assume that you are proposing that I assist in this investigation?"

Zaks refused to meet his eyes. "Well, that is, it was brought to our attention that you are compelled by circumstances to remain rather longer on Tashista than you originally intended, and we are not a world designed to provide a great deal of variety or amusement for our visitors. It was suggested that this might be an interesting way for you to pass some of what would be otherwise unprofitable time. Like Mercada, we lack the experience to deal with a criminal such as Scarab, who seems capable of avoiding our surveillance systems and who has yet to provide any consequential evidence that would aid in his apprehension. There would be a consulting fee, of course. I am empowered to negotiate the terms of such an arrangement."

Without answering, Sandor leaned forward, raised the glass to his lips, and began a long, slow draining of the liquid therein. Barely enough remained to cover the bottom when he finally set it down and reclined, letting the articulated chair adjust to his new position. "What authority and resources would be available to me?"

Zaks brightened. "Then you will help us?"

Sandor shook his head. "That remains to be seen. First I must know the conditions under which I would be expected to work. I have better things to do with my time, even here, than confront a killer while blindfolded and hobbled."

After a momentary silence, Zaks raised one hand and began ticking off points, one finger at a time. "You would have complete access to our datanet, and I do mean complete. Your clearance level would be two steps higher than my own. The compartmentalization of our public services might cause some minor difficulties; even as Kudara I don't have any legal authority to compel cooperation from the Prefect, Material Services, Medical, or the other divisions, but the victim's father will ensure that you have total cooperation throughout the Prefecture, and between the two of us, we can bring a great deal of pressure to bear upon any recalcitrant official. You will have virtually unlimited funding, including living expenses, travel, bribes, and so forth; no accounting will be required, as your word will be sufficient in all eventualities. Assistance will be provided on a full-time basis to ease your interface with our citizens, and any additional staff you require will be made available, within reason. Living quarters in Kishamkur have already been arranged, and if the location is not suitable, these can be changed. If there is anything else . . . I think you will find us more than cooperative."

"What will the authorities in Nashamata, the local Prefect, think about my involvement in the case?"

"She'll be delighted, I feel sure. Any assistance in cleaning up this matter will make her job considerably easier."

Sandor didn't reply, just kept his eyes level and unblinking. After a moment, the other man dropped the pretense.

"Of course, she may feel that it reflects a lack of confidence in her own abilities. Dunnis is newly appointed, young for that position, and somewhat sensitive about her image. Pressure will be exerted to ensure that she remains cooperative if it is required."

Sandor raised a hand. "Let's not exacerbate the situation unless necessary, Ser Zaks. Her willing cooperation, however testy, is preferable to coercion, no matter how gentle. You say she is newly appointed. She was not responsible for the investigation from the outset then?"

"No, the first two waves of killings occurred during the administration of Savram Aras, a devoted public servant although admittedly somewhat circumscribed in his abilities. He was preoccupied as well by his own declining physical condition and the aftermath of a personal tragedy. Suratic nerve disease was diagnosed while he was investigating the first series of killings, and he expended misguided effort and credit resisting pressure to resign from office during the second. A tragic story, Ser Dyle. The man's wife was attacked and received what proved to be fatal injuries many years ago. His only child, a son, disappeared shortly thereafter, apparently having run away from home. Aras threw himself into his work, which seemed to be his only solace, and then was forced to surrender that as well."

"Is he still alive?"

"Yes, certainly. Confined to a prosthetic chair, as I understand it, but still mentally alert. I believe he even provides some assistance to the Prefect from time to time, although I suspect the motivation is emotive rather than rational. His disease is progressively degenerative and incurable, although we are able to retard its development to a limited degree."

"Then he might be open to an interview?"

"He'd probably welcome it; he's the sort of man who would relish the thought that he was still of some use to society. Our culture has something of a taboo about disease, you know, particularly that involving the sura. Sura grain is the staple of our agrarian economy, an integral part of the food chain, but it is also the source of a variety of illnesses, cancers, nerve disease, rashes, and so on. With no surviving family, Aras receives few visitors and most of his contact with the outside world is necessarily through the datanet. I'm confident that an interview would not present any insurmountable difficulty."

"If sura is so dangerous, couldn't you alter your ecology to incorporate a less harmful strain?"

"It's a wedding of blessing and curse, I'm afraid. When Tashista was colonized, there were no indigenous lifeforms capable of nourishing human stock. The projected number of generations required to humaniform the planet was reduced dramatically by the discovery that the sura, at that time just one of many contending floral ground covers, was so similar in its genetic structure that it could be engineered to provide a compatible foodstuff that fit with the existing ecosphere. In essence, it created a bridge between local and imported flora. The match wasn't quite as close as was predicted, unfortunately, and a minor but pervasive mutation resulted in a variety of unexpected allergies, untoward side effects, and other unpleasant surprises. For many of these we have found solutions; even suratic cancer is almost always curable, and our researchers have indicated an effective preventive treatment will be perfected within a generation. But suratic nerve disease can only be ameliorated, never cured, and has a one hundred percent mortality rate. Even worse, its symptoms vary from patient to patient, ranging from general numbness to paralysis, from headaches to complete insanity. Aras has lost virtually all use of his legs, as I understand it, although his mind seems relatively untouched."

Still playing with his mustache, Sandor began tapping the fingers of his other hand against his thigh. "When would it be possible to remove ourselves to Soshambe?"

Zaks brightened and sat erect. "Then you find our offer acceptable?"

"Let us say I find it worthy of further consideration. I would like to visit your city, Ser Zaks, and talk to one or two people there. I will make my decision once I have had the opportunity to judge for myself the degree of cooperation and competence which I may expect."

"I'm sure you will not be disappointed, Ser Dyle. This latest incident has shocked us all. Our own petty differences have all been shelved pending deliverance from this parade of atrocities."

"It has been my experience, Ser Zaks, that there is no act atrocious enough to force human beings to truly set aside their own concerns, but a reasonable compromise between these internal conflicts is usually sufficient."

"Yes, well, my private lifter is available at any time. I can entertain myself here in the capital for however long it might take you to make whatever arrangements you deem necessary, but I am prepared to leave whenever you are ready."

Sandor pursed his lips thoughtfully. "There is nothing holding me here. I would prefer to keep my room open, in the event that I decide to decline your offer after all."

With a dismissive gesture, Zaks assured Sandor that there would be no difficulty. "As a matter of fact, the city of Soshambe insists upon taking financial responsibility for any charges you have incurred here, regardless of your ultimate decision. The room will be held until you personally terminate your occupancy. Now shall we order? I personally find my appetite much improved."

After they had eaten, Sandor made arrangements to be picked up following a short interval during which he would pack the personal belongings which he felt necessary or potentially of use. He told himself that he remained skeptical about the possibility of acquiescing to the request of Preston Zaks, but he knew himself well enough to recognize the quickening of his pulse, the sudden precision of his thoughts. Unless the situation with the local Prefect proved to be completely untenable, he was certain that he would pursue this investigation, and perhaps despite her objections if she proved intractable and obstructive. A contentious relationship with Ser Dunnis could be no more unpleasant than endless days trying to amuse himself in the capital.

Chapter Three

Night on Tashista was an ambiguous state. Two of the three moons, Lucora and Sulimar, were bloated, pock-marked companions when visible, bathing the countryside with their brilliant reflections. Sirita, their substantially smaller (although actually only more distant) sibling, appeared unblemished in comparison. When forced to contest the night sky with one or more of its rivals, Sirita was often reduced to near invisibility. Good luck was supposed to abound when Sirita held the sky alone, which happened at long intervals and for brief periods.

Within the convoluted streets of Nashamata, towering, decaying buildings stood linked by walkways; elevated tubecar lines frequently surmounted the ancient roof gardens, many of which had either gone wild or were now overrun by nasura and other prolific growths. Even the light of the daytime sun had difficulty penetrating to the lower traverseways, and the underways were shrouded in darkness broken only by the inadequate artificial illumination provided by the city.

It was the evening of the same day during which Sandor Dyle had met with Preston Zaks in the dining room of the Spherium. A front of colder air had swept into the city, bitterly chill but mercifully dry. A heavily-cloaked shape stood concealed in the archway between the lower concourse of Nashamata and a row of private dwellings that stretched from the southernmost abutment to the elevated way that wound up and back toward Tashamir. This was the uppermost reach of the lowermost class; the structures were well maintained and attractively laid out, but they lacked the amenities to be found among the more affluent.

It was late, full darkness had fallen, a brisk and cutting wind whistled through the artificial canyons of the city, playing with dust, discarded trash, dead leaves shed from desiccated plants, and other detritus which normally gravitated toward the gutters. The figure remained silent and virtually motionless: listening, watching, waiting, hating.

Traffic had been heavy throughout evening. The apparel merchants of eastern Tashamir were unhappy with the volume of business that had been transacted within their stalls, walls, and shops during the past several trading periods and had announced a single evening sale with prices so attractive that even the frugal Nashamatans had decided this was one of those rare opportunities that justified dipping into hidden reserves of hard credit for something other than urgent, immediate need. Foot traffic back and forth had been constant; the poorer citizens of Soshambe were loathe to pay for mass transit except in an emergency. Credit saved was credit invested in the future.

Now, as the tiny moon Sirita reached its highest point in the night sky, currently abandoned by its sister moons, the number of pedestrians was dropping off rapidly. Scattered groups of shoppers bragged to one another about the skill they had displayed while negotiating the price of their latest acquisitions, possibly to a figure a mere three times what the merchant had actually paid for it and twice what he was probably willing to accept. As the merchants closed their stalls, the shoppers faded away and were supplanted by smaller clusters of pedestrians, couples taking time from their work schedule for a moment of affection, occasional lone figures carrying messages, seeking work, or too restless to return home. It was much darker when Sirita ruled the sky unchallenged, and most walked rapidly as they hastened to their destinations. The air had become unseasonably chilly, and a playful wind rustled the watcher's cloak, which clung tightly along one side of the body. The figure shifted position, pressing close to a masonry wall to trap the fabric, whose flapping might betray the presence of the otherwise invisible observer.

Those who passed by never realized their peril, but they were being measured, judged, unwittingly auditioning for a part they would have universally declined to accept had the choice been offered to them. In particular, those individuals who pursued solitary business were evaluated if their paths brought them past this vantage point, and on more than one occasion, the silent onlooker moved forward a step, as though prepared to advance into the comparatively open traverseway. But on each occasion, some subtle factor caused the cloaked figure to reconsider. Perhaps there were other pedestrians too close at hand, perhaps the prospective target was a bit too powerfully built, or too alert, or it might be that some other, less easily described aspect of the situation was wrong. The silent onlooker had a unique set of standards and an abiding patience. Time and again the figure tensed, preparing to act, and time and again, it relented and waited for another opportunity, one better fitted to its purposes.

There was no need to hurry. There would be other nights, other quarry. Haste was unnecessary. In this, as in all things, the cloaked figure subordinated emotion to reason.

* * * * *

Prefect Marym Dunnis was not the slightest bit uncertain about her own reaction to the announcement that an offworld specialist had been approached about "assisting" in the Scarab murder investigation. It had been phrased diplomatically, of course; officially this Sandor Dyle was nothing more than a consultant, a pattern analysis and datanet whiz of some unspecified variety, employed to evaluate the situation and suggest possible alternative approaches to the authorities. Unspoken was a clear implication that any contravention of this man Dyle's requests would be looked upon with extreme disfavor. The truth, she suspected, was that with the killing of someone more noteworthy than the average citizen of Nashamata, particularly the son of the Prefect of Kishamkur, the job previously awarded to a troublesome, aggressive young woman had taken on a greater significance.

Despite assurances that she remained undisputed Prefect of this quarter, and that this was no reflection on her abilities, Marym was convinced that exactly the opposite was true. She had paid the full price to obtain this position, and any overt infringement upon her authority could provide grounds for punitive and substantive litigation against the city as a whole and the General Council in particular. Had she objected, however, Marym felt certain that the city authorities would have quickly found a reason to suspend her from office, possibly placing her on administrative leave while they investigated an anonymous charge of malfeasance. During the interim, a carefully chosen and trusted underling would be installed in her place, ordered to cooperate fully with the offworlder. In the unlikely event that this alleged consultant actually did contribute to the capture of Scarab, whatever credit might remain for others would accrue to her stand-in, who might even have sufficiently wealthy backing to preemptively purchase her posting even if she objected.

There was no question but that she would have to handle this situation with considerable delicacy. If she provided tangible grounds for her own removal, she would play directly into the hands of her rivals and might even forfeit the credit she had paid as well as her chance for further advancement. Chafing at the necessity to compromise for political reasons, she had reluctantly agreed to comply with the wishes of her superiors, while silently preparing to resist anything that would infringe on her prerogatives.

"When's this offworld genius supposed to be arriving? I have actual work to attend to." Tiko Parsi sat at the opposite end of her office, his comparatively slender shape stretched over a free-form articulated seat which seemed to be straining the limits of its programming to accommodate his unusually long arms and legs and unconventional posture. Although he was the best investigator available to her, Marym had to admit his inclination toward radical styles of dress and impertinent behavior interfered with his job performance, alienating witnesses and adjudicators alike. Tiko was one of those rare citizens of Nashamata who seemed to have found his niche and grown content with it; his personal credit line was nearly large enough to finance a move to Moshamadur, but he showed no inclination to change his status, perhaps cognizant of the fact that a higher lifestyle would require a greater investment of his time in the acquisition of additional credit. He was even known to spend disproportionately in the entertainment district, and Marym suspected he was psychologically unprepared to advance himself and went on foolish spending binges to ensure that he would not be faced with a credible choice about his personal future. Many citizens became troubled once they realized they would likely climb no further in society. Some became violent, others withdrawn and passive, still others refused to accept the inevitable and pretended that further advancement was imminent. Tiko's adjustment was probably healthier, and certainly more socially acceptable, although it diminished his worth in the eyes of everyone around him, and to a degree reflected poorly on his performance. He was bright enough to avoid demotion, which would reduce his living standards significantly, but his performance had remained at minimally acceptable levels long enough that Savram Aras had tagged him as "troubled," a characterization with which she agreed.

"They're moving his belongings into the Black Ark in Kishamkur. Prefect Leskar will bring him to us in his personal vehicle. We have been requested to place one of our patrol lifters and a driver at his permanent disposal. As if we weren't already straining to find enough personnel and material to cover this quarter." She took a deep, calming breath. It was never a good idea to express frustration with one's superiors in front of one's subordinates. "They wouldn't be more specific about their arrival time; we're supposed to hold ourselves in readiness for them."

"Well, there are so few crimes in this district that we certainly have plenty of time to sit around idly, don't we, Prefect?"

Tiko's penchant for sarcasm had irritated her in the past, but just at the moment, it matched her own mood so well that she even granted him the dispensation of a short laugh. "There are crimes and then there are crimes, Tiko. We should feel honored that we're being offered such extraordinary support, and without having to adjust our own operating budget."

"I'll lay you odds that there's an adjustment in our next fiscal period. The welfare of the city is one thing; the distribution of credit is entirely another." His mock good humor faded. "Couldn't you just have refused, Marym? They couldn't insist without committing a major breach of protocol."

"I'm surprised they haven't requested that I hold his hand personally."

"They haven't relieved you, have they?" The two had not always seen eye to eye during the short period Marym had served as Prefect, but against the common, outside foe, a new unity had been forged. Marym knew better than to expect that this would alter their relationship once things returned to normal, but she still relished the alliance for the moment. It was unlikely that her chief detective had any interest in actively undermining her, since he would never accumulate sufficient credit to purchase her position for himself, but he had developed a taste for minor insubordination and had tested her good nature on more than one occasion in the past.

She chose to ignore the last question. It was impertinent even if meant sympathetically. "Have you accessed Ser Dyle's file? His credentials are fairly impressive, I'll have to admit, although the evidence tends to be anecdotal."

"What there is of it. Even the Samarkan databanks are stingy with the amount of file space they allocate to offworld events. Rich, successful, and powerful, but largely disengaged of late from the businesses where he made his fortune; he should fit in quite well with our neighbors in Kishamkur."

Marym allowed a faint smile to twist her lip. "He seems to make a habit of outraging the authorities from time to time, you may have noticed. Even though he cleared up that string of cult assassinations on Vernier, he was so acerbic about the inequities, as he saw them, in their social system that they couldn't wait to get him off their planet. Confiscated a commercial vessel and had him transported as its sole passenger to the transit terminal at Vorkuta. That sort of reputation probably disqualifies him for citizenship among our elite. They prefer a more placid, less expressive type."

Tiko repeated his previous question. "You don't have to accede to Leskar's wishes, do you? He doesn't have any legal authority here; you paid for this position without his assistance. Why don't you just tell him what he can do with his dilettante friend?"

She laughed. "Tiko, you've been around long enough to know the answer to that. Only properly qualified contenders are allowed to bid for the post of Prefect, even here in Nashamata. Qualifications are judged, and periodically re-evaluated by a review board which consists, in part, of the other Prefects in the city. Leskar's opinion carries what you and I might consider disproportionate weight with some of his colleagues. He has a powerful personality and substantial personal wealth. They could abrogate my contract and probably retain part or all of the fee, particularly if they decided retroactively that I had misrepresented either my abilities or my intentions. There are other ways that they could retaliate as well. You might be correct that Dyle's fee will be hidden in our next budget guidelines, but even if it isn't, Leskar could use his influence to constrict our flow of credit. We're under-equipped and most of what we have is outdated. A reduction, for whatever reason, would only make our jobs more difficult."

"It still seems like you should be able to assert your authority. What good is it to buy an office if you're unable to take advantage of the prerogatives that attend it?"

"Since they're adopting the position that this is technical assistance being provided as a grant to Nashamata, it would be a bit difficult to refuse it gracefully, don't you think? And despite my reservations, it's not as bad as you make it sound. They won't throw their weight around much, or at least not ostentatiously. Leskar is honestly distressed about the death of his son, but not so much that he won't realize how poorly it will reflect on him if it becomes public knowledge that he's using his position to impose his wishes outside of Kishamkur. Rumor has it Zaks wants to retire next year, and Leskar is the only qualified contender wealthy enough to outbid Vascio for the position. Even in his grief, he's not going to jeopardize a chance to be Kudara. No, we'll accept Dyle's assistance and do our best to make him feel as though he's being useful. If through some miraculous leap of intuition he actually makes a useful contribution, I will accept it as providential."

Shifting his weight slightly, Tiko's voice was less bantering as he asked the next question. "How do you plan to handle the offworlder then?"

"What do you mean, handle him?" She allowed the faintest hint of an arch smile to distort her face.

He sighed. "Marym, you know as well as I that an outsider is going to be at a distinct disadvantage here no matter how intelligent he may be. There are aspects of Nashamata that even you and I don't fully understand; for someone who has only been on Tashista for a matter of days, this has to be a bewildering and insuperable problem. I'm not suggesting you obstruct him, of course, but with judicious editing of the information you provide, you could almost certainly ensure his frustration, possibly discourage him enough to cause him to withdraw voluntarily."

Marym tightened her lips. "Tiko, I'm going to pretend I never heard you say that. Whatever our personal feelings about this outside intervention, it is clearly at the behest of the General Council and we are ethically bound to do our best to support their decision. I won't conceal from you that I am offended by the arbitrary fashion in which they acted, and that I doubt this offworlder will provide any material help to the investigation. At worst, he will tie up some of our resources and confuse the issue even further. But if there is any way that he can advance the investigation, then I'll accept his assistance without reservation. There are people being killed out there, Tiko, and we don't have the faintest idea how to stop the person responsible. If it takes an offworlder to identify Scarab, then that's the tool we'll use."

Tiko Parsi did not look properly chastised, but he fell silent, and she chose to interpret that as a positive sign.

* * * * *

At about the same time Prefect Dunnis was arguing with Tiko Parsi, Sandor Dyle was being shown his new living quarters at the Black Ark Hostelry. It was a smaller suite of rooms than had been available in Samarka, the building itself older, less well maintained. Privately, he found it more appealing, less artificial. He had just recently learned to adjust to articulated chairs and still preferred the static ones, and the room contained two very fine examples, both rather ornate for his taste but properly proportioned and quite comfortable. The old fashioned morphless bed was a particularly welcome sight. While sleeping, he preferred that the furniture maintain a constant shape, and it was difficult to disable that function without affecting the bed's other automated features.

"I'm afraid these accommodations are a bit more rustic than those to which you are accustomed, Ser Dyle." Preston Zaks made a disparaging gesture with both hands. "But there is little in the way of tourist traffic to Soshambe, and merchants traveling on business generally stay in the respectable but rather characterless hostels in the Tashamir district."

"It will be more than adequate, I feel certain," he assured his host. The third person present, a middle-aged man with a thick mane of gray hair streaked with white, had crossed the room and was staring out a window, down onto the concourse.

"How will you proceed with your investigation, Ser Dyle?" The third man's voice was hoarse, low, filled with emotion. Zaks glanced thoughtfully toward the speaker, evaluating his tone, posture, and mannerisms. Dylan Leskar had lost a child only days before; petty considerations of custom and comfort were elements of polite conversation which he employed to mask the questions he wanted to ask. The elaborately detached interpersonal relationships prevalent on Tashista offered themselves instinctively to the man, who might otherwise have been too wrought to speak.

"I had hoped you might have some suggestions in that regard, Ser Leskar. Certainly I would like to review the database containing everything known about the cases to date, and perhaps speak to some or all of the investigating officers. After nearly three years of study, I imagine they have developed theories of their own."

Without turning away from the window, Leskar spoke crisply and to the point. "Considering the lack of any concrete results to date, any theories they may have developed seem unlikely to be fruitful. My suggestion would be to review the data objectively and draw your own conclusions. You could hardly do worse than they. I have a technician standing by to provide you access at the highest level whenever it is convenient. I have secured authorization for you to tap into any file maintained by the datanet, other than certain military and political information which is not likely to be relevant. Prefect Dunnis has been advised of your arrival and has been instructed to provide you with any assistance, information, equipment, or staff within her authority. If you need anything beyond her ability to provide, she will contact my office in order to obtain it. If you are in any way dissatisfied with the level of her cooperation, you may contact me directly and I will intercede. Will that be adequate?"

"Probably. You do understand, Prefect Leskar, that I can promise nothing. My talent, if you will, lies chiefly in the detection of patterns. If there are any obvious relationships among these killings, your local programming should already have turned up these correlations. If these were random crimes, there would be no helpful underlying patterns. It seems likely that they are not, that a single individual or group is responsible for most if not all of the murders. The fact that no pattern has emerged during analysis, particularly given the large number of datapoints, is intriguing, to say the least. Analysis programs have their limitations, however, and I may be able to detect tendencies that point to new avenues of investigation. That doesn't necessarily mean that this will be sufficient to ensure apprehension of the guilty party."

This time, Leskar turned toward Sandor, and their eyes met. "Ser Dyle, I have had taken from me the better half of my world. My wife died years ago and I had but the single child. For the first time in my life, I have realized that wealth and power have their limits. I can never regain what I have lost, but I would sacrifice what remains to satisfy myself that the responsible party was punished, do you understand? I will employ any and every tool necessary to do so. I can ask no more than that you do your best. You could hardly accomplish less than those who have preceded you. I have few illusions about the difficulties, and frankly I am not optimistic that you will succeed, but I am not yet entirely without hope. I hope that you will not disappoint me in this."

Sandor bowed slightly to honor the man's obvious grief. "I can only hope that this imperfect tool proves adequate for the task to which it has been set."

"I'm certain there is no question of that, Ser Dyle." But it was Zaks and not Leskar who rushed forward with that assurance. Leskar himself remained silent.

Sandor ignored Zaks, addressing himself to the Prefect. "I suppose it would be politic to get the introductions over with as quickly as possible. I should then prefer to spend the rest of the day familiarizing myself with details of the previous murders. I assume I will be able to do so from this terminal." He indicated a reasonably modern datanet link mounted on the wall in one corner of the room, far too sophisticated to be normal equipment in a minor hostelry such as this. There were fresh scrape marks on the wall indicating a recent installation. One of the two chairs stood directly in front of it.

"That can be arranged immediately." Leskar gestured to Zaks, who walked briskly to the door, opened it to admit a younger man clad in a brilliant yellow smock.

"Level one security clearance," Leskar said crisply. "I will validate when you are ready."

Nodding, the technician sat down without speaking and began running his hands along the iconographic input pad. The screen came to life, passed through several complex displays so quickly that Sandor knew the man was running through familiar sequences without waiting to read and interpret before responding. After a surprisingly short period, the technician rose and spoke deferentially to Leskar.

"If you would stare directly into the recognition field and enter your authorization code, Ser Leskar."

"Yes, yes, I know how to do it." Impatiently, Leskar sat down and pulled forward the articulated arm that terminated with a retinal recognizer and positioned the interface directly in front of his right eye. His fingers moved over the icons but no characters appeared on the screen. Almost immediately, there was a flash of green from the upper righthand corner of the display, followed by a blinking yellow.

As Leskar rose, the technician indicated that Sandor should take his place.

"Annoyingly inconvenient arrangement, Ser Dyle," apologized Leskar. "No doubt you have more civilized ways of handling this offworld."

"Actually, no we don't." He pressed his own right eye against the glass. "And in some cases, our security measures are even more odious."

"You may input your own password, Ser, up to twenty characters in length. Each password is individual and inaccessible even to others with Level One clearance. It will be synchronized automatically with your retinal scan. Any working file you create will be randomly coded unless you specifically transfer it to leveled access."

Sandor entered a series that corresponded to the commercial registration number of the family business back on Hazard. There was a second green flash and the screen cleared. The technician swung the retinal recognizer away and smiled. "That should complete the sequence. May I be of any further assistance?"

"Is this unit capable of responding to voice commands?"

The technician was momentarily nonplused. "Why, yes, as a matter of fact, in both argot and the old tongue. It can respond with synthesized speech as well, with a limited choice of voice profiles."

Sandor made a disgusted sound. "Spare me that; I'll make do with a display. But I'm slow-fingered and lazy. How do I access the vocal initialization sequence?"

"Run procedure Vocal1 for argot, Vocal2 for the old tongue from the utilities command template," he indicated a small, stylized toolbox icon, "and follow the prompts. It's quite self-explanatory."

"I shall manage quite well then. Thank you." He turned toward Leskar. "I see no reason to delay here any further."

Leskar roused himself from what appeared to be a deep reverie. At some point during the last several minutes, Zaks had unobtrusively left the room. "We'll be off then. Zaks has gone to the roof to prepare the lifter. Rolo here," he indicated the young man who now stood awkwardly to one side, lacking further purpose, "will be on call through the host downstairs if you need assistance with the terminal or have any difficulty accessing whatever you need. For that matter, you will be able to reach either myself or Zaks by the same method. The host has been advised of the importance of your mission and has been compensated in advance for whatever special services you might require during your stay. A private lifter has been assigned to you for the duration, a slightly smaller model than the one waiting for us at the moment but hopefully adequate for your purposes."

Sandor touched the disconnect icon and stood up. "Then I believe it's time that I met your fellow Prefect."

* * * * *

"They're on their way down now," Tani's nervousness was audible even through the netlink.

Marym acknowledged the message brusquely and signed to Tiko. "Shape up, Investigator Parsi. Our exalted visitors are about to descend upon us."

Tiko grimaced dramatically, but did make some effort to assume a more alert posture. The door opened a moment later and Marym got her first look at Sandor Dyle.

"Good day to you, Prefect Dunnis. It's been too long since we last talked." Kudara Zaks actually sounded sincere, but Marym was too familiar with the posturing of seasoned politicians to be taken in. A friendly demeanor was just another commodity to be leveraged in such high circles, to be withheld or dispensed depending upon the circumstances, and only after analyzing the potential benefits. Not every exchange of value involved registered credit; some were more ethereal, though no less real. Prefect Leskar made no effort to be pleasant, stood impatiently by while Zaks made the necessary introductions. She felt a tug of sympathy for his loss, but not a sharp enough tug to compensate her for this invasion of her district.

"Ser Dyle, this is Prefect Marym Dunnis, head of the Nashamata Prefecture. Marym, may I present to you Ser Sandor Dyle, who has consented to be coerced into helping with the Scarab killings." The offworlder touched his chest politely with both palms and half bowed in her direction, the latter a custom unknown on Tashista but which she recognized as being common elsewhere. Tiko, who had ostentatiously moved to a position where he could hardly be missed, was nevertheless ignored by Zaks, although Marym noticed that Dyle was eying him out of the corner of one eye.

"I am pleased to meet you, Ser Dyle, and hope that you will find this a challenge worthy of your time. May I introduce to you

Tiko Parsi, who has had primary responsibility for on-site investigation in the latest round of the Scarab killings."

"A thoroughly unpleasant task, I would imagine," Dyle acknowledged.

The social amenities satisfied, Marym invited them all to be seated, but Leskar shook his head. "I'm confident you'll have no difficulty working together, and I doubt my presence will contribute in any material way. I must return to Kishamkur, where other responsibilities await my attendance. Ser Dyle, a lifter and pilot have been provided and attend your convenience above. I will be in touch with you as time permits, but feel free to contact me at any time if you discover anything which might merit my attention, or if there is any additional assistance which you cannot obtain here. Ser Zaks, may I offer you a ride back?"

For a moment, Zaks seemed uncertain whether he wished to remain or not, but finally he smiled and stepped toward Leskar. "As a matter of fact, I don't suppose there is much I can do either, and other work awaits me as well. I will be speaking to you again, Ser Dyle. It was nice to see you again, Marym." And with nods all around, the two aristocrats were gone.

"So," Dyle spoke animatedly, a broad smile splitting his face, "that leaves just the two of you to deal with the overbearing, unwelcome, and possibly troublesome offworlder whose presence has been forced upon you, and whose ill-defined authority and all too evident unfamiliarity with your culture is certain to waste significant amounts of your valuable time. How shall we proceed, Ser Dunnis?"

* * * * *

Mikki Seurat kicked the door shut behind him and set the basket of fresh fruit on the crude table he'd built from the ruins of an old packing crate. "Shayne, it's me," he called out. "I'm home, and I have a surprise for you."

There was no reply from the inner room, the bedroom where his sister had spent the biggest part of the past two years, a situation that was likely to persist for the rest of her life unless Mikki succeeded in his ambition to move them up to Moshamadur. The silence was not unusual; Shayne frequently napped during the day to conserve her strength for those hours when he was home and could keep her company. But ever since his unwelcome discovery of the

dead man in the park, Mikki had placed sinister interpretations upon
any number of unremarkable events. After all, when the Scarab killer
prowled the streets of Nashamata, there was no way to guarantee
anyone's safety. The previous year, one of the victims had been a
subprefect on night patrol; if the Prefecture itself was vulnerable,
what ordinary citizen stood a chance?

Slowly, cautiously, he edged toward the bedroom door,
telling himself that nothing was really amiss, that it was all just a
case of an overactive imagination, that he was worrying himself
needlessly and should just call out again, loudly enough to rouse her.
He reached the edge of the doorway, which had slid partly but not
completely shut, touched the pressure plate which caused it to slide
into its recess in the inner wall. His heart thudded in his chest, an
audible beat, there was pressure against his lungs, making it more
and more difficult to breathe. Cursing his own faint heartedness, he
stepped boldly into the room.

One outflung arm dangled down the side of the bed, the
slightly curled fingers just brushing the eversoft flooring. The
bedclothes were flung to one side in chaotic disarray, the long,
slender, nearly atrophied legs crossed one over the other as her torso
lay twisted at an awkward angle on one side. His breath catching, he
stepped closer to the bed, just as she opened her eyes.

"Oh, Mikki. It *was* you. I thought I was dreaming." She
glanced up at the pattern of light splayed against the wall of her
bedroom from the single large window. "You're home early. Is
something wrong?"

When the two of them had moved into this housing complex,
Shayne had fallen so completely in love with the way the light fell
through the faceted window that it had been a foregone conclusion
that this was where she would sleep. There was a second window, on
the adjoining wall, which had originally been meant only to provide
light, since it faced directly toward the featureless rear wall of a
small warehouse. But fire had gutted the building a year earlier, and
once the wreckage was cleared away, the view was actually quite
pleasant. If one stood in the right spot, it was possible to gaze down
through the open space between two small shops, across a busy
traverseway erected above a small series of ornamental gardens
which were maintained on an erratic basis by some of the local
residents. Shayne insisted that she felt less lonely if she could see

others, even if they were strangers and at a distance, and she spent hours watching the endless traffic on the traverseway. Despite her physical problems she refused to surrender to despair, and if she felt sorry for herself from time to time, these moods were generally concealed from him. But living as she did in a very narrowly circumscribed world, she knew every aspect of it in great detail, and telling the time by examining the pattern of light on the wall was one of the least remarkable.

"No, nothing's wrong. In fact, I have a present for you. Wait right here," he admonished her unnecessarily. "I'll just be a moment."

He hurried back to the other room and approached the basket, thinking for a moment before choosing a pale green fruit with a smooth but highly irregular surface. Smiling with satisfaction, he shifted it behind his back, intending to make her guess the nature of his gift, but when he returned to her room, she was sitting up, legs over the side of the bed, so obviously anticipatory that he relented and showed her his prize without a word.

"A yuba fruit! I haven't seen one of those since you found the ones that fell off the Tashi transport last year." He had actually stolen the fruit on that occasion, having noticed a poorly secured strap at the rear of the cargopod. She accepted it from him with unusual animation, turning it slowly as she switched it from hand to hand, running the pads of her fingers over its smooth skin.

"Well this one I actually paid for, and there are three more out in the other room for you."

Shayne's face fell. "I don't understand. Just because I don't go out very often doesn't mean that I don't know how much yuba fruit costs. We can't afford that much credit." She held the fruit out to him. "Maybe you can sell it down on the esplanade."

He shook his head, smiling but also serious. "Don't worry. We're not rich yet, but I've earned more credit today than I did all last secant. We can afford a small treat for ourselves. I even bought some stale kurilic pastries."

Her face betrayed complete confusion. "But how?" She frowned suddenly. "You're not mixed up with one of the underway gangs, are you, or anything else dangerous?"

He raised his hands, palms out, and shook his head quickly. "No, no. I told you I don't work for the gangs any more." Which wasn't true, but he didn't work for them exclusively. "Don't worry about anything. Everything is all right. It's just that I'm suddenly a celebrity, sort of. Datanews sent someone down to talk to me about, you know, what I found, and I was smart enough to make him hand over hard credit before I said a word. I've stashed it already, so I can't show you, but it was a lot. Even after buying the food and paying off the money we owe Cerdas, I still put away almost a full forty units."

Shayne's eyes opened wide. "Forty units! Why would they pay you so much? You didn't even see anything really."

He shrugged. "I don't know. Datanews doesn't come down into Nashamata very much. Maybe this is the going rate in Moshamadur and they just paid it automatically, or maybe it's because the guy I found was related to one of the Hierata. I don't know and I don't care. I wouldn't have asked half that much if they'd told me to name a price, so it was a good thing I kept my mouth shut and let them do the talking. But add that to the finder's fee from the Prefect, and I wish I could stumble onto a body more often. A few more days like this, and we'll have enough to qualify for soft credit."

Looking distinctly alarmed, Shayne pushed herself unsteadily up from the bed and reached for her cane. Mikki resisted the temptation to get it for her; she preferred to hang onto what small independence was still available to her. "Don't even think that, Mikki. Every time you go out lately, particularly at night, I feel this tiny tremor inside me that says this might be the very last time I ever see you. I know it's silly and I should just ignore it, but until the end of this Secant, I won't be able to rest easy while you're gone. Maybe now that you've made so much hard credit, you can stay home for a while. At least until the killings stop."

Mikki sighed. "It's tempting, Shayne, but I can't. You know that. If I let up at all, if I start to find excuses not to go out and hustle the next credit, then our reserves will stop growing and we'll never get out of this place. My regulars will find someone else to run their messages. You deserve a better life, Shayne, and I'm responsible for you. I'm going to see that you get it."

Her mouth tightened. "I'm as happy right now as I need to be, Mikki. Even if we move to Moshamadur, I'll still be confined to a room. It might be a bigger room, and I might be able to eat yuba fruit and kurilic pastries and hurum fish and every delicacy to be found in Tashamir, but my world still won't be any bigger than it is now. And I'm afraid that if we do get there, you'll have to work even harder to keep up, and I'll see you less often than I do now. Why can't we just make a place here? I'm happy most of the time; I don't need anything else."

It was a discussion they had had before and Mikki had no good answer. He became confused and short tempered whenever she questioned his outline of their future. Surely she could see that the whole purpose of life was to better one's standard of living, to advance, to escape the stifling poverty and hopelessness of Nashamata. Accepting one's personal status quo was a kind of premature termination to life, a living death, a surrender to the forces of inertia in a society that abhorred immobility.

"Look, let's not talk about it right now. We're celebrating, remember? We don't have many chances for that, so let's not waste the one we've got."

She looked dubious for a moment, but finally allowed a slow smile to spread over her features. "Sure, sounds good. Want some?" She had split the two lobes of the yuba apart and was holding one out.

"No, go ahead. I'm already having my treat."

* * * * *

Elsewhere in the city, a cloaked figure moved covertly through the less popular traverseways, seeking opportunity. Patiently it evaluated and discarded one potential prey after another. There was no sense of urgency, no compulsion to act precipitately. The Secant of the Scarab had barely begun and there were many nights remaining, many nights in which to hunt.

The casual observer would not have noticed anything unusual. The cloak was of a common design, showing only moderate signs of wear, so voluminous that it masked sex and shape as well as identity. Someone unusually curious might have taken notice if the weather had been fair, but it was a cold night and the wind was impertinently disrespectful of class distinctions, buffeting the rich as well as the poor. The figure followed a path that was at times unnecessarily circuitous, skirting the better monitored intersections, sometimes taking advantage of a malfunctioning surveillance camera to cross a better lighted area, but no casual observer would have realized that there was a pattern to its progress.

Soshambe was not the kind of city where people were rewarded for taking interest in others. When self interest is the highest virtue, casual curiosity becomes a handicap. In Soshambe, handicaps were a source of shame because, after all, rising above one's limitations to accumulate material wealth was the entire purpose of human life. What other goal could one rationally aspire to reach?

Chapter Four

Marym was the first to respond to Sandor's unsettling question, and her reaction was to laugh with quite genuine amusement. "Is that meant as a demonstration of your powers of perception, Ser Dyle? Or is it just your way of dealing with ruffled dignities at the first opportunity?"

"Primarily the latter, an effort to clear the air immediately. It doesn't require any extraordinary talent to realize that I've been forced upon you over your objections. I've been in variations of this situation before, Prefect Dunnis. I am inevitably viewed as an imposition at best, an outright hindrance and unnecessary diversion of resources more commonly, sometimes even as a rival or as a symbol of official displeasure from above."

"And which of these many roles applies to you on this occasion?"

Sandor sighed. "It is possible that I may be able to help; it is equally possible that I will fail utterly and all the time and resources I consume will be lost to you for no purpose. I hope for the former outcome, of course, but I guarantee nothing. Pattern recognition is as much an art as a science, which is the primary reason why artificial intelligences do so poorly. They are constrained to thinking logically and in discrete, cumulative steps. The human mind, on the other hand, is capable of making leaps of logic, which we call intuition. No criminal, indeed no sustained human activity, is devoid of patterns, you see, and by identifying and interpreting these patterns, we can often trace them back to their origin."

Her smile faded. "We employ pattern analysis on Tashista, Ser Dyle. I have studied the art myself, and my predecessor was an acknowledged expert."

"I apologize for my tendency to lecture, Prefect. I did not mean to imply that you were an uneducated rustic. And I'm sure that you are aware that some patterns are culturally invisible. On the only occasion where I attempted to solve a puzzle on my home world, I failed, and it may well be for that reason. But here I am a disinterested, reasonably objective outsider, and that may give me a subtle advantage. I am an admitted dilettante but not a glory seeker. I am not interested in receiving public recognition. In fact, if it turns out that I am able to assist you, I would prefer to remain in the background."

"Did Leskar warn you that I might be touchy?" Marym's hackles rose. If Dyle patronized her, she would throw him out of her office, regardless of the consequences.

He sighed. "I know little about your relationship with Prefect Leskar; they described you as competent but perhaps faced with a situation too complex for you to solve without neglecting your other duties."

"Is the tactful phrasing yours or theirs?" Marym knew her tone was offensive, sensitive as she always was on this subject.

"A little of both. You seem to be something of an unknown quantity to your associates. It might be worth pointing out that Prefect Leskar feels that the Scarab killings are beyond his own capacity as well. If it were otherwise, he might have intervened personally. For what it's worth, I think he honestly wants to help and that his opinion of your skills is fairly high. His estimation of the talents of our mutual antagonist is rather higher."

For a few seconds, Marym struggled internally, finally decided to relax, though guardedly. "The truth is, we are no closer to a solution now than we were after the first killing. Any advice or assistance you might be able to provide would be welcome, Ser Dyle, I mean that. My ego is unbruised by your presence, but I do resent diverting resources to support you, particularly because your offworld origin presents additional handicaps. Despite your admittedly impressive reputation I just don't see how you can hope to pick anything out of the data that we haven't seen ourselves. We do have competent pattern analysts and Savram, who was Prefect before me, consulted with several offworld experts for the very reasons you have mentioned."

"I expected no less," Sandor smiled broadly. "But each analyst is bound by his or her own preconceptions, blind spots if you will, myself included. I am sympathetic to your concerns, however, and will endeavor to be as little trouble as possible."

She nodded. "It would be churlish of me to resist such a tactfully phrased offer. I understood you to be a professional trader, Ser Dyle, but you have the bearing of a diplomat."

Dyle chuckled. "The two are more similar than you might at first think. And if it is not a violation of some cultural norm of which

I am not aware, I would prefer Sandor to Ser Dyle. I find that formalities such as that interfere with understanding, and it is also contrary to my upbringing. Hazard has a very informal society; the planet is subject to violent storms and other natural dangers and the first few generations grew very close, a tradition which has lingered into the present. And I am as much a product of my background as you are of yours."

After a pause, she nodded. "It would be out of the ordinary, but I suppose the entire situation is out of the ordinary. You may call me Marym."

Sandor turned his head toward Tiko, who had remained silently perplexed during the interchange.

"Tiko, my name is Tiko, Ser Dyle." Rebel though he might be in his chosen way, Tiko found this sudden familiarity very unsettling. He and Marym hadn't begun using their first names until they'd known each other for more than a year.

"How do you wish to proceed?" Marym felt the tension slowly subsiding now that they had moved on to the case itself. "I understand you've been provided full access to the datanet." She didn't conceal her envy; even as Prefect she was only up to amber level. "Presumably you've already run through our findings to date, meager though they are."

"Actually, I've been rushed about so rapidly these past few hours, I have only the most general understanding of the situation. A broad overview would be very helpful, if you please. Ser Leskar's account was rather vague, and I would prefer some context into which to fit the few facts I possess before examining the specific data you've collected. Any undocumented theories and particularly any negative information not in the official record would be of particular interest to me. It often happens that the pattern is more readily visible in the data that is not present than in that which is."

She nodded, sat back comfortably in her chair. "Tiko, if I leave out anything important, break in whenever you wish." But Marym had been over the sequence so many times in her mind, she doubted it would be necessary.

"Two years ago, on the fourth night of Scarab Secant, a young man was murdered in the harbor area, his body mutilated horribly and concealed in an empty crate. It was not actually discovered until two days later; a sailor became curious when he noticed several of the local skitters sniffing around the container with unusual interest, apparently attracted by the smell." When Sandor raised an eyebrow, she explained. "Skitters are small carrion eaters, indigenous. Originally they were no bother because they couldn't metabolize the protein forms we introduced to the world, but eventually they mutated and they're so firmly rooted in our cities that we can't exterminate them."

"What were the nature of the mutilations?"

Marym looked uncomfortable. "The hands and feet were severed from the body. The jaw was shattered. There were multiple blunt object wounds scattered over the torso and what remained of the limbs, but most of these were apparently inflicted after the death of the victim. So was the disembowelment."

"Were the wounds cauterized?"

"No, he didn't use a laser. The dismemberments were done with a thick, short bladed weapon, probably a hand axe of some sort. That was true of the first victim and all those that followed."

"What was the actual cause of death?"

She raised her eyes and locked onto his, speaking steadily. "A metal implement of some undetermined nature was driven through the sexual organs and into the lower abdomen, causing massive internal bleeding, but that only occurred after the limbs had been severed."

"Impalement," Sandor said simply.

"That's technically correct, although the intrusive device was removed from the scene. We know of what alloy it was made from traces found in the wounds, but it's in quite common usage. The shape indicates a thin, narrow implement, razor sharp. The muscles were cleanly severed, no tearing, and the bones split and separated under terrific pressure. In one or two cases, it appears that the perpetrator required two tries to finish the job, but never more than that. He's not a weakling or he's using some mechanical device, possibly a prosthetic. If that was the case, the individual wielding the weapon need not even have been particularly powerful; a child would have had sufficient strength armed with such an effective blade and a pressure glove or similar augmentation. An adult male might even have been able to do it unassisted. The wounds bore strong resemblances to several historical cases and initially we suspected that the Sharith were making a comeback."

Sandor looked puzzled. "I don't recognize that name."

"You wouldn't run into in the ordinary course of events, even if you were Tashistan. They don't exist any more. How much do you know about Nashamata, about the underways?"

Crossing his arms, he sat back and gathered his thoughts. "You refer to the levels below the traverseways, the lower city as it is sometimes called. I know that it's the dwelling place of the poorest of your citizenry, and the openly criminal class." He smiled sardonically. "The socially acceptable lawbreakers are less predictable in their living arrangements."

Allowing the implied criticism to pass unremarked, she pursued her original question. "And the gangs? What have you heard about them? Do you understand how they operate?"

"Only in the most superficial manner. In Samarka, they consist primarily of young adults who are either frustrated by their inability to move up the economic ladder, or too lazy to do so, at least by conventional means. They group together into tightly knit organizations, stake out territory, and derive what income they can by terrorizing the inhabitants. It's not an uncommon pattern, I'm sad to say."

"That's all true as far as it goes. Most citizens of Nashamata are associated with one gang or another, even if they aren't openly members. A street vendor without protection from one of the gangs couldn't do business even in his home district, let alone peddle goods elsewhere. There are occasional battles, often about territory, sometimes just as recreation. Individual gangs come and go, but an equilibrium is maintained. They are in at least one sense the stabilizing element in Nashamata. They provide an underlying structure."

"And this has forced the authorities into an accommodation, I take it."

"Absolutely, but little force was necessary. The anarchy which would result from an absence of social structure would present problems with which the city is not equipped to deal. Keep in mind the fact that two-thirds of the city's population lives in Nashamata. If the gangs didn't exist, we would be compelled to go out and organize them or their equivalent. With the resources available to the Prefecture, we could never maintain simple order, let alone investigate crimes. There are nearly half a million people living in Nashamata, and my entire department consists of forty individuals, six of whom are clerical or support. For the most part, the gangs arbitrate disputes among themselves or their clients. If one or another group steps out of line, they either take care of it themselves or on rare occasions anonymously advise us of the situation. The Sharith wanted to change all that; they tried to unite the gangs into a single hierarchal power structure, under their leadership, of course.

"We never did learn exactly who was involved. The Sharith's membership seems to have spanned several of the underway gangs, a secret cabal of a dozen prominent figures according to some reports, trying to establish themselves as a governing body. They concealed their identities while engaging in an assassination program that lasted almost two full years and claimed scores of lives. They would kidnap an obstreperous gang leader or member, cut off both hands and both feet, and impale the victim. There were fifteen attacks that we know of, rumors of several others. None of the victims survived to identify their assailants."

"When did all of this take place?"

"It ended about four years ago; we don't know exactly why. Rumor has it that the Sharith themselves split into factions, and that several of the last victims were in fact members of the inner circle. Once the Sharith were neutralized, the rest of the gangs became less willing to share information with us, so we don't really know much about the aftermath. Things appeared to return to the normal uneasy peace."

"This new killing, it followed the Sharith pattern?"

"Up to a point. The Sharith left their victims impaled; Scarab removed whatever device was used and took it away. We know the blade is at least half a meter in length, but it's probably something that could be concealed easily under a cloak, or just disguised as some ordinary object. There are numerous possibilities."

"But no rumors of the Sharith re-emerging?"

"None," Tiko interrupted. "I have a cousin who runs with the Klerish. None of the gangs seem to be involved; there aren't even any credible rumors to that effect. Those we've managed to question insist they're as much in the dark as we are, and we're pretty sure they're telling the truth. No threats have been made against the gangs, and there's been no effort we can detect to assert any kind of authority over the underways. Most of the victims weren't gang members to start with."

"There are two other significant differences in the Scarab murders," resumed Marym. "All of the Sharith killings were of gang members; Scarab strikes in what appears to be a totally random fashion. Itinerants, merchants, the elderly, gang members, artisans, indolents, even one of our subprefects. Leskar's son just happened to be in the wrong place at the wrong time. If there is any unified purpose behind the killings, it seems unrelated to any gang rivalries. There have been no taunting messages to the authorities and no actual physical evidence. Scarab is efficient, thorough, and careful. He seems to know what we'll be looking for and he takes countermeasures."

"And the other difference? You said there were two."

"Scarab introduces nemesol into the bodies of his victims. Are you familiar with its properties? We import it from offworld."

Frowning with concentration, Sandor searched through dusty shelves of memory. "Wasn't that an experimental drug that was developed by the Kascar Medicants? It was in use briefly before some rather unpleasant side effects were discovered."

Marym nodded. "They were looking for something that would dramatically slow the metabolism of terminally ill patients. It worked after a fashion, but the side effects were, as you said, occasionally unpleasant. Introduction of nemesol into the bloodstream causes temporary paralysis and a marked slowing of normal metabolic processes, but it does not render the patient unconscious. In fact, it seems to inhibit the brain's ability to change from one state to the other. It is still in use, primarily by hunters seeking to capture live prey, because of its almost instantaneous effect and its effectiveness on a broad range of metabolic systems."

Sandor's mind was already ahead of her. "Scarab immobilizes his victims with the drug before killing them?"

She nodded. "Even worse. He does it before mutilating them. They are probably conscious until at or near the moment of death, although it's unlikely that they experience much actual pain."

Frowning deeply, Sandor interlaced the fingers of his hands and brought them to rest against his chest. "Do you see any link at all then between Scarab and the Sharith?"

"I think it's too close to be coincidental. The two favored theories are that Scarab is a surviving member of Sharith on a killing spree for reasons, sane or insane, of which we have not a hint, or that he has merely borrowed their methods, improving them slightly, because of the terrible impact the original killings had on Nashamata. If that's his intention, he's succeeded. The terror the Sharith generated seems almost placid compared to the current unrest."

"And why do you think he strikes only within Nashamata?"

"That should be obvious," Tiko spat out the words venomously. "Scarab could only elude capture for so long in this quarter."

Marym nodded. "Proportionately, Moshamadur and Tashamir have six times the personnel and ten times the budget in their Prefectures. Kishamkur has twenty times the manpower and a hundred times the budget. Flittercams cover better than ninety percent of the public ways in Kishamkur, fifty percent in the other two districts, less than ten percent here."

"When they work," muttered Tiko.

"Yes, when they work. The gangs don't like surveillance, even under the present circumstances. Shooting flittercams out of the air is an old sport in Nashamata, and fixed cams are so easy to circumvent, we don't even install them except for traffic surveillance."

"So you really don't have any online monitoring of the district?"

She shrugged. "The few operating flittercams we have are rotated around the city on a regular, though confidentially coded, basis. We're currently monitoring just under five percent of the public ways. That stacks the odds in Scarab's favor about twenty to one."

Sandor nodded. "I understand the situation, I believe. Still, after twenty-seven killings, I'm surprised pure mischance hasn't worked in your favor."

"It almost did; we nearly captured Scarab on one occasion. It was the third murder that first year, before the killer had even acquired a nickname." She paused, remembering. "The second victim had already been discovered, an elderly destitute who'd taken to sleeping in the Lucharist Society garden. I had just been transferred here from Olamphos as an investigator, reporting to Prefect Aras. We were together at the time, about to return to Moshamadur for the night, when the call came in."

"Return to Moshamadur?" Sandor raised his eyebrows.

"To our homes. It was late at night, you understand."

"But don't you live here in Nashamata? I thought this was your district?"

Marym appeared genuinely perplexed. "Any citizen with the funds to purchase a Prefect's post could easily afford Moshamadur, Sandor."

"Ah, yes," he nodded, realizing that on Tashista, few would live in a quarter lower than the highest which they could afford. "I had forgotten. Do you also live in Moshamadur?" He had addressed his remark to Tiko.

"Not yet," the man admitted, plainly uncomfortable. "I spent an injudicious youth, wasted much of the time and effort which would have bettered my circumstances. Wisdom after a fashion has come with maturity, however, and I hope to relocate within two years."

Sandor turned back to Marym. "Your pardon for interrupting, Marym, but it is important that I understand as much as possible about your social customs if I am to be of any help."

"I'm sure you wouldn't ask a question for no purpose, Sandor, so don't apologize. Prefect Aras had offered me a ride back home, as I mentioned, and we had just lifted when a flittercam alarm indicated an attack near Bodanga Concourse, which is only a short distance from here. Savram, that's Prefect Aras, responded immediately, setting us down quite skillfully in the intersection of Bodanga and Esplana. We moved immediately to the reported attack site, a storage yard, unfortunately entering from the wrong side. Scarab and his victim were at the opposite end. We were seen and although we both fired, there was no evidence that either of us caused him any hurt. Scarab escaped into the darkness, and we were too late to save the victim; he died while the medilift was landing."

"The victim was . . ?"

"A small time thief, as a matter of fact, though not officially a gang member as far as we could ascertain. A freelancer only recently arrived in the city. We speculated that he had been searching the storage yard in search of worthwhile pilferage when Scarab spotted him."

"The flittercam could not follow him then?"

She shook her head. "Even with direct control from the monitoring station, that degree of sophistication is unavailable to us. We could follow a fast walk; anything more is beyond our capability. And there were entrances to the underways within a few meters. Scarab could have eluded us without difficulty even had we been much better equipped."

"Did you conduct the subsequent investigation?"

"No, Prefect Aras took personal charge of the Scarab killings until the end of last year when illness forced his resignation."

"Is that normal? For a Prefect to take personal charge of a crime investigation, I mean."

"No, but this was not an ordinary situation. The crimes were quite brutal and had started to generate severe public criticism. I think also that Savram was deeply frustrated by our own near-miss, and was at the time looking for some emotional anchor in his life. He was known to sleep in his office chair some nights rather than expend time traveling to and from his home."

"His illness had become a serious liability by then, I imagine."

"Yes. Suratic nerve disease is ultimately fatal and completely unpredictable. Under normal circumstances, he would have been forcibly retired immediately, even though the debilitating effects did not begin to show up until the following year. He had earned a great deal of respect here, however, for his many years of devotion to his duties. The tragic loss of his family was also a factor that generated public support for his continuation in office. We're not an entirely heartless society." She met his eyes directly but Dyle thought he saw a flash of something there. Defensiveness? Guilt?

"I never thought any such thing," he assured her not entirely truthfully. "I was told that I might be able to interview Prefect Aras at some point."

"Oh, yes." She brightened noticeably. "He would be very pleased to feel that he was contributing to the investigation. His illness is intermittent and he still has periods when his mind is as fertile as ever. Although he has no official standing, we have allowed him to maintain his security access, on a read-only basis, of course. He reviews our cases regularly and sends along advice from time to time, often quite helpful. He is always willing to entertain visitors, now that he can no longer move about freely."

"He is confined, then?"

"For the most part," she responded quietly, obviously saddened. "He was such a vital man, as well as brilliant. I believe he planned to bid against Leskar for the Kishamkur Prefecture eventually, and that might have been good for Nashamata as well. He often complained that more credit should be diverted to the underways, that we should do more to encourage the economic mobility of the population. But his illness causes portions of his brain to . . . operate erratically. There are occasional lapses of memory, sometimes sensory input is confused, and for the past year, he has been unable to stand unassisted, although his legs are perfectly healthy. Apparently the portion of his brain which directs those muscles is affected. Not even his physicians know exactly what is wrong. The brain is still the organ of the body about which we know the least."

"So none of the subsequent crimes were witnessed by anyone?"

"Not to our knowledge." She gave him a brief summary of the eight additional crimes which had taken place that first year, each involving the use of nemesol: the severed hands and feet, impalement, and the severe battering of the body following death.

"How was the nemesol introduced into the bodies of the victims?"

"Hypodart. Standard equipment used by the herders of the Beatic Valley. Hundreds, perhaps thousands of such devices are available on Tashista, unregistered, untraceable."

"And nemesol itself?"

"Sold openly in Tashamir and through the Beatic regions. I imagine it would be sold here in Nashamata as well if there was any use for it."

"Does it deteriorate with age?"

"Only if exposed to the air. Sealed capsules could have a shelf life of years, decades in fact. We wouldn't have been able to trace it back in any case; nemesol is not a controlled substance, although perhaps it should be. There are and were no records kept as to who might have purchased it. We've subsequently instituted clandestine controls on the legal sale of the drug, but there are so many unofficial sources . . ." She spread her hands dramatically and shook her head. "Even a clumsy criminal could evade our precautions. Scarab would not even be inconvenienced to do so."

Dyle hesitated for several seconds, tapping his chin with the end of one forefinger. "And the killings stopped with the end of the season?"

"Absolutely. That first year, we didn't even refer to the killer as Scarab. The name came into use with the resumption of the deaths on the very first day of the Scarab Secant the following year. I'm not sure who originated it; it just seemed to fit."

"Were there any changes in the killer's methods the second year?"

"None which were perceptible to us, nor this year either, except for the unfortunate identity of this last victim."

"Did Prefect Aras change his approach during the second cycle of murders?"

"He attempted to. On several occasions, he traveled to Kishamkur seeking assistance, the loan of personnel, financing. Petitioned the Kudara as well. There was in fact a small increase in flittercam coverage that year, although at least part of that was from funds Savram donated personally." She sighed. "I wanted the position of Prefect badly, Sandor, but not in this quarter, particularly not if it meant replacing a man like Aras. But his illness was progressing noticeably last year. He became incoherent from time to time, his attention wandered, and the paralysis of his legs had begun, first just a slight numbness, finally an almost complete loss of feeling. He held on until the second series of murders ended, determined to outwit Scarab as his final official act. When the secant changed and it was clear the killings had stopped, he shrank into himself and seemed almost to welcome retirement."

"That's when you were appointed?"

"That's when I was certified and closed the deal, yes."

"And have you continued to direct the investigation personally from your office?"

"No, not in the way Savram did. He became so obsessed with stopping Scarab, he allowed the other affairs of the Prefecture to slide slowly into disarray. Even during the other secants, he remained preoccupied and distracted, although his illness was obviously a contributing factor. Tiko is officially heading the Scarab investigation, although I naturally maintain a very close liaison with him."

"Not that there's much we can do," Tiko sounded defensive. "There are never any witnesses, no clues that provide real help. If we do capture or kill Scarab, it's likely to be because of sheer luck, good on our part or bad on his, or hers."

"All of your findings have been entered into the datanet?"

"Interviews, examination of the bodies, background checks of each victim, surveillance reports of the crime areas preceding discovery of the body—such as they are, theories, ideas that didn't work out, our attempts to trace the nemesol, analysis of the metal traces from the murder weapon, intensive undercover work among the gangs. You name it, it's in the net. If you can find a pattern, I'll be the first to applaud, but I'll also be very, very surprised."

Sandor's eyes twinkled. "Actually, there are visible patterns already, but I assume you meant ones which would provide clues about the identity of the murderer."

Tiko's eyes clouded, but almost immediately cleared. "Oh, you mean the details of the murder themselves, the amputations and impalement, the use of nemesol."

"As well as the fact that each crime took place within the limits of Nashamata, always in a public place or one with easy general access. The victims were always alone, weren't they? There were no cases in which a companion was incapacitated while the murder took place?"

Marym shook her head. "Not unless the second party recovered and fled the scene without making a report."

"The murders all took place within the Secant of the Scarab. In each case, posthumous damage was inflicted upon the body. Within the mind of your killer there is a plan. It might be an insane one by our standards, probably is as a matter of fact, but the facts we have just enumerated indicate that these incidents are a part of a conscious thought process, and where that exists, there is also a controlling pattern. Once we have detected that pattern, we can predict in limited but accurate fashion the perpetrator's future actions. Even those aspects that appear random, such as the choice of victim, must fall into a pattern, however obscure, and if we can identify it, we can anticipate Scarab's activities. That is how we will solve this problem."

"If we can find the controlling pattern," Marym appended.

"When we find it, Marym. It's there for us to see if we have the wit to perceive it. Each of us has a psychological blueprint that dictates how we behave, a behavioral structure that we can mask but not alter. It's part of what makes us human."

She sighed. "Sometimes I'm not entirely convinced that Scarab *is* human."

* * * * *

Night in Nashamata was lonely in a sense known in few non-Tashistan cities. It was expensive to operate a business at night; lights required payment of credit. The traffic level dropped off sharply, and during the less pleasant secants, when chill rain or high winds plagued the traveler, the traverseways were nearly empty. The public transit system in the underways was theoretically free, subsidized by metropolitan taxes. It was the closest thing to equitable treatment in city services that the people of Nashamata received and was even maintained at a relatively high degree of reliability and comfort. It was ironic then that so few used it. After the fall of darkness, most Nashamatans left their homes for only one of two reasons—gang business, or to add to their concealed stashes of hard credit while unobserved. The tubecars themselves were closely monitored and virtually immune to crime; the accessways leading to them were among the most dangerous places in the city.

Akim Tutellatis finished counting the hard credit in his condata and smiled with satisfaction. Before the end of the secant, he would be in a position to open a soft credit line. The fees would wipe out the normal growth for the first year, but after that, if he continued to accumulate fresh credit at his usual rate, he would begin to build a base that would allow him to invest a portion of his wealth in the Tashamir Solvency or perhaps buy a share of cargo on one of the trading vessels running out of Port Tash. He was at the point in his life where he could no longer think of himself as a young man, and if he was ever going to raise the credit to make the move to Moshamadur, he would have to do it soon.

He returned his condata to the stone-lined hole in the soil which he had excavated one night nearly a year ago, then carefully moved the intact sessua plant back into place, patting the soil carefully to cover the roots he had exposed while digging it up, then smoothing the surface of the ground, redistributing twigs, fallen leaves, and other detritus to disguise the fact that anything out of the ordinary might be found here.

The Teratorium was deserted, as it usually was this late in the evening. Because it was exposed to the open air, the hordes of homeless Nashamatans eschewed its use as a sleeping ground during the cold and rainy months, preferring instead the sheltered underways. They possessed nothing worth the trouble to steal and were generally ignored by the gangs. When the weather began to turn cold this year, Akim had decided to search for a new condata; once the ground was frozen, it would be far too difficult to gain access to his horde, and a temporary second condata doubled the chance that it would be discovered by someone else. Straightening up, he brushed a few grains of soil off his shirt and trousers, glancing around nervously to assure himself that he was unobserved.

He failed to notice the unmoving figure leaning against the side of a steelcrete pylon, part of the understructure of the traverseway above. Surface vehicular traffic was not exactly forbidden within Soshambe, but the only citizens who could afford private transport dwelled in Kishamkur, and they had few reasons to visit Nashamata, even during the day. The concealed figure had approached along the overway, paused to gaze down into the Teratorium, descending only when assured that the man below was alone.

Akim moved quietly toward the southern exit, which angled away from the one who watched. The latter was motionless for another moment, evaluating potentialities, then slipped back and away, moving along the line of pylons, not hurrying but wasting no time either. When Akim reached the exit and stepped out onto the small pedway that led down toward the underways, his unsuspected companion had reached the outer wall of the structure and was moving along its perimeter.

The two figures proceeded through Nashamata, one following the other, as Akim unknowingly led the way down the convoluted pedway to the wider eastern Bodanga concourse below. The buildings on every side were silent, windows blacked out, residents either sleeping or sitting in the darkness watching the evening's holonet programs. Lighting was not one of the city's limited free services, and there were few in this portion of the city willing to expend unnecessary credit for the luxury of illumination. Akim continued across the concourse, then took the middle of three traverseways that spread out and gently downward toward the lowermost levels of the surface city where there was access to the underways.

Scarab followed his prospective prey doggedly, sometimes allowing the gap to close slightly, sometimes falling back when there was danger of discovery. Twice possible opportunities to strike were aborted, the first time when a pair of late-night strollers appeared unexpectedly, the second when Akim began singing softly to himself, unconsciously fooling his pursuer into believing he was speaking to a third party.

Akim reached the entrance to the underways a few minutes later. A high arched opening, one of many access points in this section of the city, led into the enclosed but fairly well illuminated maze of corridors and vestibules. An enormous elevated screen flashed messages so quickly that it was difficult to read them: advertisements, public service announcements, news flashes, tubecar schedules, and such. It was a general access bulletin board, used by businessmen, philanthropists, and exhibitionists alike. Pausing inside, as if undecided where to go next, actually torn between the desire to go home for the evening or use some of his remaining hard credit for a late night meal, Akim was unaware of the pressure of eyes on his back, eyes which scanned the area, alert to possible danger, seeking an opportunity to strike. Ahead, a solitary traveler was climbing into a tubecar, punching his destination into the control system even as the door dilated shut. His vehicle was whisked off into the main travel corridor within seconds.

The figure known as Scarab stepped through the arch into the underway, moving off to one side silently but taking pains not to appear furtive as he carefully remained outside the scanning range of the surveillance device mounted near the ceiling. In one corner, still watching as Akim scanned the sign, Scarab removed a very uncommon device from within the heavy cloak's interior pocket, unfolding it to reveal a small datanet screen. Entering a code, Scarab examined the display for several seconds before nodding briefly, deactivating the device, and returning it to its hiding place. When Scarab glanced back toward Akim, it was almost too late; he had entered one of the pedestrian tunnels and was headed southeast toward a junction where he expected to find inexpensive food vendors, a compromise between his stomach and his wallet.

With a soft curse, Scarab moved to follow, entering the mouth of the tunnel. The sound of Akim's footsteps was distant but distinct, each impact echoing in the confined space, and his pursuer was able to move to within a few meters in a surprisingly short time.

Scarab fired the dart as Akim was passing a series of currently abandoned stalls, occasionally used by entrepreneurs who bought low quality foods in Tashamir, subsequently marked up for resale within Nashamata. Scarab was confident that the high velocity projectile with its long, firm shaft would pierce the other man's clothing and enter his body without hindrance. The dart struck, and his quarry spun halfway around, one hand rising, but conscious control of his muscles escaped Akim almost instantly, and the turn became a slow, graceless fall to the pavement. Even before Akim had come to rest, Scarab was running forward, replacing the hypogun in the cloak. Scarab grasped the prone man by the upper arms, dragging him out of the walkway and through an opening into the closest of the stalls. It took only a few seconds to obstruct the entrance with some discarded packaging materials before turning to examination of the paralyzed victim.

Akim's eyes were wide open, bright, filled with confusion, but moved alertly when he was rolled over onto his back. His assailant's face was obscured by the hood of the black cloak. Nodding with satisfaction, Scarab rearranged the man's limbs to provide easy access to each, then reached inside the cloak once again, this time bringing forth two implements which were set down beside one inert thigh. The first was a double-faced tool, a heavy iron mallet on one side, a flat bladed ax on the other. The second was a highly sharpened plasteel spike with a set of finger grips mounted on the blunt end.

* * * * *

No one will ever know if Akim had any presentiment of what was about to happen, but posthumous examination proved beyond question that he was still alive during the amputations that followed, and that the primary cause of death was blood loss and trauma inflicted when the spike was driven point-first through his testicles and into the lower body cavity, piercing the kidney and penetrating one lung before the intrusion reached its limits. It was also proven that the massive damage to the man's head and the shattering of all but one of his ribs occurred after he had breathed his last.

The body was discovered the next day, shortly before the sun reached its highest point, when a vendor of stale kurilic pastries decided to choose the wrong stall in which to set up his wares. In the confusion, his stock and equipment were stolen, and he refused to cooperate with the Prefect's office unless the finder's fee was increased to compensate him for his loss.

Chapter Five

When the lifter pilot dropped Sandor Dyle back at the Black Ark Hostelry that evening, he identified himself as Izik and indicated that he was had been assigned another room at the same establishment, no doubt in less luxurious quarters, and would be available almost instantaneously if Ser Dyle required his services for any reason. Thanking him warmly, Sandor took his leave, descending to the appropriate floor, entering his room only after a quick blink into the recognition field released the door locks.

Despite the lateness of the hour, his thoughts were tumultuous. He felt quite intrigued by this case, and impatient to examine its more objective face, which would be contained in the datanet. The impressions, observations, and theories of Prefect Dunnis and her staff might represent informed, expert opinion, but they were necessarily subjective, colored by their experiences, filtered through their prejudices, and immune to measurement. Dyle's talents lay in analysis of the less dramatic statistical underlay, the facts and figures related to the crimes and the environment in which they were committed. If a revealing pattern was to be uncovered, it would be found among those dry, seemingly barren facts, locked away in some arcane strongbox, waiting for the proper key to be turned to reveal its secrets.

Pausing only long enough to toss his jacket onto a chair, Sandor crossed to the datanet, seated himself, and ran through the security procedure that would provide access to the information he desired. Almost immediately, he was presented with a list of choices that scrolled smoothly down the screen.

<Input Mode: Voice\Console\Other>

Sandor requested vocal input; his fingers were often clumsy on the keyboard and he was too restless to remain seated.

<Output Mode: Voice Synthesis\Screen\Hard Copy>

"Screen," he replied, and the display immediately cleared. Synthesized voice programs irritated him; machines should act like machines, not like human beings.

<Ready for input.>

"Access all files relating to the Scarab murder case and copy to Block One. Access all other files containing the names of any of the victims, the officers investigating each case, or the individual who reported the crime, and copy to Block Two. Blocks One and Two are to be coded for my use only."

<Requested files are now available.>

Much of the work he would do tonight would be a duplication of that already performed by the local authorities, but Sandor considered it necessary. Summarized reports frequently left out details that might not seem important to the person composing the analysis, but which might bear greater significance if placed in the proper perspective later on. Misplaced emphasis could distort the results, cultural biases resulted in blind spots, and these shortcomings compounded the already difficult task of determining when an avenue of inquiry had been overlooked or not explored to the fullest. From past experience, Sandor knew that the response to one inquiry might open up an entire range of new questions, but that most investigators narrowed their focus to avoid what they thought of as side issues. He invariably chose to repeat even the most elementary steps with the same care as the most complex, later comparing his own observations to the officially derived results.

Tonight he chose to begin with the most basic variables, time and space. "Display a map of the Nashamata quarter, please."

The screen filled with an elaborate, highly detailed representation of the city's main level with shading and a simulated three-dimensional overlay to indicate that there were subsidiary maps available for the underways and other features that would have cluttered the main map had they been displayed simultaneously.

"Reduce detail by fifty percent."

The screen became slightly less confusing.

Thoughtfully, planning his approach, Sandor stood up and began pacing back and forth, a habit which he insisted helped his mind to function. "Highlight the locations of the first eleven Scarab murders."

<Plotted.>

Although the small orange dots were confined to the southeastern portion of the city, the port area, and the neighborhoods adjoining, there was no obvious indication of any specific geographical pattern within those limits.

"Reverse last instruction. Highlight the location of murders twelve through twenty-one."

<Plotted.>

The ten new lights had shifted very slightly toward the center of the display, but again with no discernible relationship to one another.

"Reverse last request. Highlight the last six murders."

<Plotted.>

These few seemed totally random, and Sandor ordered the map cleared almost immediately.

"Replot all twenty-seven murders, in chronological sequence, with a two-beat pause between data points. Commence now."

Slowly the map filled with orange dots, but the final result still appeared to be a random distribution, nor had the progression indicated anything out of the ordinary. There seemed to be no pattern in the selection of crimes sites, but he made a mental note to use interpolative geometry and other methods later to determine if there was some less obvious correlation that would not be noticed during a cursory physical examination.

"Clear screen. Until canceled, all queries are to be considered as applicable to the same distribution of data points, in chronological succession, one year at a time and then in summary. Confirm this instruction."

<Instructions confirmed. Four-step query procedure following previously established format.>

"Very good." At least Tashistan heuristic programming seemed up to civilized standards. "Now, summarize the nature of each location for these data points."

<Please rephrase.>

Sandor made an annoyed sound but complied. "Provide descriptions by functional type of data point physical locations."

<First sequence, in descending order of frequency: pedways seven, parks one, gardens one, storage yards one, underway platforms one. Second sequence: pedways four, underway platforms three, underway stalls one, parks one, concourse one. Third sequence: parks two, pedways two, concourse one, underway stalls one. Summary sequence: pedways thirteen, parks four, underway platforms four, underway stalls two, concourse two, gardens one, storage yard one.>

Other than a hint that Scarab might be changing his preferred hunting ground, Sandor saw nothing noteworthy in the data. It went without saying that he would choose ill-frequented, poorly monitored regions, and the site analysis provided no immediate further insight into the killer or his methods. "Graph plot. Relationship between degree of Prefecture surveillance of crime sites by type and actual frequency of crimes by site."

He had expected this to reveal that Scarab was able to somehow anticipate where surreptitious surveillance would be concentrated, either through deduction or because of a pipeline into the Prefecture. Even given the low level of municipal financing available, it was surprising that a series of crimes of this magnitude had taken place over such an extended period of time without the perpetrator making an error. Prefect Dunnis struck him as intelligent and thoughtful, and even if she labored under severe budgetary constraints, she would have leveraged what she had to its best advantage. It seemed likely then that Scarab possessed some means of anticipating and circumventing her efforts to apprehend him.

The results were most perplexing, and Sandor pursed his lips, his eyes skipping around the screen. If there was any relationship at all it was inverse, a slight tendency to strike in the type of setting most likely to be under surveillance. The data had a relatively low degree of confidence and might just be chance, but he filed it away as of potential interest anyway. If it wasn't just a statistical fluke, then Scarab might almost be flaunting his ability to evade detection.

"Clear screen. Graph plot. Relationship between average pedestrian traffic at estimated time of crime at site by type and frequency of occurrence."

This time there was a very clear relationship. The lower the traffic level, the higher the likelihood that a Scarab killing would take place. That seemed only logical, but Sandor had learned not to assume anything until it was proven. And sometimes not even then.

"Were any of the sites enclosed?"

<Rephrase; define enclosed.>

"Were any of the sites protected against weather at the estimated time of the crime, either by natural or artificial means?"

<Negative.>

"How many sites were open to the sky?"

<Twenty.>

"Identify seven sites which were not open to the sky."

<Underway platforms four, underway stalls two, park one.>

That was puzzling. "Explain park site not open to sky."

<Event sixteen site was a covered sitting area in Skuna Park.>

So much for space as a variable; Sandor turned his attention to time. "Scatter plot. Estimated time of crimes measured in terms of standard Tashistan day."

<Range or midpoint?>

"Midpoint."

The screen displayed a very clear trend this time. Sandor had to make some mental conversions; he still had trouble with the twenty-hour Tashistan clock. The earliest incident had taken place comparatively early in the evening, the latest shortly before dawn.

"Identify extremes."

<Lowest point, third event in sequence. Highest point, seventeenth event in sequence. Expansion?>

"No." Sandor had stopped pacing and stood squarely in front of the screen. "Replot using full projected range." The datanet complied, but the data became, as Sandor had expected, fuzzier, less useful, and he cleared the screen after a moment.

"Calculate correspondence between estimated chronology against site for all events."

<Peshwar Exponential Ratio 1.083. Do you wish enhancement?>

"No." Sandor cleared the screen again. If there was any correlation, it was so minuscule it could be ignored.

"Graph plot. Percentage of surveillance of each class of site during each event. Pause each data point until input is 'Go.' Display first graph now." Sandor stood thoughtfully, commanding the series of displays that followed.

Once again, Scarab appeared to be totally ignorant of or unconcerned with the degree of surveillance allocated to each category of crime site, even though they varied considerably. "Graph plot. Degree of surveillance of all crime site categories by day starting with event number one and terminating today."

The graph which appeared consisted of several short lines separated by enormous chasms. Sandor immediately recognized his mistake. "Amendment. Delete all data points which do not fall within the Secant of the Scarab." When the graph reformed this time, it was an irregular curve, generally trending upward, but with occasional dips. The increases in surveillance were a clear response to the crimes, but the dips puzzled him.

He examined the scale across the bottom of the graph. "Explain difference between data point seventy-four and seventy-five." That was the largest single decline in coverage, a trough from which the graph did not completely recover for what amounted to six full days.

<Surveillance declined 1.44 percentage points.>

"I know that," Sandor muttered, then ignored the subsequent request to rephrase the question. "Search mode, all files. Locate references to decline of flittercam surveillance in Nashamata during the time frame displayed."

This time it took a while, as the datanet accessed and searched every file stored in its database.

<Seventeen records found.>

"Display first record." For the next few minutes, Sandor found himself reading an increasingly acrimonious series of exchanges between Prefect Aras and, initially, his maintenance department; later, Prefects Leskar, Horus, and Gylph; finally the Kudara himself. Working with outdated, limited, and rapidly failing equipment from the outset, Aras had impressed into service all of the marginal and backup equipment he could find, only to discover that it had an extremely high failure rate. He had urgently requested the loan of additional equipment from Kishamkur and the other quarters, along with emergency funding from the municipal administration. Some of each had been forthcoming, but too little of either to make any difference. At its high point, surveillance had not quite reached ten percent of the potential crime sites, at least not until the night following the most recent murder, at which point it had jumped to thirteen. At its lowest point, it had been barely above one percent. Sandor shook his head sympathetically.

"What are the shortest, longest, and average intervals between events in each subset, disregarding intervals between subsets, to the nearest full day?"

<Minimum interval three days. Maximum interval twelve days. Average interval eight days.>

"Graph plot all intervals except those between subsets."

The graphic revealed nothing; he hadn't really expected it to.

Sandor shifted his attention to the victims themselves. "Table plot. In chronological sequence, ages of all victims." Once again, he had to convert mentally to units of measure with which he was more familiar, but the spread varied from very young adulthood to one individual who was impressively long-lived for such an otherwise backward planet. "Change color of all female victims to red." Of the twenty-seven victims, nine were female, starting with victim three and ending with victim twenty-four.

For the rest of that evening, until his eyelids were too heavy to continue, Sandor explored various profiles of the victims. Educational background, occupation, medical histories, the articles of clothing they were wearing when killed, organizations they belonged to, and hobbies or other activities they were known to be involved with. None of these provided any promising hints for further lines of inquiry, although there were a few questions he wished to pursue in more detail later. Sandor reviewed whatever was known about the movement of each victim on the day of their respective deaths, then the previous day, even the previous week. As far as he could tell, there were no correlations.

At one point he asked for a graphic display of all known interactions among the victims. Twenty-seven data points appeared on the screen, followed by a web of small solid lines which joined several of them. The final result was a display of three tenuous sets of linkages. Only four individuals had no known interaction with any of the other victims. One of these was a mountain hunter who had fallen on hard times and entered the city only a few days before his murder. After studying each of the other links, Sandor was inclined to disregard them all as apparently inconsequential, although that might not prove to be the case once he had more data. There might also be other interactions of which the datanet was unaware. Some of the deceased were simply neighbors, others had done business together, none were related by blood or marriage except at some degree so remote that they were probably unaware of it themselves. The largest node of interactions included two members of the Carcieri gang and one from the Sundluns, all of whom had been arrested together after a particularly violent street brawl. There was no record of any further contact except between the two Carcieris.

The last area he explored that evening was the incidence of murder and other violent crime excluding the Scarab cases.

Soshambe turned out to have a slightly higher than average murder rate, even with Scarab factored out, but still not as high as Samarka or some of the more industrialized cities. Theft was an unusually high motivating factor in these cases, at least by offworld standards, but just about average for Tashista. Violent crime for non-material reasons was more frequent in the hotter, drier weather of the Raptor, Star, and Shadow Secants, a situation which held true for the planetary population as a whole.

The amputation of hands and/or feet was peculiar to Scarab, at least in recent years, although nemesol had been used once before, in Soshambe as a matter of fact. A merchant in Tashamir found with his throat cut was discovered to have been initially subdued with the drug. Mutilation of any sort was rare; Tashistan culture de-emphasized the physical body as a cultural icon in favor of material wealth and the physical being therefore lacked much of the psychological significance that it held on most other worlds. There were no other evident similarities to the Scarab case that he could detect in this last crime, other than the fact that it remained unsolved. The attack had taken place during the Secant of the Rapier shortly after the first series of Scarab murders had ended, and the Prefect of Tashamir had been in a panic that the serial killer might have shifted his hunting ground. There had, however, been no recurrence and it was assumed to be an unrelated event. Sandor tentatively agreed with that assessment.

Although he had many more questions to ask, he found himself yawning and seriously doubted that he retained the clarity of mind to recognize a pattern if it should appear. Reluctantly, he signed off the datanet and turned in for the evening.

But his relentlessly churning brain did not allow him to sleep for a considerable time thereafter.

* * * * *

Marym rolled over on the sweat-soaked sheets, the delightful numbness already beginning to fade and the nagging frustrations of the day manifesting themselves as a tightness behind her lower ribs, a throbbing pulse in her forehead, a feeling of impatience that jumped from subject to subject, without a clear focal point. In the other room, Kruzer, the only man with whom she was currently involved sexually, was fixing himself a light meal. Sex always made him hungry, or at least so he claimed. Normally it made her languorously sleepy. But not tonight. Too many unsettling things at once, she realized. The perplexing and irritating introduction of Sandor Dyle into her affairs, Leskar's aloof attitude and callous interference, and her own inability to find a way to cope with Scarab gnawed at her composure. And at the same time she felt a tug of guilt about resenting what was at least to a degree meant as an honest offer of assistance. Leskar had lost his only son, and if he had become somewhat intrusive in his desire to bring the murderer to justice, it was certainly an understandable reaction. For his part, Dyle had been employed to perform a job, one at which he was reportedly somewhat skilled, and he certainly couldn't be faulted for agreeing to use his talents to bring Scarab to heel. She had accessed his file and knew it was not a question of the credits he had been promised, nor did he appear to be fond of publicity. And on top of everything else, she found that she even liked the man; he radiated an honest, open enthusiasm that she found quite disarming.

"Want some?" Kruzer spoke around a mouthful of what appeared to be doldren bread and mordred cheese.

"No, thanks. I wouldn't want to spoil the climax of your evening." She knew it was petty, but he could at least have demonstrated enough tact to lie there with her for a few minutes before catering to his next desire.

Kruzer raised an eyebrow and stopped chewing. "Listen, Marym, if you've had another bad day, don't take it out on me. It's not my fault, you know."

She sighed. "You're right; I'm sorry. It's beginning to wear me down, I suppose."

"You seemed unusually preoccupied tonight, as though your body was here with me but your mind someplace else."

"It didn't feel that way to me." She smiled and rolled onto her side as he sat down on the edge of the bed. They were both still naked. "But I do have a lot on my mind. Sorry if I was sarcastic; there aren't many outlets for frustration in my position."

"It's forgotten," he grunted. "I'm not complaining. Is there anything I can do?" He frowned. "Silly question. It's that Scarab thing again, isn't it? Still no clues?"

Kruzer had earned his way into Moshamadur by playing professional netball, had been the second rated player on Soshambe's intercity team for two years running and something of a local celebrity. Retired now, he earned a small amount of credit coaching, but lived primarily off the income from the astronomical credit reserves he'd acquired from wealthy patrons during his brief but glorious career. Kruzer's strong but inexplicable contempt for those he had left behind in Nashamata was a sentiment which had occasionally caused friction in their relationship over its four-year course. He boasted openly that he had not entered the poor quarter since the first day he had accumulated enough credit to leave. "They're losers," he insisted whenever the subject came up. "The ones who are worth my time will earn their way out sooner or later. Those who can't are of no interest to me."

His question hung in the air. "Mostly," she admitted. "Anxieties building up, I guess; it's not going to help my career if I don't find a way to stop the killings. The fact that I lack the proper tools is irrelevant. Now, on top of everything else, there's talk of another budget cut because of the drought. I have two officers down with Scabrous Fever and Wiltner down in properties accidentally destroyed some evidence we needed to clinch a verdict in the Yoshema Credit Embezzlement. My lifter isn't holding a charge and needs servicing, the medicator tells me I'll probably need a corneal implant within three years, and my investment income declined four percent during the first half of the secant." She shook her head. "Talking about your problems is supposed to make you feel better, they say, but it doesn't seem to work in my case."

"You could always change professions. You have enough credit to bid for an administrative position with the Kudara or at the collegium."

"Kruzer, you know how much I paid to get where I am now. Not just credit either." Her voice rose, filled with emotion.

"Doesn't matter if you're not enjoying it," he rejoined almost offhandedly.

"Well, there's a turnaround for you. What happened to the man who insisted anyone willing to accept the responsibility of an honest job will find a way to accumulate the credit to move up to a better standard of living?"

He shrugged and took another bite. "I don't see any contradiction. You've made it; you're here. It would be nice to break into Kishamkur, but we all know most of the credit there is inherited, even though they pretend otherwise, and even if we did, we'd be considered *parvenu* and socially shunned. You could move into another profession, or even live off your interest. We could combine households; neither of us has much stuff and there's plenty of room here, or at my place."

Marym frowned and pulled slightly away. "Kruzer, we agreed right from the outset that we would not give up our separate lives. Neither of us is prepared to make the kinds of accommodations that would be necessary for a full-time relationship to succeed."

"I'm not suggesting a radical change in our situation. I don't want permanent bonding any more than you do. But almost every night that we're not here, we're both at my place. We could save space, effort, and some credit by combining our resources, at least for so long as we can stand each other's proximity."

"Kruzer, I don't want to talk about this right now, all right?"

There must have been something in her voice this time, some fine edge of steel, that warned him off. With studied casualness, he changed the subject. "This Dyle character they foisted on you. What's he like anyway?"

"Impressive, disarming. He's a little rough around the edges, too blunt to be a real charmer, but straightforward enough to be refreshing. What we've been able to pull out of the datanet about him is impressive; his personal fortune is larger than the entire Samarkan budget. Pattern analysis, particularly slanted toward recognition of criminal activities, is more or less a hobby; he's largely disengaged from his business interests, which are managed by a combination of artificial intelligences and hired hands. Published a few papers on the subject of pattern analysis, said to be working on a book. He's rubbed a few diplomats the wrong way from time to time, even those he's helped. Egotistical, but with some justification."

"Good looking?"

"Hardly." She laughed, her good humor restored. "You don't have to worry about a potential rival, Kruzer. He's twice my age, I'd guess, lean and bony, tall although not by his own standards, I suppose. There's something exotic about him but not enough to make him sexy. Still, he has an aura of authority and intelligence that's independent of his official status. He's not the kind of person who's easy to ignore, and I wouldn't be too complacent if I was a criminal and thought he was after me."

"You think he'll solve the case then? Capture Scarab?"

She was silent for a long time, never having really wrestled with that question. "I don't know," she admitted at last. "We've been through the data a million times ourselves. Savram was . . . is a pretty good pattern analyst; you can't be an effective investigator without some grasp of the principles. It's possible that there's something we've overlooked, and if there is, I'd bet on Sandor to find it. I'm just not convinced that there is anything there for him to find."

"How will it affect you if he fails? Or if he succeeds for that matter?"

Marym lay back and pulled the coverlet up to her chin. "Frankly, I wish I knew. If he succeeds, they'll pay him whatever fee they've settled on, pat me on the head, take back all the equipment they've loaned, and I imagine we'll be pretty much back to the status quo ante. If he fails, we'll just have to keep trying until something happens. Luck seems to side with Scarab, you know; even with the poor surveillance coverage we've been able to implement, the chances of his having been picked up by now are slightly better than even."

"Which would you prefer? Success or failure?"

Her eyes had been drifting shut, but now they snapped open. "I want Scarab stopped, no matter how it's done!" She modulated her voice, which had been rising toward a shout. "I can't believe you even asked me that question, Kruzer."

He made a pacifying move with one hand, the one that didn't hold the small remnant of his meal. "Okay, sorry. I didn't mean to upset you. It just seemed like, careerwise, it would be better if he packed up and left. You'll catch Scarab sooner or later, like you said, and if you do it on your own, that's your ticket to qualifying for a better posting. Didn't you say Zanur wanted to move back to Samarka?" Zanur was currently Prefect in Tashamir.

"I buy my positions with work and credit, Kruzer, not with human lives. Not even the lives of Nashamatans." She felt a cold anger that struggled for release, but her professional training asserted itself. Maintain control, she thought silently; don't let your emotions interfere with your actions. "If Zanur does in fact retire to his home city, I'll succeed to his post on my terms and because of my accomplishments or not at all. The decision won't be based on the outcome of a single case."

But she knew that it might well happen that way, particularly now that Leskar's son was numbered among the victims. If Scarab wasn't caught soon, he'd be looking for someone else to blame once the initial grief faded and turned to anger, someone to punish. Leskar's influence over the Board of Qualification was significant.

"Well, if that judgment is based on intelligence and hard work, you're certain to get it," Kruzer replied diplomatically and set the uneaten portion of his meal down on the floor beside the bed. "I'm stuffed. Want to help me work up the energy to finish?"

Marym closed her eyes and turned her head away. "Not tonight, Kruzer. I'm not mad, really, but I need to work things out in my mind for a while."

Kruzer sat on the edge of the bed, nearly motionless, for a long time after that, staring down at the back of Marym's head. He was not smiling.

* * * * *

Tamara Stoat had known for years that she would never escape the confines of Nashamata unless it was through some extraordinary stroke of good fortune. That's why she had finally agreed to a permanent bonding with Ramis Marchok, the man she'd been sleeping with ever since adolescence. Ramis was a hard worker, diligent but not bright, capable of performing manual labor and following simple sets of instructions, but with periodic lapses of memory that she sometimes suspected might be more serious than they appeared. He had been earning a subsistence-level income as a day laborer in Tashamir for years, and when they had moved into common quarters, her own wages had enabled them to actually raise their standard of living somewhat, although they had so little hard credit at any one time, neither of them had ever bothered to establish a condata.

Having surrendered whatever dreams she might have entertained of moving to a better part of the city, Tamara had resigned herself to her present environment and set about making as pleasant a life as possible for the two of them. But now, as they moved toward late middle age, she was worried once again. Ramis complained more and more frequently about muscle aches in his back, and periodic fierce headaches as well. The latter was more immediately worrisome, since even minor treatment from the medicators was very expensive, but the backaches might also endanger his portion of their joint income. If Ramis' physical condition deteriorated, if he could no longer perform at his best, the assignments would begin to come at greater and greater intervals and then stop entirely.

Without mentioning anything to her bondmate, Tamara began to look for additional work. She had always had a good visual sense, so she purchased access time for graphic interfacing on the datanet, and worked out a number of designs she had been carrying in her head or drawing in the sand at Skuna Park. The finished file she transmitted to a clothier in Tashamir, where it had initially seemed to disappear into the void. Long after she had given up hope of a response, she returned home one day after cleaning suba fish on the wharf to find a note on her door requesting that she use a public datanet to access a specific coded terminal. Two days later, she was hired on a trial basis designing patterns for the autoweavers at a base salary which slightly exceeded the average she and Ramis had been able to earn together.

In addition to paying well, her new position was interesting and presented a pleasant working environment. Her employers were unusually considerate of her feelings. She was the only Nashamatan they employed directly, although they used street vendors to distribute some of their wares in the poor quarter, a practice technically a violation of the law, but one which every merchant ignored in quest of marginal credit. Unpopular patterns, discontinued styles, slight misweaves or miscolorings, anything which could not be peddled easily in the mercantile quarter or elsewhere on the planet at standard prices was distributed through Nashamata by whatever means were available.

Tamara responded to success by working even harder, often staying long after the owners had returned to their own homes in Moshamadur. Ramis had chided her about this on more than one occasion, pointing out the dangers of walking the traverseways at night, with underway gangs constantly on the prowl for sport, to say nothing of this new string of murders. He had frequently insisted that she wait until he could walk out to meet her, providing an escort home through the darkened streets. But Ramis had been so tired and discouraged of late, experiencing great difficulty relaxing the muscles in his back, and she felt increasingly guilty about dragging him out, particularly on those infrequent days when he had found work of his own.

She was walking home alone that evening, keeping to the better traveled pedways wherever possible. There were still large numbers of people about, although her route occasionally took her through less populated areas. Normally she avoided Cassio Traverseway, home to a number of unsavory establishments which, while legal in themselves, were focal points for violence. Some dispensed drugs, supposedly under controlled conditions, not releasing their clients onto the streets until a neutralizing agent had been administered. Others exchanged credit for other vices: sex of various varieties, cortical stimulation, banu root baths, more bizarre services and products about which she knew little and cared less. But tonight she was exhausted, and anxious to be home. They had accumulated enough credit now that she felt it was time to urge Ramis to visit the medicator, get treatment before something went seriously wrong in his back. He disliked discussing the subject, always claimed they could not afford the fees involved, but today she had steeled herself for the confrontation and wanted to get it over with before her resolve melted away.

So she took the shorter route through Cassio.

The right side of the traverseway facing the garishly lighted establishments was lined with tallow trees, whose upper branches had arched to either side forming a canopy under which she walked. Under which also stood a large, cloaked form, with clothing uniformly black, motionless, staring across at the lights.

At first she thought she was staring at a prospective client, perhaps waiting to meet someone, more likely trying to summon the nerve to cross and enter. New customers were often shy about making contact. But there was something else, a stealthy watchfulness that made her pause, one foot half raised. She hadn't been seen yet, and suddenly she felt certain she did not want to be. Not by this man. Instead, she slowly replaced her foot on the pavement and moved quietly to one side, concealing herself behind the trunk of a tallow.

This tableau continued for an extended period of time, long enough for Tamara to consider risking a quick cross to the opposite side of the traverseway, even though this meant advancing along the front of the shops until she had bypassed the lurker in the darkness. Proximity to mundane sins seemed somehow preferable to coming within arm's length of the figure ahead of her. After all, he might be a thief or some maniac, possibly even Scarab himself.

With that thought came irrational certainty. Quite by chance, she might have stumbled across the key to future happiness. The newly announced finder's fee for evidence leading to the capture of Scarab was enough to support two people in Moshamadur for the rest of their lives. All she had to do was reach a datanet station and alert the Prefect.

The only immediate problem was that she didn't know of any datanet stations within several blocks. She was biting her lip, trying to decide whether or not to chance slipping away and finding one, when the man moved.

He stepped away from the lights rather than toward them, moving along the retaining wall that separated the traverseway from the access tunnel down into the first level of underways. Tamara felt determination rise within her; she would not, could not, allow this opportunity to slip away. As silently as possible, she began to follow.

Her quarry moved directly and unhesitatingly away, with such evident purpose that Tamara was soon forced to walk at a rapid pace just to keep him in sight. There was no time to spare for concealment, but fortunately, he showed no inclination to look back in her direction. They left the underway access behind and climbed the steps to the concourse above, crossed that, then passed through a series of small gardens and public spaces, down another set of steps and along another traverseway to a larger open space where public assemblies were occasionally held. In one corner, a small private lifter stood with its running lights off. The man she pursued walked directly to the lifter and, while she was hastily concealing herself behind a badly vandalized statue of Luchar, turned on its running lights and floods, climbed inside, and closed the outside door.

As it lifted away, she ran out into the open, trying desperately to pick up some distinguishing mark which would allow her to identify the lifter or its occupant, any little detail which might be translatable into credit.

Fate was kind, in its fashion, because as the vehicle turned west toward Kishamkur, an emblazoned symbol was briefly illuminated by the running lights along its underside. The two stylized wings and the pattern of crosses were unmistakable.

It was the insignia of the Prefecture of Kishamkur.

Chapter Six

Marym Dunnis stood in her office, staring down into the maintenance yard, amusing herself by drawing parallels between the disreputable scene below and Nashamata as a whole. A broad expanse, filled with the artifacts of society, some of which operated adequately enough for the purposes to which they were set although generally lacking the flexibility to be modified when new situations arose, many others functioning in a more haphazard fashion, kept in service only because there was no choice, no standby equipment, no hope for replacement with updated models. Some of the latter were so totally dysfunctional that they were slowly subsiding into piles of discolored metal and circuitry. A few wildflowers had sprung up where human and machine traffic were sparse enough to allow such growth, pinpoints of beauty which exaggerated rather than ameliorated the ugliness of the area as a whole. For the foreseeable future, the maintenance division would persist in its operation through momentum enlivened by occasional bursts of innovation or some idiosyncrasy of outside funding, but there was no happy solution to its entropic slide toward chaos. Perhaps that explains Scarab, she thought. He's an agent of chaos, a warning of the disaster to come, a forerunning shadow of our collective future.

Each decade, a smaller percentage escaped Nashamata than had during the previous ten years, even if the figures were adjusted to compensate for the general population rise. For the past three years, there had even been a sharp decline in the real numbers of those who made the transition to Moshamadur. The decline had been blamed on the economy, which had suffered from a combination of poor weather, an intermittent trade war with the cities of the southern continent, and the comparative relaxation of import quotas from offplanet. There were more diverse and abundant goods available in Tashamir at relatively stable prices, but although the people of Nashamata had been able to eat better than ever for the same amount of credit, acquisition of the latter had become more difficult as the merchants tightened their belts. There had been a mini-exodus to nearby industrial cities where the chance for advancement seemed greater, but this had simply bled off the more talented and ambitious; the enormous mass that remained was churning with suppressed anger and frustration, a steam engine with no safety valve. Even in Moshamadur, there was growing anxiety. Many there had been forced to trim their living styles back into balance with reduced income levels. If the economic climate did not improve soon, some would inevitably fall from grace, slip back below the minimum subsistence level for Moshamadur. The psychological effects of retrogression were well known: an increase in suicides, depression, frustrated anger, and violence. Almost no one who slipped back ever made it out of Nashamata a second time. And progress from Moshamadur forward was increasingly rare, and many of those few who qualified refused to uproot themselves, preferring to stay in familiar surroundings where their wealth brought them respect they would forfeit if they should leave.

A shadow crossed the side of a nearby building and Marym instinctively glanced upward, even though the angle was too acute for her to see the sky. A lifter had landed on the roof, almost certainly Sandor Dyle arriving for his appointment.

Tani's voice a few seconds later confirmed her suspicion. "Ser Dyle is here, Prefect. Shall I send him in or would you prefer that he wait?"

"Send him through, Tani, and would you have Jenilla come up as well?"

"Certainly. Is there anything else?"

Marym replied negatively and crossed to the door, was standing there when it opened to admit Sandor. He was dressed in a much more practical fashion today, baggy pants and a heavy, water resistant top. He was smiling broadly, his slightly too-large mouth emphasizing the narrowness of his face.

"Good morning, Prefect, although I confess it would be far better if the weather were somewhat more pleasant. It's too bad this killer of yours didn't choose the Secant of the Scepter. I understand that's the warmest season of your local year. Hazard is a much hotter, drier world than Tashista; the equatorial deserts are still basically uninhabited, as a matter of fact. I find this chilly dampness quite depressing."

"Come in, please." She cut through the effervescent flow of words. "Scepter is a little too warm for my tastes, I'm afraid. That's when we have most of our violent crimes. Domestic quarrels get out of hand, the underway gangs are at their most active, and everyone's tempers are frayed, including those among my staff."

Sighing melodramatically, Sandor collapsed into a non-articulated chair. "Behind every pleasant facade, the ugly reality. Conquer war and disease, overpopulation rears its ugly head. The universe is the fulcrum of an infinite series of opposed characteristics and influences; the best we can hope to do is keep ourselves as level as possible."

"Isn't that from Pantagria's *Patterns and Principles*? The introduction, I believe."

"The preface, actually, but I'm impressed nonetheless. Pantagria is a bit rarefied for casual reading; her philosophy is frequently intriguing, but has little application in the real world, I'm afraid."

"Any good Prefect will have some familiarity with the classics of pattern analysis, Sandor, even the theoretical side. But the truth is, I read it only at the urging of Savram Aras. He has an excellent holobrary and taught me a long time ago not to rely completely on the datanet and its programmed analytics."

"I like him already. Give me a good, solid holobook over those flat, characterless screens any day. I have nothing against technology, Marym, but when we become too dependent upon a tool, we cause a muscle to atrophy." He pressed the tip of one finger against his temple. "Exercise is as important to the mind as it is to the body."

Marym seated herself behind the desk. "Have you decided whether or not you want to start with a tour of Nashamata? I've arranged for someone to spend the day as your guide."

"I think this would be an excellent time for me to do so. I have ingested a surfeit of dry facts; I need some context, some background, if they are to acquire dimensionality. I don't have any specific agenda, but I'd like to walk the streets for a while, perhaps visit a couple of the actual murder sites, particularly the most recent one, if that's possible. I promise not to be conspicuous or interfere with any of your own investigations."

"I don't see any difficulty. The quarantine shield was lifted yesterday so you don't have to worry about interfering with anything. The park is generally empty; few of our citizens have the leisure to use it. I've already sent for Jenilla, the woman whom I've assigned to you. She's local, patrols along the docks most of the time but knows the quarter thoroughly, one of our best subprefects. She was part of the follow-up team in the park, as a matter of fact, so she can probably answer any questions you might have. If there's any additional assistance you require which is beyond her authority or capacity, she has a priority clearance to reach me at any time on your behalf."

"I apologize if I'm putting additional strain on your department. I'm aware of the personnel limitations under which you operate. Even relatively crimeless worlds have a more favorable staff level, if only for crowd control and traffic modulation."

She shook her head. "Please don't apologize any further. If there is any chance of your turning up something that will help, it will more than repay us for the investment. If not, we're no worse off, and to be truthful, I've spent time and credit on wilder ideas."

"Under those circumstances, I accept as gracefully as my awkward body will allow." He stretched his spidery arms wide in illustration.

"Are you still interested in talking to Savram Aras? I might be able to arrange a meeting this evening, if you're going to be available."

"I've made no specific plans. I would very much like to speak with Ser Aras at the earliest opportunity. Now that I've exposed myself to the raw data, comparison of his thoughts and theories to my own could be very helpful. Differing viewpoints often lead to solutions because of their divergences rather than their similarities."

"All right, I'll speak to him today and see what can be arranged. A late afternoon appointment might be best, though. The illness saps his energy and he often retires at dusk."

"I will arrange my schedule to suit his convenience. Nashamata as a whole does not, I assume, retire at dusk. I would like to sample its flavor in darkness as well as in light."

"As soon as I've spoken to him, I'll contact you through Jenilla, your guide." She paused, then continued somewhat uncomfortably. "Would you mind if I went along with you? To see Savram, that is." She bit her lip. "I've rather neglected him lately. There have been so many problems, distractions, reasons not to go. And frankly his deterioration has not been a pleasant experience for me either. He's a man I've admired for a long time, and this inability to do anything to help him is almost as frustrating as trying to stop the killings."

"There is no problem at all, Marym. I wouldn't have presumed to ask you to invest your time, but I'm delighted to have you. Your presence will bridge those awkward moments which inevitably arise between complete strangers."

It was at that precise moment that Marym's assistant indicated that Jenilla Kanark had arrived.

"Send her in."

Sandor rose courteously as the door slid aside to admit a woman whose bulk was unusual even for a Tashistan. Jenilla was almost a model for healthy athletics, her body solidly muscular, her gait confident, her eyes alert and active. On a world whose founders had used genetic manipulation to ensure a population physically capable of standing up to a gravity pressure somewhat above what was ideal for its colonists, Jenilla still stood out from among her fellows. Oddly, she wore her hair long, below shoulder length, a surprising variation from the local fashion. Sandor doubted that anyone would dare to make an unfavorable comment about her unstylishness, at least not in her presence.

"Jenilla, come in please." Marym made the introductions, while Sandor and the newcomer touched their chests ritually.

"I'm very honored to meet you, Ser Dyle. I hope that I may prove worthy of this association." Her words were formal but not unfriendly.

Sandor made a gesture of self-denigration. "You flatter me unnecessarily, Ser Kanark. I'm just as much an employee as you, and I have yet to prove that my services have any value."

"Jenilla has been released from her normal duties for the day," Marym interrupted. "Please feel free to alter your plans as you wish. Jenilla has full authority to provide you with whatever assistance might be necessary." The two Tashistans exchanged a look that excluded Dyle.

Nodding, pretending not to have noticed this confirmation that he was an outsider, Sandor turned back to Marym. "To a great extent, I'll rely on her judgment then." He smiled disarmingly. "I would like to get a general feeling for life in Nashamata. As an offworlder, I'm naturally ignorant of a great many things which you both take for granted. The basic facts of existence in your city are available through the datanet, but none of that really conveys any idea of how it feels to walk your streets, haggle in your markets, live in your homes. I don't expect to be able to assimilate much of your culture during my entire visit, let alone a day's wandering through the streets, but I hope at least to sample its flavor."

Jenilla and Marym exchanged another glance, and there was a barely perceptible nod from the Prefect before Jenilla spoke.

"Nashamata is the largest and most populous quarter of the city, Ser Dyle. Perhaps if we visited representative sections, you could interpolate from that."

"I place myself in your hands, Ser Kanark. Or is it Subprefect Kanark? I'm not certain of the proper forms."

Unconsciously glancing at the attenuated symbol on her chest, Jenilla shook her head. "The first thing for you to learn, Ser Dyle, is that not all of us are as formal in Soshambe as in most regions of Tashista. Our forebears believed that the relationships among individuals should evolve from their experience with each other rather than from some artificially imposed system. Although the modern view is more relaxed, some of us still believe that experience is more important than the dictates of authority."

"Ah, then you are a relationist?"

"I am a member of the Lucharist Society, if that's what you mean. There are some distinct differences between our philosophy and that of the Relationist Union as it exists elsewhere."

"I don't mean to engage you in a philosophical debate, however rewarding that might be, but how do you reconcile your disdain for titles with the stratification of society here in Soshambe?"

She smiled with obvious relish. "An excellent point, Ser Dyle. You must understand, the Lucharist Society is opposed to the class system which has evolved. Any constraint working to reduce the widest variations in human interaction prevents the reconciliation of social forces . . ."

At this point, Marym broke in. "The official position is that there is no class system. Mobility between classes by completely measurable criteria, credit level in this case, is assumed to render the artificial distinctions irrelevant." She didn't sound as though she believed what she was saying. "That was one of the underlying principles of the Accord."

Jenilla's eyes flashed. "The Lucharist Society was not a signatory to the Accord of Alyshambo. In fact, we opposed it as an attempt to avoid dealing with the real issues."

Marym appeared ready to respond, but Sandor raised his hand. "Excuse me, but I'm afraid that this is one area about which I am almost totally ignorant. Every society has artificial divisions of wealth; you seem to be implying that there's a deeper chasm here."

"It is a confusing issue," Marym explained apologetically. "Theoretically, there is no barrier to movement from one district to another except the financial wherewithal to support a better lifestyle. There are, however, elements in our city who feel there should be other criteria for advancement, or no criteria at all." She glanced at the other woman.

Jenilla nodded and took up where her superior had left off. "In our parents' lifetimes, there was an attempt to solidify class divisions. The wealthy district, then known as Kishamata, changed its name to Kishamkur."

"And this was significant?"

"Subtle, but laden with meaning. Kishamata means the 'people who live where luck smiles upon them;' Kishamkur means the 'people who wed luck to hard work.'"

"It sounds innocuous enough." But Sandor thought he knew enough about the way things worked on Tashista to intuit what was to come.

"It is hard to translate into offworld terms," Marym interposed. "But the implication was that there was a requirement to earn a way into Kishamkur, where before it was possible through simple luck to accumulate enough credit to buy admission to Kishamata."

"And it didn't stop there." Obviously this was a topic upon which Jenilla was prepared to expound for quite some time. "Having established the principle that admission into Kishamkur was no longer simply a matter of one's credit balance, certain interest groups decided to place further limits on the social mobility of the citizenry. The then-current residents of Kishamkur redesignated themselves as 'Hierata,' or 'the lofty ones.' The distinction is a difference of kind rather than degree. Legislation was enacted setting an upper limit to the total number of citizens who could be a part of the Hierata, which effectively cut off virtually all further migration from Moshamadur. If it had remained unchallenged, the Mosham would have been forced to establish similar restrictions of their own."

"But as I understand it, the Kishamkur make up only about eight percent of your total population. Surely they lacked the sheer numbers necessary to enforce their will on the legislature?"

Both women laughed and it was Marym who answered first. "You forget, we don't have elected officials here. Every public position is auctioned off to the highest-bidding qualified contender, and the qualification process is administered by the Kisham themselves."

"Ah, yes, an interesting variation. But these restrictions were overturned, I take it?"

"Their impact was at least blunted," admitted Jenilla. "For two years there were escalating riots in Soshambe, primarily in Moshamadur, although the unrest spread ultimately to Nashamata as well. It was this latter fact that forced the Hierata to agree to a general conference which resulted in the Accord of Alyshambo. The name 'Hierata' was officially dropped, although the wealthy quarter retained its new name and many of its residents use the term among themselves. Quotas restricting the numbers of individuals who could migrate from one level of society to another were revoked, although the rise in the cost of living accomplished almost the same thing."

"Much of that was beyond local control, Jenilla," Marym interrupted wearily. "You can't blame a secret cabal of wealthy Kisham for everything. Essentially we returned to the status quo ante. I know the Lucharists wanted to abolish the barriers entirely, but that just isn't possible under the present circumstances. The resultant disorder would have torn the city apart. There has to be some stratification of society; if everyone lived the same lifestyle, there would be no incentive for improvement or enterprise."

Jenilla's eyes betrayed momentary anger, but her voice remained level. "With all respect, Prefect, the specters of social stagnation and chaos have been waved in our faces every time we, or any other segment of society, has proposed a change of direction. We cannot forever refrain from improving our culture for fear that change results in unrest. Life itself is restless."

Marym sighed. "Jenilla, we have worked together for a long time now. Will you please stop resorting to formality whenever we find ourselves disagreeing? I respect your position even if I cannot accept it."

For a moment, Jenilla was silent, considering the proposition. Then she relaxed, even allowed herself to smile. "Actually, Marym, I rather hope you end up in Kishamkur. I think you're too willing to accept that the way our affairs are conducted at present is the way they should be conducted in the future, but at least you have always been willing to give my unpopular views a fair hearing. I apologize for the stiffness."

"Was this unrest planet-wide or confined to Soshambe alone?" Sandor interjected.

Marym seemed relieved by the interruption. "Every major urban center has the same basic stratification, but Soshambe was the first—and so far the only—place where a codified limit on migration was imposed. It was in a sense a test case for our entire planet, although the resolution was so ambiguous, the issues remain unresolved to this day."

"Well, despite the fascinating content of this discussion, I fear we are occupying too much of the Prefect's time, Jenilla. As worrisome as Scarab might be, I find it hard to believe that he is the only criminal at large."

"Of course," Jenilla took a short step toward the door. "If there are no other instructions, Marym?"

Marym stood up and glanced from one to the other. "No, none that I can think of. I hope you'll both have a pleasant and constructive day."

Sandor rose and joined his guide at the door. "If not, it won't be for a lack of effort. Until this evening."

And then they were gone.

Marym Dunnis stood staring at the closed door for a long time after the two of them had left, still trying to reconcile her conflicting feelings about Dyle's presence.

* * * * *

The tour that Jenilla Kanark had arranged for Sandor was comprehensive and well organized. On the flight from Samarka, Sandor had noticed that Soshambe presented an odd silhouette even from a distance. There was a lopsided cant to the skyline. The western end, Kishamkur and portions of Moshamadur and the commercial district, Tashamir, consisted of row after row of low buildings, often only a single story, gradually increasing as the residential areas gave way to the markets and factories of Tashamir. There they grew to two, three, four stories in height, and some of the major industries were housed in even taller structures.

But it was in Nashamata that Soshambe actually began to resemble an offworld city. As one moved eastward, approaching the port to the south and the foothills of the So Mountains to the north, the buildings grew larger and larger, massive edifices towering into the sky, intersticed with winding pedestrian traverseways and pedways, some wide enough to handle powered vehicles although there were few hovercarts or surface lifters in evidence, and most of those they did see that day were service or supply vehicles. The architecture was obviously influenced by the now discredited Brutalist School, which had enjoyed immense popularity during the period in which Tashista was first colonized. The markets and public places were spacious and practical, although adequate allowance had been made for parks and gardens of various sizes, small backwater concourses where street merchants could set up their carts or where the rare citizen who had time to spend other than in pursuit of credit might find an opponent for kubits, ultima, or any of the other games popular on Tashista.

The dwelling places and public buildings themselves consisted of massive fabricated blocks, consciously designed to appear crudely made and randomly arranged. Floor plans branched and rejoined with reckless abandon, and with little consideration for efficient utilization of space. When Soshambe had been under construction, it had never occurred to its creators that there would come a time when the availability of virgin land upon which to construct new buildings might become an issue. There were small, widely scattered open spaces which were so difficult or inconvenient to enter, they had become dead spots on the city's face. The detritus of years which had accumulated in many of these testified to the city's lagging commitment to maintenance and sanitation.

Ever eastward the city marched until the ocean and mountains made further progress impossible. And ever higher stretched those towering buildings, housing greater and greater numbers of people. It became a sign of social standing in the community first, to live as close to the ground floor as possible, then to reside in smaller buildings, with fewer neighbors. In Kishamkur, no one would even consider building above three stories, and even those were largely split-levels built into the contours of the ground below and adjoining hills. Although there was more than enough open space to expand the rich quarter westward toward the Beatic Valley, social pressure had raised such an outcry against diminution of what was perceived as the quality of life that expansion had effectively come to a halt.

When they had completed a brief aerial overview, Izik set Jenilla and Sandor down in a public lifter park near the eastern city gates.

"Shall we walk for a while, Sandor?" They had progressed to a less formal relationship during the flight.

"Whatever you think best, Jenilla. Despite my appearance, I'm surprisingly hardy and I've had time to adapt to your gravity. I've traveled with miners in the Dushalt region of Copernica, scaled the precipices of Gellatis, and hunted silicon tigers with a full ecopack in the jungles of Vulnea."

"If you still insist on visiting the underways, you might find yourself in a different kind of jungle, one even less forgiving."

"I was given to believe that your abilities were sufficient to cope with any problems we might encounter."

She smiled wryly. "Don't believe everything you hear. But we should be all right. It's more dangerous at night, of course, but even then most of the gangs are fairly well behaved, at least when faced with serious opposition. They prey on the defenseless for the most part and rarely oppose the Prefecture with anything stronger than harsh language. There's an understanding between parties," she had the grace to look uncomfortable, "that should afford us ample protection."

"As I said, I am in your hands."

Jenilla was silent as they left the lifter park and crossed a wide, sparsely occupied concourse toward rows of buildings which established an even more noticeable line of demarcation than the official city wall to their rear. At this point, most of the structures around them towered over eighty stories into the air. Pedestrian traffic grew moderate, but never heavy, which Jenilla explained as normal for this time of the day.

"Those who haven't found themselves day work here or elsewhere are over in Tashamir exchanging credit for the goods they can't find locally. For the most part, necessities can be obtained from the street vendors: food, clothing, fuel credits, that sort of thing. If you're not fussy about exact specifications or high quality, you can live your entire life without ever leaving Nashamata, despite the theoretical rules limiting trade to Tashamir. But there are always a few things that don't seem to be available, although for most people I think it's just an excuse to leave, even if only for a few hours. They get to glimpse a better lifestyle, a taste of what they might be able to experience if they scrimp and save for the greater part of their lives."

"You don't seem to be particularly enamored of your political system."

Jenilla laughed. "Please don't patronize me, Sandor. You're from offworld; you recognize how ridiculous and repressive a striated social structure must be. We sell our public positions to the highest bidder; how can we expect excellence in their performance under those circumstances?"

"That's not quite as rare as you might believe. You're not as out of step in that regard as you might suspect. Certainly Tashista has formalized the process a bit oddly, but as much as I'd like to say that the rest of the universe—even my own world of Hazard—chooses its public officials in a less arbitrary manner, the truth is that wealth often does play a significant part in determining who holds public office. There have been cases where opposing candidates have claimed with some justification that the winner purchased his or her position, even if there is no formal procedure for doing so."

Jenilla looked doubtful, but didn't argue the point. Instead she began to describe their surroundings.

Soshambe had been planned as a series of modules, islands of residential housing separated by parks, commercial and pedestrian accessways, and public buildings. Sandor and Jenilla emerged from between two particularly ugly residential structures at the top of a slight decline, the foot of which broadened in a fan shape toward the next, somewhat smaller unit. To their right, a large garden complex had been broken up into a series of small green and blue islands of verdure by a graceful weave of pedways, mostly abandoned. The gardens were maintained only in the sense that the plant life was roughly cut back to allow easy use of the pedestrian paths; otherwise it was untended. Sandor was no expert on cultivation or agriculture, but he guessed that much of what grew here at present consisted of hardy weeds, that the original ornamental plants had been overwhelmed somewhere along the line by less desirable growth. Certainly the garden was still a pleasant contrast to the whites, dull grays, blues, and browns of the surrounding buildings, but viewed from close proximity, it was untended, dirty, most of the plants attenuated and out of balance, and much of the foliage diseased or damaged.

To their left was an open concourse, and a handful of street vendors had set up their carts in its center, hawking bruised fruits, miswoven scarves, stale doldren bread, even a few no longer popular holobooks. Their bantering trade talk was without enthusiasm and the handful of loiterers and through travelers who passed within the sound of their voices seemed generally unimpressed. Near the outskirts of the concourse, which overlooked a narrow waterway running under this part of the city, a dozen or so board games were in progress. Most of the players were elderly, those who had grown too old to consider themselves in contention for promotion to Moshamadur, but who had accumulated sufficient credit that they could conduct the remainder of their lives in indolence if not luxury.

Directly in front of them were two large traverseways, obviously designed to support vehicular traffic, although the relatively dense throngs using them consisted of pedestrians interspersed with occasional slow-moving scootsters.

"What are these buildings?" Sandor gestured ahead and slightly to the right, where a small cluster of shorter structures huddled under the shadow of the larger dwelling complexes.

"They're owned by private groups, most of them non-commercial. We do have a few opposition political movements, although they are generally ineffectual. It was a massive public outcry that led to Alyshambo, not the work of any of these. There are a few social clubs and private societies as well, and some administrative offices. The underways in this section of the city are administered from there," she pointed to one side.

"But all of your industry and most of your marketing is confined to Tashamir. It seems rather inefficient. If you mixed the four quarters together, wouldn't that help break down the barriers between classes?"

Jenilla thought before answering. "The Lucharist Society has suggested a number of radical alternatives, including a transformation of the city. Such a change seems impractical, though. Even if the Kishamkur could be induced to surrender their physical separation from the rest of the population, the cost of rebuilding would be prohibitive. And the Moshamadur would side with them."

"Why should that be? Surely they are as isolated as the Nashamata? And even if that were the case, the vast majority of the population resides here."

"Moshamadur makes up about one fifth of the city; they are no small force to contend with."

"But Nashamata is over seventy percent, and I still don't understand why the Mosham would side with Kishamkur."

"Moshamadur borders Kishamkur, Sandor. They can look out their windows and see into paradise. Although most of them will never live to see the day when they can cross over, the possibility exists in theory at least for all of them, and they are loathe to throw away that dream. The truth is, even many in Nashamata support the stratification, at least those who consider themselves upwardly mobile and capable of taking advantage of the system."

They passed into an artificial canyon between two opposing buttresses, pressing ever deeper into the city. For the rest of that morning, they moved from one aggregation of buildings to another, crossed gardens, concourses, traverseways, and narrower pedways. Sandor saw the grimier side of a grimy city, the areas where sex, drugs, and neurostim were sold with or without the tacit approval of the authorities. They passed numerous underway access stations, although Jenilla seemed reluctant to lead him below the surface. Sandor chose to ignore that for the time being, although he did not intend to allow that portion of the city to go unexplored, relevant to the case at hand or not.

They ate at mid-day, a pastry filled with meat paste called stouffa that was sold to them by an elderly one-legged man who called Jenilla by name. The food was hot and fresh, surprisingly good considering the poorly maintained and clearly old-fashioned equipment the man was using. They devoured several apiece, their appetites stimulated by the long walk, washing them down with yuba juice another vendor squeezed fresh for them from bruised fruit.

Early in the afternoon, they turned to skirt the low wall that separated Nashamata from Tashamir, heading south toward the border with Moshamadur. Sandor considered suggesting that they cross over through one of the many gates which pierced the wall, but Jenilla showed no such inclination and he made a mental note to explore this interface at a later opportunity. Just now, there was a higher priority on his agenda.

"Jenilla, are we anywhere near Nashamata Park, the place where the last victim was found?"

She nodded. "It's not far ahead. I assumed that you wanted to visit there last."

"I don't imagine I'll see anything that your investigators haven't already noticed, but I would like to examine the crime scene."

"The next concourse has a stairway which leads down into the park. We should be there shortly."

But as it happened, they never did reach their destination.

They had just stepped out into the concourse when Jenilla abruptly stopped, cocked her head as though listening to a sound inaudible to Sandor. As indeed she was. He had seen that same reaction enough times before to know what it was; she had a receiver embedded in her earlobe.

After a brief pause, she turned toward Sandor, her face impassive, but her fingers curling and uncurling in a nervous gesture which he noticed immediately.

"I am afraid we'll have to forego the park for today, Sandor. Something else has arisen which requires my . . . our attention."

He arched his eyebrows questioningly.

"Another Scarab victim has just been found, concealed in an underway station not far from here. A lifter is being sent to pick us up immediately."

Chapter Seven

The scene at the murder site was a study in organized chaos. Prefect Dunnis and her chief investigator, Tiko Parsi, were already present, along with what seemed to Sandor to be the majority of the Prefecture of Nashamata. Certainly there were close to twenty people within sight, using various arcane devices to examine the area for clues, fingerprints, sweat samples, DNA traces, anything else which might provide some means of identifying who was responsible and what had happened the night before. Later he was to learn that most of the technicians were freelancers who contracted to the Prefecture whenever a crime was committed, exchanging their services for credit.

The body had been discovered by one Egan Nopes, an itinerant vendor who specialized in consensual medications. His cart, partly unloaded into the stall adjacent to that in which the body of Akim Tutellatis still lay, was piled high with painkillers, stimulants, sensory enhancers, muscle conditioners and relaxants, skin dyes, hair coloring, follicle ointments, dietary supplements, mineral additives, neutralizers, and other bottles, packets, and syringes whose labels Sandor could not read, and whose purposes were probably even less discernible. He recognized at least one offworld product, a tablet which was supposed to improve sexual performance, although it had been banned or restricted on a number of worlds when its manufacturers had failed to prove its effects to be anything other than psychological.

Marym had noticed their approach and, after a brief conversation with two non-uniformed women who were holographing the scene, crossed to greet them.

"Sandor, Jenilla," she nodded to each in turn, voice pitched low. "It looks like our friend has wasted no time striking again."

"Is it certain this is a Scarab killing?" Sandor's head moved from side to side, quietly observing all that was taking place.

She nodded. "We won't have the test results for a while yet, but I believe so. The mutilations are the same; I'm pretty sure we'll find nemesol in the body. There's an appropriate entry wound."

Sandor nodded solemnly. "If I wouldn't be in the way, I think I should take advantage of this opportunity to look around. We had planned to visit the park site, but this is obviously more likely to be unchanged."

"Be my guest," she stepped slightly to one side. "But I hope you have a strong stomach."

As it happened, Sandor was able to maintain his composure, although the pungent mix of odors that assailed him moments later caused his gut to churn. No stranger to violence, he was nonetheless shocked at the savage nature of the attack.

Akim Tutellatis lay sprawled on his face at the back end of the stall, a space large enough to hold the half dozen technicians currently engaged in their respective specialties. Each of the four limbs was outstretched, although the right arm was slightly crooked to accommodate the wall dividing this stall from the next. Both hands had been severed at the wrist, the amputations obviously performed with an edged weapon of some sort rather than a laser. There was no cauterization of the wound and although the area of trauma did not display a particularly ragged separation line, one wrist in particular showed quite clear indications that two blows had been necessary to effect the separation. The feet had also been removed, and in both instances it was obvious that multiple blows had been inflicted, the heavier bones obviously presenting more of a problem. The hands and feet had been lined up neatly along the left wall of the stall. There was a small pool of blood there, a larger, irregular one under the body, and a third, the largest yet, on the open ground between the body and its severed portions.

"You get used to it after a while."

Sandor roused himself and recognized Tiko Parsi, who had moved silently to his side. "Inured, perhaps. Numbed, more likely. When was this reported?"

Tiko indicated a time just shortly before Jenilla had received the call. "We sent for the technical people immediately. Normally we request quotations before choosing a site team, but Marym has suspended the usual procedures for the Scarab case. These are the best people available in Nashamata. Olag there even came over from Moshamadur and he's so good, he's likely to end up in Kishamkur before the year turns." He laughed shortly. "Yet another reason we struggle here; all the first-rate talent is elsewhere."

"It looks to me as if the amputations were done at this spot," Sandor pointed to the open space, "and the body moved afterward."

"I'd say you were probably correct. If you'll notice, the head and chest have been struck repeatedly with some heavy object; the chest cavity is caved in, at least seven broken ribs, the jaw and nose have both been shattered as well as the right cheek. We'll know more when we move the victim, but judging by the relative amounts of blood, I'd say the blows were administered after he was already dead. They look purposeless, possibly an outburst of rage when the victim finally died."

"Which matches the previous cases. And I agree with you about the final series of blows. I've seen a similar case."

Tiko nodded and smiled unpleasantly. "Except that this is the first instance in which the head was severed as well." He leaned forward and pulled back the dead man's collar, revealing the damage to the back of the neck. "Cut it off and then replaced it." He shook his head. "Scarab is developing a decidedly bizarre sense of humor. The decapitation followed all the other injuries."

Sandor nodded restrainedly, keeping his voice low. "Which means either that Scarab has changed his style or that some other factor is involved. If we're right that the blows to the torso were the result of an outburst of rage, then why would Scarab have waited around long enough afterward to calm down, then methodically sever the spinal column and replace the head? If this is in fact his handiwork."

"A copy cat?"

"That possibility always exists. In exotic cases of this sort, where there is massive media coverage, it's not unusual for other latent murderers to jump on the cathartic bandwagon. Some even believe themselves responsible for the earlier atrocities. The Iceman established a secret code with the authorities on Lothar so that they'd know which victims were actually his. A very fastidious killer he was. I don't suppose there's any aspect of Scarab's activities which have been successfully withheld from the datanet? Perhaps the use of nemesol is as yet not a matter of public knowledge?"

"We've tried to get the various services to use some discretion, but they haven't been particularly cooperative. It took the threat of legal action to keep crime scene pictures off the videonet, as a matter of fact. Nemesol has not been specifically mentioned, but there have been reports that the victims were drugged prior to their deaths, and the specific nature of the drug is probably widely known."

Sandor sighed resignedly. "By now so many people have been involved, it would be folly to assume that much of anything has truly remained secret. I could tell you stories of planetary security directors who knew less than many of their citizens at large."

Marym, who had been talking quietly with Jenilla, beckoned to the two men. Carefully avoiding interfering with the technicians, they left the stall and joined her at the edge of the underway platform.

"There was nothing on the surveillance flittercams," she spoke directly to Tiko, but clearly for Sandor's benefit as well. "Not surprising. Preliminary estimate of the time of death places the incident between the seventeenth and eighteenth hour last night, but the last clear survey we have was during the afternoon. A flittercam was scheduled to pass through this tunnel during the twentieth hour, but it was . . . interfered with."

Sandor's head snapped up. "How so?"

She shook her head. "It's unlikely to be related. Apparently it was spotted by a couple of rousters at the Galen terminal. They cracked a lens and damaged a steering vane. It was retrieved from a maintenance accessway this morning, apparently got caught there because it couldn't distinguish between it and the exit. We have the attack on tape and it looks pretty casual and straightforward."

"Any chance the witness removed anything from the scene before reporting it?"

Marym shrugged. "I suppose it's possible, but we have no reason to suspect anything of the kind. Once he realized what he had stumbled on, he even abandoned his cart to make certain he was the first to report to us. The finder's fee for a Scarab victim will buy him a brand new cart filled with prime merchandise if he's so inclined."

"How much would the finder's fee be for the capture of Scarab himself?"

Marym looked surprised. "Don't you know? Why did you involve yourself in this investigation if you had no idea of the reward?"

Pursing his lips, Sandor made a slight, disapproving sound. "Marym, my interest here is diversionary, if you will pardon what may sound cold and uncaring. The accumulation of credit is no longer a matter of interest to me. In your terms, I am quite well off. Certainly I will not live long enough to exhaust the wealth available to me no matter how flamboyant a lifestyle I choose to lead."

While Jenilla and Tiko exchanged expressions of obvious disbelief, Marym gathered her wits and named a figure. Sandor remained unimpressed. "So little? I had expected a much larger figure."

"Until Prefect Leskar's boy was killed, it was only a tenth as much. You forget, Sandor, that Scarab is killing Nashamatans, people whose economic value to the community is very low. Leskar himself increased the fee the day before you arrived here. It represents a substantial amount of hard credit, enough to support a Nashamatan family for the rest of their lives, or a single Mosham for the same period, two if they were frugal."

A uniformed man approached deferentially. "Your pardon, Investigator Parsi, but we are ready to move the body."

Sandor wasn't really sure that he wanted to watch the operation, but he decided it was necessary.

* * * * *

Marym Dunnis diverted the lifter toward Moshamadur before returning to her office. Ever since arriving at the underway tunnel and seeing the body, her skin had itched and it had felt as though her clothes were stiff and soiled. Although it was still comparatively cool, sweat had broken out all over her body, and the dried salts and chafing clothing irritated her skin. She knew that this feeling of dirtiness was psychological; she had had similar physiological manifestations on previous occasions. But knowledge of the cause did nothing to dissipate the effect. She would be unable to concentrate on her duties until she had washed and changed into a clean uniform.

Kruzer was not there when she arrived. Ever since leaving the sporting world, he had confined his "work" to occasional inept manipulations of his credit portfolio, which were almost always accomplished through the datanet console in Marym's rooms. He was unwilling to pay the rental to have one installed in his own quarters, and sometimes she suspected he came to visit her solely to have an excuse to use her equipment. Not that their relationship was unsatisfactory, at least on a purely physical level. Kruzer was an attractive and inventive lover, and occasionally quite amusing in an unsophisticated fashion, but Marym never fooled herself into believing that their relationship held any serious level of emotional significance despite his periodic suggestions that they combine house holdings. The truth was that Kruzer was not particularly bright, and if he had not been endowed with the perfect body for athletics, he would almost certainly have been doomed to a life of futility in Nashamata, among those very people for whom he expressed such thoroughgoing contempt.

She was not happy with his political leanings either. For reasons which she had never quite understood, Kruzer was a member of the theoretically disbanded and marginally legal Hieratic party, and he supported restrictions on relocation from one quarter of the city to another and all of the other repressive positions of that organization. Since it was quite clear that he lacked any potential for further advancement himself, it was hard for her to understand why he would sympathize with a group from which he was forever barred, but she had long since given up trying to understand how his mind worked.

Empty though it was, her apartment was far from silent. The datanet screen was blinking insistently as she entered, and she crossed to activate the playback.

Four of the seven messages were advertisements, which she dismissed by touching the override icon; obviously it was time to upgrade her screening program. One of the remaining was a brief message from Prefect Leskar's secretary indicating that he would appreciate a call at her convenience, presumably to deliver the latest volley of suggestions, complaints, and questions. She suppressed an upsurge of irritation; Leskar obviously had a legitimate reason to be interested in the investigation. He rarely talked long, and a few of his suggestions had been quite provocative, although none of them had turned up anything useful. The next message was an automated notification from the Prefecture, indicating that her active link to their databank was being severed. She must have forgotten to sign off the last time she used it, although she would have sworn that she had broken the connection before going to bed. The same thing had happened on three or four previous occasions, and she had begun to wonder if there might be a fault in her equipment. Without her passcode sequence, no one else could have made the connection, and only Kruzer had physical access to the unit. Even if he had some bizarre reason for wanting to tap into the Prefecture databank, he lacked her access code. Perhaps the pressures of the Scarab killings were affecting her memory; certainly she had never forgotten to terminate a restricted link before this season.

The last message was a reply to one she had sent earlier. Savram Aras would be honored to entertain both his respected successor and the distinguished offworld pattern analyst. His recorded image mentioned a time early that evening. The latest killing created a host of new demands on her time, but she would not reschedule; the possibility of a productive chemistry between Aras and Sandor Dyle was an opportunity she could not afford to delay.

* * * * *

Although the technicians were still hustling about busily long after the body of Akim Tutellatis had been removed, Sandor saw no point in remaining. His examination of the dead man and the surrounding area furnished no particular insights, and when Tiko informed him that the preliminary tests had confirmed beyond question the presence of nemesol, he wasn't particularly surprised. There are patterns, and then there are patterns, he thought to himself.

"Jenilla, I don't see that we're accomplishing anything here. Is there any reason why we shouldn't complete our tour? There are still a few things I'd like to see."

She glanced up at the sky, apparently judging the time of day. "There's still some time left before dusk. We can use the stairway at the end of this tunnel and cut across to the park."

"No," he shook his head. "I don't think there's anything to be gained from visiting the park just now. I would much rather see the underways, the deeper levels."

Making no effort to conceal her displeasure, Jenilla moved restlessly, retreating into cool formality. "Ser Dyle, the underways are dangerous at the best of times, and it will be getting dark soon. Nor do I understand your interest. This," she gestured toward the row of stalls where Tiko stood pensively, staring at the bloodstains, "is the closest Scarab has gotten to the underways. They would appear to be irrelevant."

"I don't want to expose you to unnecessary danger, Jenilla," he replied, hoping that a hint of condescension would do the trick. It did.

Her back stiffened. "Ser Dyle, I was not concerned about my personal safety."

He raised both hands placatingly. "I never meant to imply any such thing, Jenilla." Which was a lie. "Excuse my clumsy phrasing. It was just my enthusiasm to develop a complete picture of Nashamata, you see; in order for me to understand your culture, and use that understanding to draw conclusions about how Scarab thinks, I must have a reasonably complete picture of life in this city. The very fact that Scarab has avoided the underways may be significant in itself, don't you think?"

After a hesitant moment, Jenilla nodded. "I see your point. Nor did I intend to overemphasize the physical danger involved. The underways are the spawning grounds of the gangs, but there is an accommodation between them and the Prefecture. So long as you stay close to me and we restrict ourselves to the public ways, the level of risk should be within acceptable limits. But I must insist that you take no action without confiding in me first, and if we do run into any difficulty, you'll let me do the talking and follow my instructions. There's a very narrowly-defined series of limits on our activities below."

"I am at your disposal, Jenilla. You know the rules here; I trust your judgment."

Despite her apparent capitulation, Jenilla remained motionless, still gathering her thoughts. "Sandor, I don't want you to think that I can be manipulated so easily."

Considering the available options, he decided to drop his eyes contritely. "Sometimes enthusiasm overcomes my sense of proportion. I apologize if I have given any offense."

She seemed to accept that response. "No apology is required. We both have the same goal, even if our routes sometimes diverge."

* * * * *

The underways of Nashamata were unlike anything Sandor had ever experienced on any of the several score settled planets he had visited in his lifetime. Not that he was unfamiliar with underground or otherwise contained societies. He had conducted business in the orbiting complex of Mechania with its seemingly endless levels of biotechnics laboratories, where over one million sentient beings existed in a totally artificial environment. On Waldemar, he had been given a tour of the Soto colonies in the caverns of the southern continent, and had even visited one of their remote probes studying magma temperature gradients. During the investigation of the Norsuko credit fraud on Pollicanthrus, he had spent extensive time in the Catacombs, a city which had expanded downward into the planetary crust to escape the seasons of incredibly devastating winds which had scoured the surface to a uniform vista of rolling dunes, bare rock, and hardy, but stunted, plant life. None of these had prepared him for the squalor of the underways of Nashamata.

The first impression was of ceaseless noise. It was insidious at first, a sensation almost tactile rather than auditory. The heartbeat of the city, its pulse and breath, shook the air and the floor with increasing force as Sandor and Jenilla descended through a series of tunnels into the bowels of Soshambe. The decline was so gradual that Sandor was unable to estimate how deeply they had penetrated, but he suspected that they were already at least a dozen stories below ground level when the rumbling became so insistent it could no longer be ignored. They were forced to speak more loudly in order to be heard, and when they finally leveled off in what Jenilla described as the Service level, he was suffering from a mild sympathetic headache, a throbbing directly behind his forehead. He began using advanced biofeedback techniques to suppress the pain.

The second impression was one of incredible filth. The upper tunnels had been disorderly, littered with transient trash, but no worse than he had seen many times in the past on other worlds. There were areas even on his home planet, Hazard, which amply demonstrated the human race's proclivity toward fouling its own nest. But as they moved deeper, the change was more than just a matter of degree. It was also of kind. This was not the discarded trash of unthinking passersby. There were open pools of lubricant fluids and other substances that bore a chemical stink which did not invite closer examination. Stains on the walls created grotesque silhouettes, some caused by leakage from the piping above, others of less obvious origin. There were fresh bloodstains on two occasions, an attenuated line that almost certainly indicated someone had pissed against a wall, and clumps of decaying matter which he initially thought the result of some sort of animal infestations, scavengers of some variety. Jenilla disabused him; it was human excrement. The few examples of domesticated fauna which shared Nashamata with the human race were uniformly wary of the tunnels. Under certain conditions, humanity established itself as a predator with no peer; underneath the city of Soshambe, the environment was so foul and artificial, only humankind and a few parasites could dwell within it.

Most of the people they encountered either moved away furtively, crossing the tunnel to pass at as great a distance as possible, or stiffened their backs assertively. The latter were generally younger men and women, frequently talking in near shouts, sometimes trading uncomplimentary remarks to one another or addressing the world in general. More than one made a disparaging remark about Sandor's spindly frame, which he pretended not to hear. The sense of despair, desperation, and danger was obvious. Here were those who had given up any hope of progressing to better standards of living, or even maintaining the minimalist lifestyle that characterized Nashamata. Human derelicts of all ages and descriptions hovered, most of them poorly dressed, a few wearing little more than loin cloths and shawls. Even the rebellious ones, presumably gang members, used garish and bizarre clothing and adornment to disguise their poverty.

It had grown warmer as they descended, almost unbearably hot by the time they reached the Service level. Jenilla and Sandor had both loosened their clothing in gradual stages. Although his expression remained impassive, Sandor grew increasingly enraged as he realized that the people he was passing, huddled in side tunnels, wandering aimlessly, often speaking aloud to non-existent companions, included mental defectives, the physically disabled, and many who just found themselves psychologically unsuited for the unrelentingly competitive world into which they had been born. On almost any other planet with which he was familiar, even those with governments generally considered repressive or unconcerned, most of these people would have been the beneficiaries of at least some minimal form of public support. Food, lodging, the bare necessities of life were considered basic rights almost everywhere that humankind had settled, and even among most of the sentient species with which they shared the universe. Even the ruthlessly brutal Nuomi culture made provisions for those with mental and physical impairment.

There was another breed of human here as well, one with which Sandor was far more familiar. They had seen several obvious gang members early on, individuals and even small groups, but now they encountered several clusters of young men and women with cicatrices emblazoned on their foreheads, and a sense of purposiveness that was clearly of a different order. Jenilla identified them as Strakans, a relatively noncombative group which enforced its territorial prerogatives through bribery more often than bloody clashes. They were rumored to have clients among the Kishamkur and Moshamadur, who ventured anonymously to the underways to indulge in outlawed drugs such as penta, vircosium, or even the frequently fatal neurosima.

Time advanced inexorably and they passed more gang members as they proceeded; although the artificial lighting—spotty as it was—was designed to mimic that of Tashista's primary, Sandor didn't need to refer to his chrono to realize that night was rapidly approaching the city above. Down here there was an eternal metaphysical twilight, independent of the natural world, sustained by energy channeled from the fusion plants embedded in the So Mountains. There was a bewildering variety of insignia differentiating the members of one group from another: tattoos on the forehead, peculiarities of clothing, heads shaven in unusual patterns, even one group which supported unusually large and almost certainly uncomfortable headgear surmounted by a spear point. In most cases, Jenilla was able to identify the gang, although a couple were either too small or too recently founded for her to recognize. She explained to him that the territories, membership, leadership, names, and appearances of most gangs were in a constant state of flux, although a few had managed to remain relatively stable throughout her adult life. She knew several of the individuals they encountered by name, although most of these studiously ignored her presence, or yelled some obscure insult before disappearing into another passageway. "They cooperate in private sometimes, but publicly, we're still the enemy. All authority is the enemy."

"Yet they intermingle. We must have seen members of a dozen different gangs."

She nodded. "Around here they do, even though this is Strakan territory. There is a fair amount of reasonably amicable intercourse among the gangs, even some trade. But there are clear lines of authority and control, and any intrusion into the area where the Strakans live would evoke an instant and violent response."

The tunnels were often lined with empty stalls and crumbling shop fronts, although occasionally some foolhardy or well protected entrepreneur was actually conducting some sort of business. Barter seemed to be the order of the day rather than the exchange of hard credit. In most cases, the goods involved were foodstuffs, fruits so bruised or otherwise damaged that Sandor would have been loathe even to consume juice pressed from their pulp, but there were other items as well, some clearly drugs, others weapons: knives, hand axes, punjata sticks, karis chains, spiked fumaroles. There were no gasjet weapons or lasers in sight, although it would not have surprised Sandor at all to learn that such things were also traded somewhat more clandestinely.

"Wonderful city you people have here," he muttered at last, unable to suppress his distaste.

"There's not much that we can do about it," Jenilla replied defensively. "The staff we have available couldn't even begin to police this area. If we tried, we'd have a virtual war on our hands, and we'd lose it. At best, we restrict the trouble to the underways, and most citizens know better than to venture down here. The unofficial position is that if the gangs want to try to exterminate each other, that's their concern. So long as they keep their depredations against the rest of the population to a minimum, their existence is tacitly accepted. They do, after all, maintain a measure of order."

"I think I've seen enough, Jenilla. What's the quickest way out of here?"

Events pre-empted her answer.

They had been making their way along the Service level, ignoring the periodic exits to the next lowest, which Jenilla identified as Maintenance. "Even the gangs stay away from there most of the time. The heat and noise are enough to drive you out of your mind if you spend any length of time down below. Human maintenance workers come in environmental suits with sound baffles, but they're rare; most of the work is taken care of by remotes with real-time monitoring capability." At each junction, pedestrian traffic seemed to pick up slightly, although it never approached the density common above. Sandor suspected the population was actually much greater than was officially admitted, that large numbers of people remained concealed in the strings of small cubicles that opened off the main tunnel or down the scores of side passages. Most of the former had closed doors labeled in the original Tashistan script, and Jenilla identified them as designed for storage, access to power lines, water supplies, datanet trunk lines, and other facilities. They passed several stairways leading up as well as other main trunk lines similar to the one they were using. They had just reached a sharp bend in the main tunnel where signs indicating egress to the surface remained barely legible under layers of graffiti. Sandor was more than ready to ascend, but before they could do so, he and Jenilla found themselves facing six resolute gang members, each adorned with a complex, feathery pattern tattooed across one shoulder and down to the opposite hip. None carried weapons, but menace was obvious in their posture and expression.

"Slee, I didn't know you were still alive." Jenilla's voice was firm, but Sandor detected underlying tension.

One of the six took a step forward, not the largest of the group, but the one most clearly self-possessed. Sandor tagged him as the leader even before he spoke.

"Prefect Jenny. Long time no see. I thought you had forsaken us in favor of the paying customers."

"If I don't visit this settling pit once in a while, how will I know how good I have it? And it's Prefect Kanark to you, Slee."

Maintaining his sarcastic grin, the man named Slee let his eyes move slowly from Jenilla to Sandor and back.

"To what do we owe the honor of this visit, Prefect Kanark?" The last two words were emphasized with obvious sarcasm. "Nobody called you. We can't. The datanet stations here are all out of order." One member of his entourage laughed nervously, cut it off almost immediately. "And who, or maybe what, is this thing you've brought along with you?"

"We have business here."

"No, no, I don't think you have." The humor was rapidly vanishing. "This is Stiletto territory, Kanark; Straka ends at the last westway junction. Stiletto takes care of its own problems. We don't ruffle the Prefect, the Prefect doesn't ruffle us. Why now?"

"This is no ruffle, Slee, just a walk-through. Move along, or I'll call a scramble."

"Don't pull that on me, Kanark. By the time they could respond to a scramble down here, your bodies wouldn't even be warm any more. They might not even bother."

Despite the threat, Jenilla seemed calmer, spoke with greater confidence than before. Sandor hoped she knew what she was doing. "With this crew?" She waved one hand casually toward the other five, three men and two women, who seemed uncertain how to respond. "Stiletto must be hard up for new members if this is what they assign to a vice-marshal to use for push."

"I'm full marshal now," Slee's back stiffened. "Your information is out of date."

"Oh, I'd heard that days ago, but I figured even Stiletto was smart enough to have corrected its mistake since then. Guess I overestimated the council. Still, if this is typical of your membership, I'm surprised Scarlet or Avenger hasn't wiped you out by now. Even Straka might have a chance."

There were murmurings of anger, and Slee scowled and turned to flash an angry glance at the others before turning back to Jenilla. "All right, Kanark, we've pissed on each other. What's the real problem? Why the visit? Who's the offworlder?"

"He's under my protection, Slee. We're not here to ruffle you. Leave it there and walk."

Slee shook his head. "No, I don't think so. Give me something, Kanark; this is straight between us. I've always been straight with you. Wait." He turned and said something to his companions in some argot Sandor couldn't follow. They looked uneasy, and one of the women was openly rebellious, arguing in the same abbreviated language until Slee snapped at her. Silently, the five turned and walked slowly toward the opposite end of the tunnel. Slee turned back to Jenilla. "See, no push. What's going on, Kanark?"

"You're not involved, Slee. Probably none of the gangs. The offworlder is here on a special assignment. You know my word is good; this isn't something you have to worry about."

Slee's posture eased slightly, although it remained alert, watchful. Sandor suspected that it would be very easy, and very dangerous, to underestimate this man. "Scarab?"

Jenilla hesitated, then nodded.

"Bad data, Kanark. Scarab is a surface problem. Not gang style, not gang targets. Why here?"

"The last victim was found in underway tunnel 144."

Slee shook his head. "Surface tunnel, underway by definition only. He stays out of our territory. Why are you here?"

"I requested the visit," Sandor interrupted. "I wanted to see what conditions were like in the undercity."

Slee turned toward Sandor, considered a response, but when he spoke, he had already turned back to Jenilla. "Why an offworlder?"

"That's our business, Slee. You keep your distance, we'll do the same."

"You don't look so distant to me right now, Kanark."

"I plan to correct that as soon as possible, Slee. You don't suppose I enjoy spending time down here, do you?"

He smirked. "It has its good points. No pressure, no Prefect."

"But plenty of push, right? Don't buzz me, Slee; I know the neighborhood."

The young man was silent, his eyes still moving back and forth between Sandor and Jenilla. When he finally spoke, he seemed more accommodating, if no less unfriendly. "Truth, Kanark. Tell me we're clear and you walk, no problem."

"You're clear," she replied immediately. "As far as I know. Like you say, Scarab isn't gang business."

He faced them a moment longer before resettling his shoulders and stepping back. "All right then, it's been a pleasure." His tone belied the words. "Stop back again when you have more time but right now, sorry you have to leave in such a hurry." He gestured to the other five, who moved back to join him, although not in a threatening fashion. With an exaggerated flourish, Slee waved to the two intruders and led his followers off toward the near end of the tunnel.

With an almost audible sigh of relief, Sandor turned to his companion. "My congratulations, Jenilla. That was well handled, and I see now why you were so reluctant to bring me here. Did I not notice a hand laser concealed within the folds of their leader's cloak?"

She nodded. "And two of the other four carried gasjets. If Slee had decided it was worth the risk, our bodies would be lying in one of the unused storage rooms by now. But he's smart enough not to bring down heat without good reason."

"You obviously knew how to handle the situation. Slee seemed to have a great deal of respect for you."

"He should. There's a scar on his left side that I gave him several years ago, while I was running with the gangs."

Sandor allowed himself to be surprised. "You were a gang member?"

"That's right, Sandor. I was vice-marshal of Stiletto for almost a year. That was before I joined the Prefecture, of course, back when I believed there was no chance to escape this place." She gave the tunnel an all-encompassing glance. "Speaking of which, I would like to return to the surface now, if you've seen all that you wish. Slee is one of the more reasonable leaders, and I'd rather not chance bluffing our way again."

"More than ready," he admitted. "Lead on. Or rather, lead up."

Chapter Eight

Marym Dunnis tried several times during the afternoon to reach Kruzer, with whom she had tentatively scheduled a dinner engagement, to let him know of her change in plans. The visit to Savram Aras, for both professional and personal reasons, now took precedence. Despite leaving messages on her own terminal and with the housekeeping program at Kruzer's residence, she learned from Tani that no acknowledgment had been received. Kruzer might have forgotten or simply ignored her request for a response, might be sulking because of the last-minute change in his plans, or might genuinely not have listened to his messages. The lack of resolution was just another minor irritation in a steadily growing list. Tiko Parsi had returned, scowling and frustrated, reporting that nothing new had been turned up at the site of the latest killing; surveillance, physical evidence, DNA testing, and a house-to-house canvas of the adjoining surface area had been equally unproductive. No physical evidence, no witnesses, cooperative or otherwise.

"Tani, leave a message at the Kishasta Club in case he stops by. If that doesn't catch him, then I'll apologize to him later. If he insists on being so unpredictable, he'll just have to deal with the inconvenience."

"Very good, Prefect." Brief pause. "Officer Kanark and Ser Dyle have just entered the building. Do you want them sent up to your office?"

"Let Jenilla go off-duty unless she wants to see me. She's already pulled more than a full shift today. I'll see Dyle immediately if he wishes. Wait. Where is he now?"

"Staff lounge."

"Tell him to wait there and I'll go right down."

* * * * *

The Prefecture lounge was one of those rare places of leisure in Nashamata that provided for the dispensation of a number of minor luxuries, including tailored drugs and an entertainment module, the first Sandor had seen since coming to Soshambe, although they were common in the tourist areas in Samarka. He had refrained from using artificial stimulants ever since early adolescence, but compulsively played solanka squares whenever the opportunity afforded itself. He preferred genuinely intelligent opponents to artificials; at their highest setting, the latter could defeat even the best human player in less than three dozen moves and he always felt as though he was cheating when he handicapped them. He was squandering some credit playing, or more precisely, losing an advanced-level game, when Marym entered the lounge.

"So you have human vices after all. This didn't show up in your files, Sandor."

He straightened, momentarily distracted, and the cursor square rebounded from the royal blue bumper field and caromed out of play. "I am found out, I fear, my guilty secret visible for all to see. Actually, I could probably justify this as a useful mental exercise. The secret to a high score is to analyze the pseudo-random field that shifts the border areas. They use a seed pattern to generate the sequence, but after a few rounds, it is possible to predict deflection angles and general strategic predispositions if you have a good enough eye."

"Sounds suspiciously like a rationalization to me," she replied archly. "Did you have a profitable day?"

"It's too soon to draw any conclusion. Certainly I've learned a great deal more about your city than I could have gleaned from the datanet. Some of it rather unpleasant, I'm sorry to say. And nothing immediately relevant to our purpose."

"Yes, you went into the underways, I gather." He raised an eyebrow inquisitively. "We routinely monitor the location of our staff, so we knew where you had gone."

"A disgraceful situation down below, no offense intended."

"None taken. It is a disgraceful situation, and the fact that some of the residents there are at least partly responsible for the abominable conditions that prevail is no excuse. But neither you nor I created the problem, nor do we have the means to correct it." She changed the subject abruptly. "Have you determined how you will proceed from this point?"

Sandor responded with animation. "It's too soon to formulate a definite plan of attack. Tonight, I hope to integrate the specific information involving the murders with a number of other measurable elements and conduct a second- and third-level correlation with staggered offsets. Logarithmic graphing of each

series with point-by-point comparisons may turn up a relationship."
He paused. "I apologize for descending into jargon."

"That's perfectly all right. I understand and enjoy
enthusiasm, particularly when it's directed towards the solution of a
problem like this. I went ahead and made arrangements for a visit
with Savram Aras this evening, if you're still up to it."

"By all means. Do we have time to dine first or do we wait
until later?"

"Beforehand would be best, although we'll have to be fairly
prompt about it. Savram's illness makes him tire easily, and he
becomes less coherent as he grows more fatigued."

"Your day is longer than I am used to and my stomach is
already complaining. We should leave as soon as possible then. I
believe my lifter is still above."

"Yes, but I've given Izik permission to deal with some
personal matters. We can use my private vehicle; I know a place in
Tashamir whose cuisine should match anything you can find in
Samarka, if not offworld. We're not unsophisticated in all matters."

* * * * *

The meal was every bit as good as she had promised, and
Sandor felt completely satiated as Marym piloted the lifter to a two-
story building in the Moshamadur district, landing in a small
adjacent lifter park, one which allowed them to disembark onto a
covered walkway, protected from the evening's drizzle, and remain
dry as they crossed to the main entrance. They were admitted by the
door program to a small vestibule, where a wide stairway led up to
Savram Aras's private residence. "Because of his disability, Savram
moved here from a single dwelling over toward Kishamkur. His
medicators thought it unwise for him not to have human assistance
near at hand."

Marym stepped in front of the scanner at the top of the stairs
and the door opened silently, sliding back into the wall, revealing a
large, open area beyond. Tashistan rooms were generally smaller
than those to which Sandor was accustomed, with close-set walls,
narrow hallways, and low ceilings, almost as if these people needed
a tightly closed environment so that they could reach out and touch
the physical limits of their lives. Possibly because of his medical
condition, the former Prefect of Nashamata lived in an atypical
environment. Some of the interior walls had been removed entirely,

others cut to half height, forming discernible but largely ineffectual visual barriers between different portions of the room.

The far corner was filled with an oversized bed adjacent to which stood a battery of specialized equipment that included a barely recognizable datanet console with videoscreen, a musical synthesizer, and several other units whose purposes were not apparent. Near at hand was a sitting area, with old fashioned non-articulated chairs and a small, oval, pastiche crystal table. Across from the bedroom toward the left wall, a large cubicle had been closed off, probably containing oversized bathing facilities. Just beyond was the mouthpiece of a delivery tube through which Aras obviously received his meals and other items he could order through the datanet. A holographic projector stood against the left wall, which was covered with shelves whose purpose was pragmatic rather than decorative. Savram Aras possessed one of the larger private holobook collections Sandor had ever seen. There were easily four of five thousand, most neatly arranged, a few piled in haphazard fashion.

Aras greeted them from the depths of an elaborate cyberchair, a prosthetic device which had become obsolete on most other worlds. Dynamically powered artificial limbs were routinely substituted for missing or dysfunctional legs, and, except for the brain itself, any organ in the human body could be replaced with an artifice. The cyberchair moved rapidly across the floor toward them, automatically adjusting its course to avoid objects even when its passenger failed to allow sufficient clearance. Having accessed the former Prefect's datafile, Sandor had expected an older-looking man, frail, possibly with a wandering mind. That wasn't the case at all; Aras had obviously used the cyberchair's conditioning programs to keep the muscles in his arms well toned and flexible, and although his useless legs were concealed by a bright yellow cloak thrown across the lower half of the machine, Sandor suspected he also used regular massages to maintain them as best he could.

"Come in, come in. Marym, it has been too long since you last visited. And you must be Ser Dyle; you have no idea what a great privilege it is to meet you."

"It is my pleasure entirely, Ser Aras. Marym has told me a great deal about you, and the high regard in which you are held. The case resolution ratio during your administration has also given me reason to look forward to making your acquaintance."

"Flattery, Dyle, rampant flattery, but I love every bit of it. At the time, I was too busy to pay much attention to the opinions of those around me, but in retirement, I find that I was something of a minor hero, and that rather pleases me, however belatedly. But please, sit down, both of you."

"You're looking well, Savram. Thank you, incidentally, for the tip on the Rozzi embezzlement. You were absolutely right."

"A lucky flash of insight; think nothing of it. She might have gotten away with it if she hadn't gotten so greedy toward the end. Provide enough data points and the pattern emerges."

As Sandor eased into a chair, he found himself automatically anticipating a mechanical adjustment to the contours of his body.

"Waiting for it to move, are you?"

Sandor glanced up at his host. "Yes, as a matter of fact. Very perceptive of you to notice. I don't care for articulated furniture personally, but it's obviously become the fashion almost everywhere."

"Old habits persist. I'm not anti-technology, but I do believe that we become overly enamored of it at times. There's a tendency to become excessively dependent upon our inventions. Once they've taken responsibility for our physical actions, the next step is to allow them to do our thinking." He glanced down at his prosthesis. "Recent events make me particularly conscious of that fact. I was attracted to the Prefecture because of a fondness for problem solving, you know, the same urge that led me to pattern analysis. A field in which you have made a considerable reputation for yourself, Ser Dyle."

"Exaggerated, I'm quite certain," he replied deprecatingly. "A few papers published, but nothing more substantial. I can offer embellishment, but the main structure can only be erected by greater minds than my own."

"I have thought at times of fashioning a paper based on my experiences here. There are applications which seem seriously neglected in the scholarly press. Alas, without formal credentials, I cannot imagine anyone taking my poor ramblings seriously."

"There's always room for new thoughts, Ser Aras. Pantagria acknowledges the contribution of many amateurs in her *General Theory of Scope*."

"But with thinkers of the stature of Parnell, Borovin, and Karis Korkova dominating current discourse, I admit it's hard to imagine even the most talented dabbler contributing anything revolutionary to the existing body of thought."

"You have read Korkova then? I thought him unknown outside of the Patternological Congress."

"This isn't quite the backwater planet it sometimes appears, Ser Dyle. I have to confess that his *Treatise on Absolute Matrices* is sometimes too abstruse for me, but I found his discussion of interpolative overlays very useful."

"I'm afraid you're both speaking well over my head," laughed Marym. "I had to struggle with Parnell's *Basic Principles*."

"Marym is too modest," Aras assured Sandor. "She's actually quite a fine intuitive analyst in her own right. It's almost impossible to function as a Prefect without a general grounding in pattern analysis; our society is so thoroughly wedded to the datanet, everything we do, every interaction we have with our environment, is recorded in some fashion, and those recordings, that data, can be analyzed, used as a predictive tool as well as a deductive one. The mass of data is daunting in its quantity, but it provides a means through which we may detect tendencies of which the individual himself or herself may well be completely unconscious. And the automated internal analytic programs, no matter how sophisticated, only pick up the most obvious patterns. It requires human intuition to bridge the gap between potentiality and actualization."

"Absolutely true, although a surprising number of individuals and governments refuse to admit that fact."

"No one likes to be told that they are predictable. Here on Tashista, the climate was particularly open to pattern analysis during the years of the initial colonization. Relationism implies that every act is a reconciliation of two or more partially opposed forces, so it follows that the resolution of these divergent elements will create patterns which can be detected and, at least in mass terms, measured with some degree of accuracy."

"I thought relationism was rejected following the death of the original founders?"

"Well, it's true that the official status of the Lucharist Society changed following Luchar's death, and it's now more of a debating club than a political force. But there is no way to completely eradicate the founding principles of a civilization, and there is a lingering acceptance of the basic tenets of that system, even if the terminology and much of the more rigid conceptual structure has been rejected."

"Sometimes a concerted effort to rebel against an unfashionable philosophy results in a society just as thoroughly shaped, although negatively, as by an unconditional embrace."

"You're thinking of the Bunderkind on Trammela IV?"

"Actually, no, I had in mind the Dosidian Heresy, but the Bunderkind are also an excellent example."

Marym shook her head. "Lost again, I'm afraid. Would either of you like something to drink?"

"Pardon me, both of you," Aras spoke hastily. "It's been so long since I've had company, I've forgotten the duties of a host. I have tannis brew and aquavitalia at hand, and the service here is quite prompt if you'd prefer to order something else."

"Tannis is fine with me," Sandor replied agreeably. "If I drink anything stronger, I start to fall asleep in the middle of conversations."

Aras started to turn toward the far corner but Marym rose, forestalling him. "I'm supercargo here, Savram. Go on with your conversation while I get the drinks. You still favor aqua, don't you?"

He nodded. "Tannis seems to react poorly with the medication they're giving me. Not that anything seems to react favorably to it, including my body."

Marym paused, her expression serious. "There's no progress then?"

"Neither progress nor decline, they tell me. I have these periodic lapses of memory, but they pass. The paralysis hasn't affected anything but my legs, and some of the sensation has returned there, although I still can't stand unassisted." He sighed. "At least this enforced retirement has given me an opportunity to catch up on my studies. Nor can I really say I miss the everyday pressures of the Prefecture. It's much easier accessing only the files I find interesting, rather than trying to stay up to date on everything. I can already see where you've aged prematurely, Marym; don't take the job too seriously. That's what I did, and you see what happened to me."

Emotion tugged at the corner of Marym's face, but she maintained her composure long enough for the moment to pass, and when she turned to fetch their drinks, the movement seemed almost natural.

Sandor and Savram Aras discussed pattern analysis a short while longer, enough for the former to realize that the retired Prefect had much more than a broad general knowledge of the field, was in fact quite up to date in a number of areas which had application to law enforcement, economic management, political science, and other fields. He was familiar with a number of the more abstruse theoreticians, and had read summaries of many significant case studies, including most of those Sandor had written. The ensuing discussion started to drift off into a comparison of mathematical formulae and correlating philosophies, and it was with some regret that Sandor finally brought the subject back to the matter at hand.

"I understand that you conducted most of the investigations of the Scarab killings yourself."

"While I was still in office, that's true. And I routinely review the new cases even now. Marym may have told you that I was granted the privilege of maintaining my security access, so that I might make suggestions from time to time even though I have no official standing."

"I've told him how helpful some of your insights have been. It's like having a talented consultant service at no charge."

"You're kind, Marym, but since Scarab is still at large, Sandor can hardly believe that my assistance is invariably productive." They had dropped the formality of last names long before.

"Don't denigrate yourself, Savram," she objected. "Neither of us has had any degree of success with Scarab. But your analysis resulted in the capture of Ador Alinth, we probably would not have stumbled across the mechanism for the Cyberscan embezzlement without your help, and I still don't understand how you knew Dolann was responsible for the sabotage at the lifter assembly plant."

"Magic," he responded wryly. "It actually wasn't much more than a lucky guess and the process of elimination. He was the only floor worker whose leisure activity time showed a noticeable decrease, and it was only logical to assume he'd been returning to the plant during off-shift hours." Then, more seriously. "Sandor, I struggled with the Scarab killings for two years; even during the other secants, I spent a disproportionate amount of time trying to find some lead, a pattern, a predictable tendency, a flaw in the killer's methods. Random violence has always bothered me, although I suppose we should call it pseudo-random, since there is pattern to all behavior. I can accept the urge to steal, particularly here in Nashamata; I don't like it, but it arises from a perfectly understandable human emotion: greed, survival, ambition. With reservations, I can even accept the organized violence among the various underway gangs. They are, after all, protecting or extending their territories, and that's an urge that has been a part of the human species ever since our primitive ancestors arose on Earthshrine. But every so often, there is a crime so pointless, so destructive of human life, I just cannot accept that the perpetrator is entirely human. Three times now random violence has struck my life, and three times I have failed to resolve it. I assume you have reviewed my personal datafile as well as my professional one?"

Sandor nodded. "As much as is in the public record. Your involvement made that necessary; I include every conceivable piece of data in my analysis, you understand."

Aras waved away his explanation. "No need to explain yourself. I would have done the same; there is no way to discern patterns without filling in as complete a background as possible. You are aware then of the circumstances surrounding the loss of my family?"

Sandor felt uncomfortable but indicated assent. Marym was looking distinctly ill at ease as well, although Aras himself seemed stoic enough. "Your wife was slain in what might have been a kidnap attempt here in Nashamata, while watching a kubits match. It was badly bungled if so, possibly because of the proximity of so many witnesses, possibly because her attackers never meant anything more than assault. They were never identified. I believe your son disappeared into the underways just about three years ago, and has since been presumed dead."

"Correct on both counts. Oh, the two young women who assaulted Dorinda might have planned to exchange her for hard credit if such a thing had occurred to them, but I'm fairly convinced by now they were more interested in proving their prowess than in enriching themselves. Dorinda and I had gone through the old fashioned permanent bonding ceremony, you know; it's quite out of fashion here on Tashista, but not completely unknown. The blow was quite severe." He remained silent, staring into space for some moments, and neither Sandor not Marym chose to interrupt his reverie.

"My son's situation was rather different," he resumed at last, apparently unaware of the awkward lapse. "He was strongly affected by his mother's death. We had been quite a close family, unfashionably so. For almost a year, he brooded endlessly, occasionally erupting into fits of almost violent despair. He overindulged in neurostim until I forced him to undergo stabilizing therapy. When that passed, he became fascinated with the underways, spent most of his waking hours studying everything which had been datanetted on the subject. His trips beneath the surface became more frequent, more prolonged. At first he told me that he was searching for some clue as to the identity of his mother's attackers, but as time passed, I knew there was more to it than that, that somehow he had become entranced with the place, its lifestyle, the bizarre manners of its inhabitants. I don't know if he ever fully understood his own motivations, but eventually it became irrelevant. He joined one of the gangs and then . . . just disappeared." Aras turned away, his voice threatening to crack. Tactfully, Sandor chose that moment to finish his drink, providing Aras with an excuse to absent himself momentarily.

"Let me refill that for you, Sandor."

When his cyberchair had carried him out of earshot, Sandor spoke in a whisper. "No evidence of his son's fate was ever discovered, I gather. There was nothing in the file."

Marym made a negative gesture. "There were rumors that he had been killed during a gang war, but never any proof. He just dropped out of sight. Savram himself spent many of his free hours searching the underways, at considerable risk to his own life, until his physical condition made such forays impossible. But there are so many opportunities to dispose of a body down there, many of which leave no trace at all . . ." Her voice trailed off as Aras turned and started back in their direction.

They talked for a considerable time thereafter, elaborating on details of the earlier investigations. Sandor learned little new. Aras reviewed the physical methods he had used to gather evidence, the intelligence he had attempted to glean from the citizenry at large, his frustration with the shortages of manpower and material, and a general outline of his efforts to use pattern analysis to find an underlying order to the apparently orderless crimes. In general, his work paralleled the initial analysis Sandor himself had conducted the night before, but Aras had explored more recondite areas as well, including a few that Sandor had not yet considered. He added them to his mental agenda and simultaneously noted that Savram Aras had been wasted here on Tashista, that he had an untrained but obvious talent that might have made him a wealthy man elsewhere. Or rather even wealthier. It was evident from the accommodations that Aras was not short of credit. Then Dyle remembered the ailment which had brought the man's career to an end, and wondered if a cure were possible offworld. Suratic disorders were specific to Tashista, of course, but there were far more sophisticated research and treatment facilities elsewhere.

When Marym and Sandor finally took their leave, full darkness had fallen outside. Each of them was caught up in private thoughts as the lifter rose and headed for the Black Ark Hostelry.

"A most impressive man," Sandor acknowledged finally.

"Yes, he is that. As much as I wanted this position, I wish I could have gained it under other circumstances."

"His condition really is incurable then?"

"Treatable perhaps, curable no. Suratic nerve disease is still a mystery, Sandor. It affects each individual in an unpredictable fashion, particularly when the infection is in the brain itself. Savram's paralysis, for example, appears to be at least partly psychosomatic; his brain is convinced he cannot walk, therefore he cannot walk. But the reason he believes in his disability is that the cognitive portion of his brain which interfaces with those muscles has been affected; the motor nerves themselves are still functional. There are other symptoms, less obvious but more frustrating. He has brief periods of partial amnesia; on one occasion when I visited, it was obvious that he knew me, but could not remember my name. There are occasional extreme emotional shifts—hysterical laughter, inconsolable grief—although he might have had those even without the disease. Certainly he has more cause than most. His life has had enough real tragedy without phantom attacks like these. When he resigned, it was because he knew that the Kudara and the city council were preparing to remove him from office. They leaked the information to him so that he could salvage what remained of his dignity."

"But he still advises you."

"That's right, and I wasn't soothing his ego when I said his assistance was valuable. When his mind is under control, it's a finely honed tool. He has provided the key to the solution of several major and countless minor crimes. I only wish there was something I could do to repay him for his kindness."

"Is that why his son's case has been reopened?"

She started so violently that the lifter jumped from its course, momentarily causing the horizon to sway. "How did you know that?"

"You forget, I have unlimited access to Prefecture files. One of the first queries I conducted was a string search for every investigation involving a proper name linked in any fashion to the Scarab killings."

"Including my own?"

"Certainly." He refused to be embarrassed. "You were proven innocent of accepting a bribe, as I recall."

Marym flushed. "The offer was made, but I refused. On Tashista, it is almost tacitly assumed that all public officials accept credit in consideration of special favors, but I have never been that desperate for advancement."

"So your dossier would indicate. I saw nothing about which you have any reason to be ashamed, Marym."

She relaxed, but only slightly. "It remains a bit unsettling to know I am a subject for investigation as well as an ally, Sandor."

"A subject perhaps, but not a suspect. You and Savram are, as far as we know, the only people to have knowingly seen Scarab, however briefly, and survive."

"A lot of help we've been in that regard. We saw a large, huddled shape, almost certainly a man, but otherwise indistinguishable from tens of thousands of others, millions if we accept the possibility that Scarab is a transient."

"You don't keep records of outsiders visiting Soshambe, do you?"

"No, it's an open city, Sandor. We're not a primitive world. And before you ask, we did check the killings against registered visitors, even though less than ten percent of the transients in the city at any given time actually register their presence. There was no correlation whatsoever against any specific outsider, or group of outsiders."

"That would have been too easy," he admitted. "It was on my list only because I believe in being thorough in all matters. Never ignore the obvious; some criminals are incredibly narrow-minded. Unfortunately, Scarab, whatever he may be, is not stupid. He would not have left such a clear trail."

"He'll have to make a mistake sometime, if he's human."

"If he continues to kill, he certainly will. No one can refrain from making an error indefinitely. He has been lucky so far, either in not leaving a useful pattern for us to find, or leaving one obscure enough that we have yet to recognize it for what it is. Probably the latter. We are all prone to fall into patterns so faint, so hidden, that we cannot see our own effect on the ripples of the universe. That doesn't mean the ripples aren't there. It is for us to refine our senses adequately to spot the misplaced element, the slight alteration in timing, the displacement of the fabric of reality. Sooner or later, we will have him."

"But how many more will die first, Sandor? How many data points must we have?"

"That, Prefect Dunnis, I cannot tell you."

* * * * *

Back in his room, Sandor activated the datanet, reopened the files he had created or accessed previously, and scanned the displayed information in a desultory fashion, trying to determine if there was any significant change now that a new data point had been added. Every so often, he would enter a new question, manipulate the display in some fashion, pursuing every possibility as it suggested itself.

"Display graphic analysis of the intervals between each incident."

<Bar, line, syslog, or custom style?>

"Bar." The screen filled with red bars of varying lengths. "Define limits."

<Maximum interval, 12 days. Minimum interval, 3 days. Average interval, 6.875 days.>

"Derive second-order function and display." The graph shifted, smoothed itself out, but still seemed random. "Clear screen."

Sandor began pacing again, unsatisfied. Serial crimes of this sort always had a pattern, some underlying shape. Sometimes the elements of that pattern provided no immediate assistance in solving the crime. The fact that a criminal only struck during certain hours of the day was only helpful if there existed a way to increase surveillance during that same period. Proof that a murderer was righthanded or had black hair or was nearsighted was of little assistance in a population that was predominantly righthanded, had black hair, or suffered from myopia. But even the inconsequential patterns seemed faint or non-existent in this case; it was almost as if there were no single murderer. Scarab might be no more than a random series of events with multiple causes, if it wasn't for the specific way the victims had been subdued and mutilated.

"Access all information pertaining to Akim Tutellatis."

<Data available.>

Sighing heavily, Sandor seated himself and began perusing the various files, credit transfers, vital statistics, employment record, family structure, political involvement in a trade union movement, health statistics. There was already a surprising amount of data pertaining to the murder itself. Tutellatis was a small-time entrepreneur who lost credit about as often as he gained. He seemed perfectly ordinary, although there was one interesting coincidence that surfaced when Sandor did a cross-reference between the latest victim and all of the other names connected to the case. Akim Tutellatis was known to have employed Mikki Seurat on at least three occasions and he had sold art supplies to Tantra Brach. It might be nothing, no more than a coincidence. There had been casual connections among several of the other victims. But it was interesting.

Several attempts to recast the existing data in new ways proved unproductive and Sandor found his attention wandering, frustrating his ability to concentrate and approach this problem systematically. For some reason, his mind refused to respond to self-discipline this evening.

"Query. During any of the Scarab crimes, was there ever evidence of physical resistance, an attempt to flee, any positive action on the part of the victim?"

<Negative.>

"That was certainly terse enough," he muttered. After a few seconds of thought, he called for information on nemesol and its availability in Soshambe, discovering nothing that contradicted what he'd already been told.

"Were the amounts of nemesol found in the victims identical?"

<Negative.>

"Display range of amount of nemesol found in victims." The bar chart that resulted was almost flat, the differences in dosage obviously insignificant except in the third case. This one entry dipped to about two thirds of that which held true in the other cases. "What's the story with data point three?"

<Please rephrase.>

"Disregard. Access Prefecture summary report for data point three."

Sandor reviewed the file he had already read twice before. Savram Aras and Marym Dunnis had spotted the attack in progress and intervened. Aras broke off pursuit when it was obvious they had no chance to overtake the fleeing suspect, directed Marym to request immediate full coverage of the area by flittercams, lifter patrol, whatever could be brought to bear, while he attempted to render assistance to the victim. By the time the medicopter arrived, the man was dead. Despite the interruption, Scarab had already wounded his victim mortally. Their interruption would not account for the lesser amount of nemesol because the killer had already proceeded beyond that point at the time he was discovered. The report Aras had included in the file was uncharacteristically personal and bitter, and announced that he was taking personal charge of the investigation.

"Not necessarily a good idea, my friend Savram. Sometimes our own feelings alter the pattern." He caught himself yawning and sat back. The problem was too complex to attack with dull wits. "Save and exit."

But he sat staring at the darkened screen for a long time before finally going to bed.

Chapter Nine

Tamara Stoat emerged from troubled dreams to find that Ramis was missing from his half of the bed. In itself, his absence was not particularly alarming. Despite the best efforts of the bed to mold itself to his body shape, Ramis frequently had difficulty sleeping because of the sporadic pains which raced through his back. He was stoic about it, never complained, was always careful not to disturb her own rest while he rose, sometimes sitting in the front room of their small apartment watching the videonet with the sound turned very low, or just staring off into the darkness. She knew he was disturbed by the fact that her income now exceeded his own by a quite substantial amount; in fact, even when he had been able to work regularly, he rarely brought home the amount of credit she routinely earned with her design work. In a society where the sole arbiter of social standing and personal worth is wealth, Ramis had suddenly found himself slipping backwards.

Tamara lifted her head, still troubled by unspecific dreads with which her unconscious had been struggling, straining to hear the whispering of the videonet, some evidence of normality. But neither light nor sound was evident from the other room and she had an uncanny sense that she was alone, absolutely and irrevocably. She bit her lip, telling herself she was being foolish, trying to decide whether or not to attempt further sleep. Rest would be elusive until she confirmed that her fears were groundless, she realized, torn between conflicting desires. If he was there, she would feel immense relief; it not, she would toss restlessly until she heard him returning sometime between now and sunrise. Impatient with her own dissembling, she chose to act. Slipping silently from the bed, she crossed the room on bare feet, not wanting Ramis to know she was spying on him. She might as well have saved the effort; he was not in the front room, nor anywhere else in their quarters.

Perhaps he's just gone out for a while, she told herself. Ever since the pains had begun to affect his mobility, Ramis had taken periodic nocturnal walks, and they had grown more frequent with the passage of time. The exercise helped, he'd told her, shaking the vertebrae back into place, or stretching overly tense muscles, or working whatever therapeutic magic was involved. But on each occasion, his eyes were slightly averted, and she knew that he was lying; Ramis was reacting to an internal drive to do something, anything, to remedy the situation, even as pointless an activity as walking the city streets in the darkness. He'd always been the kind of man who acted rather than observed; although he'd played strikeball as an adolescent and still went curling down by the docks from time to time, he had never shown interest in watching any of the professional interurban sporting leagues, even when Nils Kruzer was leading Soshambe to a planetary championship. She wouldn't have minded his solitary wanderings, the fact that he sought solace outside of her arms, if she'd thought he gained some peace of mind as a consequence. Inevitably, he returned in a preoccupied, mildly irritable state that caused her to retreat into a shell of busy work, waiting for his nerves to untense along with his body.

Tamara returned to the bed, but she sat up in the darkness for a long time, staring into the unknowable future, bitterly regretting the unfairness of life. She resolved to make one more effort to convince Ramis to seek assistance from the city medical facilities. They could afford it now, even if she had to allow them to garnish her wages. They couldn't continue this way any longer.

* * * * *

Although the hour was quite late when Marym Dunnis returned from dropping Sandor Dyle at the hostelry, she remained filled with restless energy. The lights were off in her apartment, and a quick check of the bedroom ascertained that Kruzer had not used his entry code and fallen asleep during her absence. More than once in the past, she'd discovered him snoring in her bed when she thought she was returning to solitude. Theoretically they alternated their liaisons between apartments, but the ex-athlete's was always in such a state of disarray that Marym usually tried to arrange things so that they used her place. Not that she was such a flawless housekeeper herself, but she at least made rudimentary efforts to keep things in order, and hired a cleaning service to give it a thorough going-over three times in every secant. Kruzer may or may not have noticed the disparity, but he never voiced any objection to the arrangement. At the entrance to her den she called "Lights," then crossed the suddenly illuminated room to her datanet console. A quick tap activated the screen, which indicated there was one message waiting for her.

"One pissed off Kruzer, no doubt," she leaned forward and keyed it for viewing. "Well, if you were a little more predictable . . ."

Surprisingly, the screen displayed not a message from Kruzer but instead the abstract of a Prefecture datafile containing details of the Sian Pashoti case. The adolescent boy's wealthy parents had purchased privacy for their wayward son over a year previously, assuring then-Prefect Aras personally that they would oversee his rehabilitation and keep him away from neurostim in the future. The boy had reacted with flashbacks and wild mood swings, a rare but not unknown side effect, and since his dream fantasies were particularly violent ones, there had been several unpleasant episodes during which he could no longer distinguish fantasy from reality. His attack on a neighbor's thirteen-year-old daughter would have been even more serious if he'd struck her across the eyes instead of the forehead, and as it was, the anti-scarring treatment had been expensive and time-consuming and the girl was still in therapy. The file was confidential Prefecture material and should not have appeared on an unprotected datanet viewer under any circumstances.

Marym slid into the seat, split the screen, and used the right side to input her access code and connect directly to Prefecture headquarters. Almost immediately the clasped hand symbol appeared, paused a beat, then defaulted to a menu screen. She tapped for the Night Officer.

A young woman looked up from the desk where she'd been intently studying a printout. "Yes, how may I help you?" Her fatigue-heavy eyes suddenly became alert and her posture straightened. "Prefect Dunnis. I wasn't expecting . . ."

Marym made a brushing away motion with her hand. "Don't worry about it, Sileva. I remember working night duty." She paused a second to let her subordinate regain her equanimity. "Sileva, I just arrived home to find a confidential department document on my terminal, transmitted . . ." She glanced at the left side of the screen, repeated a series of digits which indicated the transmission had taken place early that same evening. "What in the world is going on? I could query the control program from here but I'm not certain how to proceed. Could you please find out immediately how security was breached? Call in Data Services if you have to; we pay enough for their retainer, they might as well earn it."

Sileva nodded. "I'll look into it right away, but I think I can tell you. We had a problem here just after you left. One of the big maintenance carriers lost its guidance system just as it was turning into the yard, ran right into the building. No extensive damage but there was a brief power interrupt. The backup took over but there was a lag; Data Services has two people here now going over the tracking log."

"Damn it!" Marym had tried unsuccessfully to convince the Kudara to upgrade the obsolete power backup system at the Prefecture. "How much memory loss?"

The younger woman seemed startled. "Why, none. Someone would have notified you immediately if we had lost data integrity, Prefect."

Marym nodded to herself. "Yes, of course, I'm sorry. It's late and I probably need to get some sleep. But I do want to know how that file got transmitted."

"I'll have them look for that specifically when they run their diagnostics. We did have strange results for a few seconds. Some procedures aborted; file access pointers shifted to different fields or even different files."

"All right. I guess it'll keep until the morning." She was about to end the conversation and break the connection when something else occurred to her. "Thanks for the help, Sileva. Have a pleasant shift." A second later she had returned to the menu, where she now tapped into the data queue for her private office terminal, suspecting that Kruzer might have left a message there. But although there were over a dozen items awaiting her attention, mostly routine reports she had requested from her staff, there were no personal transmissions whatsoever.

Nor was there any answer when she subsequently punched in Kruzer's private terminal code. After a momentary hesitation, she broke that connection as well, and without leaving an entry. "Enough for tonight, Marym. You can sort things out in the morning," she told herself, but as she started to turn away from the console, a fresh anomaly presented itself.

To one side of the console, on a level spot of the housing, lay a fragment of uneaten sandwich.

The bread was starting to go stale, but the cheese and meat paste inside were still moist.

* * * * *

A sleek, state-of-the-art lifter set down in an out-of-the-way lifter park not far from the Cassio district of Nashamata. Moments later, a single figure emerged, a heavyset man of average height wrapped in an expensive black cloak made of the finest material available for that purpose in Tashamir. In the unlikely event that anyone chanced upon the lifter, and happened to pass it on the side which had thoughtfully been placed facing the steelcrete abutment, they would have noticed that it bore the symbol of the Kishamkur Prefecture on its driver's side door.

The figure proceeded directly from there to the very same street where he had unknowingly been observed on a previous occasion by Tamara Stoat, taking a position concealed from view by several potted chiruga trees. It was an excellent vantage point from which to watch the quietly busy commercial establishments just opposite without being seen in return. The figure settled back into as comfortable a stance as possible, anticipating a long wait.

Customers came and went with some frequency, almost always unaccompanied. Although visits to such places were legal, more or less, there was a degree of social reproach, not because of any prudish objection to pleasures of the flesh or mind, but born rather from the sense that expending credit on transient experiences reflected a lack of seriousness, a failure of commitment to exert all efforts toward upward mobility. Nevertheless, there were enough Nashamatans weak in their economic resolve to support more than a dozen drug, stim, and flesh parlors in the Cassio sector alone, and there were three similar districts scattered through the neighborhoods of Nashamata.

Whenever a customer emerged from the darkness to enter through one of the dimly lit doors, or subsequently emerged, the lurking figure became instantly attentive, only to resume its former position once the stimulus was out of sight. If a process of selection was taking place, the criteria involved were not readily discernible. A significant amount of time passed in this fashion before the pattern altered.

A taller than average figure strode into view, passing quite near the unseen observer, moving along the traverseway to stop behind a stanchion supporting the elevated path above. Based on stature and stride, the observer judged the newcomer to be male, but

in the darkness, details were impossible to determine. Its behavior
was circumspect, if not specifically furtive; the stanchion provided
almost as much cover as the chiruga trees.

The comings and goings continued, now witnessed by two
sets of eyes. This situation persisted until the emergence of one
particular customer, a young woman dressed in a red robe, who
paused, glancing in each direction before turning to her left. She
walked briskly along the traverseway, never noticing either of the
two figures she passed. The newcomer had become instantly alert at
her appearance, the change in posture obvious even in the cloaking
darkness, and now surreptitiously set off in pursuit, falling into step
just far enough behind to avoid arousing suspicion. The cloaked man
stiffened, waited for them to pass, then followed suit.

The strange procession continued to the limits of Cassio,
across an arched bridge to an elevated garden, then along its outer
perimeter to the second set of stairways, where the woman chose a
route that would bring her down to a narrow pedway, which in turn
wound up toward the more respectable Tenduri Park area. The first
of her pursuers hesitated at the top of the stairs for only a second
before following; the trailing figure was less precipitous, but still
descended so closely that he would inevitably have been seen had
his quarry turned to look back up toward the traverseway.
Fortunately his focused attention upon the woman ahead allowed
him no opportunity for other observations.

Both gaps continued to close on the lower pedway, which
now wound left and right in tight, small semi-circles around statues,
pylons, and chaotic garden islands. There were branching paths as
well, and both pursuers were narrowing the intervening gaps,
determined not to lose sight of the person they followed. Discovery
was inevitable in these close quarters, and when it occurred, it was
the woman who spoke first.

"Who's there?" If there was any trace of fear in the voice, it
was not audible to either of the other parties, both of whom had
instantly frozen in place. "Come out where I can see you. I have a
stinger and I know how to use it."

"Amina? It's me, Dorstan." The first man had a deep,
gravelly voice, and he sounded angry.

"Dorstan? What are you doing here? Why are you following
me? I told you I didn't want anything more to do with you!"

"Right, you'd rather squander your credit on neurostim than continue the life we had together."

"Listen, we've argued this out before and neither of us is going to budge. You have your dreams, and maybe someday you really will get to be a Mosham. But I'm tired of putting off the good things year after year. I want them now. Why can't you just accept the situation and go your own way and find pleasure in life like I have?"

"Neurostim isn't reality, Amina. Everything you experience there is a lie, an illusion created by artificially generated impulses."

"I know that. I'm not stupid. But if you can't tell the difference, it doesn't matter. When I'm under stim, I'm rich and popular and beautiful."

"Yes, it does matter . . ."

But the hidden figure heard no more. Disappointed once again, he had turned and walked off into the darkness.

* * * * *

In the depths of the underway system below Nashamata, there was a stirring. A powerful figure slipped silently through the passageways, leaving behind secured gang territory and heading for the upper levels. The man named Slee had avoided donning most of the symbols of his position and his affiliation, choosing instead a nondescript cloak he'd stolen from a merchant who'd unwisely chosen to travel alone one evening. Under that garment, he concealed as well a metal fiber bag whose contents were the purpose of tonight's excursion.

Although he moved constantly upward, his route was circuitous, avoiding the more densely traveled areas as well as those which were known as prowling grounds for rival gangs. He passed scores of recumbent forms, alert to any sign of recognition or even interest, but these were the ultimate dropouts of Tashistan society, those who no longer shared any hope of advancement, who were resigned to marginal survival in a brutal and degrading environment. Slee's avoidance of the local gang's turf was not a concession to fear but rather a desire to escape notice. He was fully prepared to kill to preserve his anonymity in this instance, but he would much rather avoid the necessity.

Slee preferred to choose those he killed rather than have them thrust upon him.

* * * * *

Tantra Brach stepped back from the canvas and cocked her head to one side. "Better, but still not right," she muttered to herself, setting the autopalette down on the benchtop to her right. She'd been working on a series of twelve paintings commissioned by the Merchants Union, external views of each of Soshambe's gated entranceways, a project that had been proceeding well until she discovered that the perspective on the Central Tashamir Gate was subtly wrong. Twice now she had stripped the canvas and started fresh, each time coming closer to her vision, but still not quite there.

"Enough for tonight," she decided, directing the autopalette to seal and save its contents. Fatigue hit with a rush and she rubbed her forehead with the back of one hand, walked slowly from her undersized makeshift studio into the main room. A homogeneous selection of reasonably attractive furniture was scattered about; although as single-minded about frugality as any Tashistan, she preferred a somewhat elevated minimal standard of living. Ground floor apartments like her own were larger than those higher in the building as well as more convenient, and although she hoarded her credits judiciously, she had moved to this more expensive living space three years previously because she realized she could rearrange the internal walls to provide a minimally adequate work area and save the credit she was expending renting a warehouse studio that was only slightly larger.

She crossed to the videonet screen and touched the power icon, hoping to catch a weather report for the following day. If the clouds cleared during the hours of darkness, she'd take the time come sunrise to walk out to Tashamir and do some fresh sketches of the troublesome scene, perhaps even a holo. The screen, however, remained dark even when she tried to activate it a second time. Frowning, her first thought was of a power failure, but then she realized the overhead lighting was still functioning.

She slapped the console angrily with the palm of one hand. Now she'd have to notify municipal services, which meant either a long journey to the administrative center or an expenditure of credit to make a call from a public station. Even worse, the backlog for service was notoriously long and continually growing as older equipment was constantly patched and jury-rigged rather than replaced. If she wanted to jump up on the maintenance list, she'd have to pass a few credits around to the right people, and the wait in line at the center would take half a day in itself, which would effectively postpone her return to Tashamir Gate no matter what the weather might be like.

She could do without the videonet for a while, but the same circuitry provided her datanet connection and access to all city services. Even if she didn't care about the expense of using public installations, she was unwilling to go outdoors every time she wanted to order merchandise, check her softcredit account, query the library, or send a message to friends or business associates. The Tardis Club would want a progress report on the triptych she had promised to complete, and she had recently updated her on-line catalog of unsold paintings. It would be just her luck to miss a sale because she couldn't sign onto the ordering queue to record an acceptance-of-contract statement. She wasn't so vain that she didn't realize potential patrons would simply choose another artist if they couldn't deal with her on a timely basis. She was talented, but not so talented that people would allow themselves to be inconvenienced to acquire her work.

But any action would have to wait until morning. Even if the municipal offices had been open, she was unwilling to walk the streets of Nashamata unaccompanied after dark. There'd been an upsurge in street crime, petty theft, and sexual assaults during the past two secants. The neighborhood council had already protested to the Growlers, the underway gang supposedly responsible for security in this area. She supposed they'd do something eventually, track down a few of the culprits and provide some object lessons to the others. But the Growlers weren't one of the major powers in the undercity, and they'd just experienced a setback in a major confrontation with one of their adjoining rivals. They had ceded a large block of territory after a street brawl, and were currently licking their wounds, more interested in sorting out internal problems and healing injuries than attending to surface world obligations.

As she was about to douse the lights and retire to her bedroom, Tantra was startled by the beeping of her apartment door.

She felt no alarm as she crossed the room; the security rating for this unit was comfortably high. The door could not be forced without alerting scores of people that something was amiss. A quick touch of an icon and a circle of transparency irised open, revealing the hall beyond.

A nondescript man stood there, hands at his sides, shuffling his feet restlessly. He wore the uniform of the municipal maintenance department.

"Yes? Who is it please?"

His pacing abruptly stopped. "I apologize for the disturbance, Ser Brach. My name is Jedgar; I'm from city services. We're having a problem with the netlines in this building."

"I know," she replied testily. "My unit's out of service."

"We realize that, Ser Brach. We're trying to restore it as quickly as possible. That's why I'm here."

Instantly suspicious, she paused thoughtfully before speaking. "I don't understand. How did you know about my problem? It just happened and I haven't had time to report it to anyone." And what could possibly inspire city services to react in such a timely fashion?

"It's not just your problem, Ser Brach. This entire building is cut off, and the one adjacent as well. We've been tracing junction circuitry to isolate the problem and it appears to be a malfunction in one of the consoles that's knocking out the entire grid every time we try to bring it back on line. The fault has been isolated to the ground floor of this building and we've been checking each unit in turn. I promise it won't take more than a few minutes. I just need to test the current flow from your unit to determine whether or not the fault is here or elsewhere."

Ordinarily she would have checked the man's story through the datanet, but that was obviously impossible in this instance. Tantra was still wary about admitting the man, particularly at this hour, but he seemed innocuous enough. Just to be safe, she retrieved a tearspray tube from a drawer before replying.

"All right, I suppose you can take a look. It'll have to be quick though; I was just about to retire for the night."

She tapped the admit pad and the door slid slowly to one side. The man stepped into her apartment, now carrying a large toolkit she hadn't seen from her earlier vantage point. The tearspray lay concealed against the palm of her hand.

"Just have to pop the side panel and test the circuit. If this isn't the one responsible, I'll know that right away. If it is, I can still replace the faulty component and be gone almost before you know I've been here." He set down the toolkit and popped open the lid, reaching inside.

"Saves me a trip uptown, I suppose," she was saying as the man lifted the hypogun from the toolkit and fired a dart directly into her chest. Tantra Brach's fingers clutched the tearspray reflexively, sending a thin stream of noxious fluid spurting out across the floor before she crumpled bonelessly and without saying another word.

The false repairman returned the hypogun to the kit with studied casualness, then removed a fuser. Ignoring the limp body, he walked back to the door, crouched, and used the tool to melt through the housing of the recorder, then thoroughly incinerated the memory disk mounted inside. Metal and synthetic components bubbled and seethed, droplets falling to the floor where they sizzled and immediately began to cool. He used the fuser until there was no trace of the unit, and even the outer surface of the door was breached. Satisfied, he replaced the fuser, then leaned down to his victim's recumbent form. Crossing her legs at the ankles, he rolled the woman over onto her back. Brach's chest continued to rise and fall regularly, though at a somewhat slower pace than normal; her eyes were wide open, and although they responded slowly to his movements, she was quite obviously watching him.

After spreading her arms and legs to each side, Scarab took up a heavy metal spike and the tool he had previously used on Akim Tutellatis and Prefect Leskar's son, among many others. "I told you I'd find you," he said softly to no one in particular. Then he returned to Tantra Brach's side and bent to his work.

* * * * *

When Marym Dunnis reached the Prefecture the following morning, those closest to her could tell from her expression and demeanor that she was in a foul mood even before her curt greeting confirmed it. Two subprefects hastily found reasons to absent themselves from the outer office, and the senior investigator who had been waiting for her in order to voice his complaint about the newly instituted time reporting procedure suddenly decided that he could see the wisdom of more detailed records. Only Tani seemed unaffected by her superior's mood, greeting her with customary enthusiasm.

"The night officer's report is on your data queue; she had a quiet shift for the most part." Marym nodded abstractedly and started to walk past her assistant's desk to the entrance to her private office. Tani raised a hand, offering a department sealpak. "She left this hard copy for you as well." The young woman's expression was openly curious, but Marym ignored her, taking the proffered message. She pressed her thumb against the release and slid out the contents, a single sheet which informed her that the confidential file that had been transmitted to her private datanet had, according to the controller program, been specifically and personally requested by Marym Dunnis, Prefect of Nashamata. Sileva had appended a handwritten message.

"I looked over the results of the diagnostic. All files and procedures have been properly restored at a factor of ninety-nine point seven reliability. I took the liberty of requesting a specific analysis of the possibility that the transmission in question fell into the error range. Diagnostics could not be absolutely certain, but no matter how I manipulated the variables, the highest probability of it being a transmission error was less than two percent. The controller program suggests that you may have miskeyed an entirely different request."

Marym crumpled the note, handed the empty sealpak back to Tani. She hadn't requested anything from the Prefecture on her personal terminal in several days. Miskeying was not a possibility. "I don't want to be disturbed for a while, Tani."

Inside her office, she unfolded the crumpled note and read it twice more before destroying it in the disposall. Then she sat at her desk, staring at the far wall, idly tapping her fingers across the surface of the inset screen.

* * * * *

As it happened, Sandor was with Marym Dunnis when word of Tantra Brach's murder reached the Prefecture. He'd arrived at mid-morning, modestly asked if she might have a moment or two to spare him.

"Of course, Tani, send him right in." The truth was, Marym was pleased at this distraction; her thoughts this morning had been disturbing and depressing. The facts seemed inescapable; Kruzer had somehow learned her access code—perhaps by watching her input it in a unguarded moment—and was using it to examine confidential files. To what purpose, she had no idea. There had been no answer when she netted him again that morning. He seemed to have dropped completely out of sight.

"Good morning, Marym. I hope I'm not intruding on urgent business."

"And good morning to you. No, I was just wrestling with a problem. And losing. Please, sit down and talk to me for a while."

He eased into a seat, which began to move sinuously of its own volition. "Personal or professional?"

"A little of both." Marym didn't want to have to deal with the Kruzer issue just at the moment. "Will you want a guide again today? We've assigned Jenilla light duty for the duration of your visit, so she can be made available at short notice."

Sandor acknowledged the change of subject tactfully. "I don't think so. I have an admittedly superficial but fairly good overview of the environment. Today I'm interested in the physical evidence, such as it is—the nature of the wounds, the metal fragments, the drug that was introduced into the bodies."

Her expression was clearly one of mild confusion. "All that information is in the database, Sandor. There are no additional files or tests available. Or did you find some irregularity in the data?"

"No, no," he protested. "I'm sorry; I didn't make myself clear. Your technicians seem to have covered all the bases, or at least they filled in all of the blocks. What I'm concerned with is the methodology. To put it bluntly, the mercantile nature of your criminological services makes me a bit wary. Up until recently, the tests were performed by the lowest bidder, as I understand it, and not always by the same individual. The files I accessed rarely explained the equipment and methods which were used to obtain the data, and it occurred to me that there might be something we're missing there."

"I see. Well, we do keep dossiers on all the contractors with whom we deal, and we require that they provide us documentation of their individual training and equipage. That won't necessarily prove that they performed the tests adequately, but there's never been any reason to believe otherwise."

"I'm not being critical of your methods, Marym, but there are different techniques available elsewhere which yield slight variations in results. There's something of a trade-off in DNA testing, for example. Collier-Quillem is more reliable but has a higher positive threshold than some of the alternatives . . ."

Sandor might well have discoursed for some time on the subject, but a light began to flash on Marym's desk. With a nod of apology, she touched an icon and Tani's voice was instantly audible, uncharacteristically tense.

"Sorry for the interruption, Prefect, but there's been a murder in the city."

"Scarab?" She glanced up at Sandor as she spoke.

"There's no confirmation at this point. The preliminary report seemed to indicate a strong possibility and the control program assigned the case to Inspector Parsi. But the reliability factor is very low."

"Another decapitation?" asked Sandor.

Tani responded to his voice. "No, Ser Dyle, at least not according to the preliminary report. A woman was attacked in her apartment sometime close to mid-darkness, then dismembered and mutilated."

"The fox challenges the hounds. I should have expected something like this." Sandor made the comment so low that Tani could not possibly have heard him. Marym did, however, and the look she gave him was decidedly odd.

"What was the victim's name, Tani?"

"Brach, Tantra Brach. She is . . . was an artist of some renown."

Sandor's head jerked up and back, and now he looked as nonplused as Marym had ever seen him. "That name sounds familiar, Tani. Do we have anything else on her?"

But it was Sandor who answered. "She was with Mikki Seurat when he reported the body in the park, Leskar's son. Suddenly we have gone from no discernible pattern at all to entirely too many cross-connections. I suspect this is partly my fault. Scarab knows that you are employing me."

"Do you want to go to the crime scene?" She was already rising from her desk, strapping on her belt pouch.

Sandor sighed. "I don't want to, but I think I should, yes. Not that I have any doubts about the competence of your people, Marym, but . . ."

"Another set of eyes, another experiential background. Yes, I know. Tani, have my lifter ready. We're on our way upstairs."

"Already done, Prefect."

They gained considerable altitude over the city before turning to the southeast, a concession to the unusually windy weather. Sandor took advantage of the fact to refresh his memory of the overall layout of the metropolitan area; representative diagrams were one thing, reality was another. Although the three inhabited quarters of Soshambe were remote from one another socially and philosophically, from this vantage they were surprisingly close physically. There were definite discernible borders, but they were extremely permeable in terms of casual movement, defined by the curve of a traverseway, bordered on one side by untended gardens and apartment complexes, on the other by uniformly trimmed hedgewalls and individual dwelling units with adjoining shelters for personal lifters. The real barriers were invisible, of course, and far more effective.

They passed over parkland and esplanade, concourse and building complex, and from this distance, the dissolution and squalor were almost invisible. The illicit marketplaces were clearly defined and uniformly busy, the overgrown and untended gardens appeared to be pleasant islands of foliage breaking the sterile expanse of the city, and the lack of vehicular traffic was only noticeable if contrasted to the other quarters. It was Sandor's experience in fact that on most worlds, private vehicles were banned from urban centers as a matter of course. Another Tashistan anachronism.

Only moments later, they descended vertically into an urban canyon, among some of the tallest buildings in Soshambe. Peering out the side window, Sandor saw the fluorescing outline of the sequestered area the Prefecture had already established, encompassing the main entrance to the apartment complex and the adjoining traverseway to the end of the block in both directions. Three lifters had already grounded in the cordoned-off space, neatly aligned against the front of the building opposite, and Marym brought them skillfully to a halt at the end of the row.

A crowd of the inevitably curious had already gathered beyond the limits of the cordoned area, where they blithely ignored the half-hearted attempts of a handful of subprefects to convince them to move along. One uniformed man met them as they approached the building and led the way inside.

Tantra Brach's apartment was through the main lobby and down the first branching corridor to the left. A panel had been removed from the wall at the corridor junction and three preoccupied men were examining what lay behind: a complex of wires, nanocircuitry, and monitoring devices. Sandor noted in passing an apparent complete absence of molecularly engineered data transmission in what was clearly a communications module. Tashistan information management was at least a generation behind the norm for worlds at this stage of development, a product of their insularity. Marym's steps faltered and she glanced inquisitively at their guide.

"The victim's datanet was cut out of the circuit. We thought it was just a malfunction, but when we tried to reconnect, we found the control circuit had been deliberately reprogrammed to exclude only her unit. Whoever did it knew what he was doing."

"Scarab didn't want her to be able to reach help." She glanced at Sandor for confirmation, but he frowned.

"Considering the manner in which he has incapacitated his subjects in the past, that seems an unnecessary and atypical complication. Why risk discovery by tampering with the circuitry?"

"Then you don't think this is Scarab?"

"I didn't say that; I don't have an opinion yet."

They reached the apartment; the door was open, a small hole visible near the base, an armed subprefect stationed there. He glanced curiously at Sandor but didn't object when the two of them entered.

Tantra Brach lay on the floor, or at least for the most part she did. Hands and feet were standing in a line on the seat of an adjacent lounge chair. Technicians were still recording everything they could examine with their equipment, and another pair were kneeling just inside the door, examining its inner workings. Marym advanced past the body to where Tiko Parsi stood quietly, apparently lost in thought, but Sandor turned and stared down past the two men working at the door. The inner mechanism was melted into an indistinguishable mass.

If anyone had been watching his face at that moment, they would have seen him nod slightly, as though something he suspected had just been confirmed.

While Marym and Parsi were talking in hushed tones, Sandor walked slowly around the room, carefully not touching anything, occasionally peering closely at one object or another before moving on. His examination seemed casual but its intensity was betrayed by a startled twitch of the shoulders when Marym spoke to him.

"Find anything useful?"

He shrugged. "She was quite talented. Some of these pieces would command respectable prices offworld." He raised an arm to indicate the row of paintings that marched around the circumference of the apartment.

Marym suppressed a twinge of annoyance. "Tiko doesn't think this was Scarab, that someone is copying his technique."

Sandor shrugged a second time. "He might be right. Is there evidence of nemesol?"

"Not confirmed, but a clear entry wound in the abdomen and the areas of trauma, the wrists and ankles, seem to be identical to the earlier cases." She grimaced. "They keep telling me I'll get used to this."

"The damage to the door was after the fact; it was melted through from the inside, not from the corridor," he observed. "So she must have let him in."

"Or he was waiting in the apartment."

He shook his head. "Not likely. If he'd been inside, he wouldn't have needed to risk disabling the datanet unit from the corridor access. He could have disconnected the power supply a lot more easily."

"If she let him in, he must have been someone she knew."

"Not necessarily. He might have talked his way in somehow. And then he had to destroy the door recorder, which would have provided a voiceprint even if he disguised or otherwise concealed his physical appearance." He reached up and massaged his chin with one hand. "I confess your suggestion is likely however. Unless she was an extraordinarily stupid woman, I can't imagine her allowing a complete stranger to enter without a very good reason."

"If this was Scarab, he may have made his first mistake. We can have a list of everyone with a known connection to Brach within minutes."

"Perhaps, but not necessarily. I don't think he'd have risked attacking someone he knew personally unless he was certain it would not help us."

There was a sudden flurry of activity at the opposite end of the room. Without a word, Sandor moved quickly in that direction. A man and a woman were both recording the presence of a small, crushed cylindrical item lying against the wall.

"Tearspray module," Tiko Parsi had come up behind them. "We expected to find it somewhere. There was a fresh stain on the carpet; the analysis was easy."

"How old?" Sandor already knew the answer instinctively but needed confirmation.

"Not very. Falls right within the preliminary window for the assault."

Marym made a frustrated sound. "If she felt it was all right to let him in, why did she use tearspray? Or did he use it on her?"

The investigator shook his head. "No evidence in her lungs or eyes, and definite traces on her right hand. She was righthanded. I'd say she was the one who discharged it, but judging by the spray lines on the carpet," he pointed back to a dark, attenuated triangle, "we think she was holding it at her side when she squeezed."

"Paralyzed by the hypodart, no doubt."

"That's our preliminary assumption."

"What about surveillance? Isn't there a monitor in the lobby? I thought I saw a circumferential recorder in the ceiling when we came in."

Parsi raised his hands and began ticking off points one finger at a time. "First, it's a cheap copy designed to look like a circumferential recorder; in fact, it's an intermittent model, revolves every few ticks for a full pan. Second, this particular one is so badly maintained, your mother could walk through its field and you wouldn't be able to recognize her. Third, the resident system supervisor neglected to reload the host unit in the control room, so the input just kept overwriting previous data over and over again. And finally, the intruder didn't enter through the lobby, although he might have if he'd known the rest."

"How did he get in?" asked Marym.

"System supervisor entrance. And he didn't break in; he had a passcard. No door recorder there, of course, and if there was, he probably would have slagged it. There is, however, a power interrupt log, and the door was opened twice last night, bracketing an interval long enough and at the right time for him to have accomplished everything here."

"How hard would it be to get a passcard?"

"Not enough to help us," offered Marym. "They're not keyed to individual buildings, at least not in Nashamata. They provide emergency access for city services so they're interchangeable by law. Hundreds of city workers have them, hundreds more system supervisors, and every subprefect in the city." She reached into her beltpouch, withdrew a slim cardholder, picked quickly through the contents, and extracted an electronically coded yellow card. "Here's mine. I'll bet there are six of them in this room." There were twelve people in sight.

"Not to mention how many of them are lost, stolen, or counterfeited." Parsi made a wide gesture encompassing the entire room, perhaps the entire city. "If we want to follow that lead, we only have to check out the alibis for about half a million people." He made a disgusted sound. "And we don't even know if this was indeed Scarab. Even if nemesol is involved, it's not a certainty. There have been so many people brought into this investigation by now," and he carefully didn't look at Sandor as he spoke, "it's inevitable that most of the details have leaked."

Marym and Sandor left the site a few minutes later, lifting off in a steep vertical climb. The wind had died down slightly, and they made much better time returning to the Prefecture.

"Any thoughts?" Marym had been quiet throughout the flight, speaking only once before the rooftop landing area was in sight.

"I think our friend Scarab is a lot smarter than we thought he was, but more foolish as well. First there was no pattern to his activity, which is in itself a pattern. Now he strikes on consecutive nights, where before he staggered his intervals. In the past he has invariably chosen remote, public places, outdoors, away from recording devices, striking suddenly and impulsively; now he claims a victim in her own apartment, after carefully engineering his approach, gaining entry through some presumably elaborate pretext, and departing. And instead of choosing his victims at random, he has now struck three consecutive times at associates of this Mikki Seurat."

"I'd forgotten about that." The lifter touched down and the power died, but neither made a move to exit. She turned to face him. "Do you think it would do any good to bring him in for questioning?"

"It wouldn't do any harm, but I don't think it will help. Protective surveillance might be more profitable."

"I'll see what I can do, but it's unlikely the other Prefectures will loan their staff to watchdog a Nashamatan. Why would Scarab change his methods now? Nothing we've been able to do has given us the faintest hint of his identity. Why take the risk? Does he want to be captured?"

"Quite the contrary. Scarab is merely adapting to a change in his environment."

She looked puzzled. "But what has changed? The situation is the same as it has always been."

"No, we've added a new element." He turned and met her gaze squarely. "I've been brought into the situation, and our quarry has become aware of me."

Chapter Ten

Marym and Sandor ate a quiet, thoughtful lunch in the Prefecture's
autoteria, after which Sandor politely took his leave, announcing his
intention to return to the hostelry and add his personal observations
and the data on the new case to the projections he had already made,
hopefully interpolating something useful. Marym frankly didn't
know whether the sudden alteration of Scarab's method of operation
was a help or a hindrance. On the one hand, it suggested movement
and certainly greater risk on the part of the killer, but at the same
time, it indicated an even more pronounced level of unpredictability.
Theoretically, disparate data should make pattern analysis easier, but
her knowledge was so rudimentary, she could not intuitively
understand how further chaos would help. She had ordered Mikki
Seurat brought in for questioning, although that decision was
dictated by procedure rather than serious hope of a breakthrough.
Unfortunately, he had yet to be located. His sister knew he had found
work for the day, but if her knowledge was more specific than that,
she was unwilling to volunteer the details to the subprefect who
questioned her. Either she was genuinely ignorant of his
whereabouts or the work in question was illegal and the girl was not
about to compromise him.

Back in her office, she reviewed the message queue
cursorily, deleting most of what she found there, transferring others
to a holding file pending further action, attending to a few issues that
she could resolve easily or for which time was an important factor.
Most of this she performed automatically, her mind on other matters.
Periodically she opened a link to her apartment, but there was no
indication that her terminal was engaged. There continued to be no
answer at Kruzer's place in Moshamadur and she even considered
contacting that quarter's Prefecture. Caution overrode that
inclination, but by late afternoon, she was edgy and had to exert
control to avoid snapping at her staff. Finally she accepted the
inevitable and walked into the outer office.

"Tani, I'm leaving for the day. I've taken care of everything
that couldn't wait. When Tiko files his preliminary report, net me a
copy at home, will you? I'll be there if anything urgent comes up."

She parked her lifter in its assigned space behind the complex of small houses where she had moved following the death of her parents five years previously. Although they left her a small inheritance, she had already earned her way into Moshamadur by rising rapidly in the administration of an investment cartel and carefully developing her own fortune by selectively participating in trading ventures both on Tashista and, to a necessarily limited extent, offworld. After studying both the structure of municipal government and the personal files of the leading administrators in all areas, she had chosen the Prefecture as the area most likely to allow rapid advancement, studied those areas required before she could be certified as a valid contender, and bought herself an administrative post in Tashamir. Her strong organizational skills and quick grasp of procedure had come to the attention of her superiors, who supported her bid to be Assistant Prefect of Kishamkur, and, although Vernek Tarramore had made a higher offer and ultimately moved into that position, her credentials had been officially acknowledged and she later assumed the same title in Tashamir.

Technically, she should not have been able to afford to bid successfully for a full Prefect's position, in Nashamata or anywhere else. Even before the advent of Scarab, Nashamata was considered a dead-end or hardship post; Savram Aras had surprised everyone when he assumed the posting, since his own meteoric rise in the city of Lashamar had seemed to indicate a bright future. Her own career plans had never involved an assignment in that quarter, but pressure was brought to bear, from Leskar among others, and it was made quite clear that if this ambitious newcomer wished to receive the support which might eventually lead to a major position in Soshambe or another city, it would first be necessary for her to accede to the needs of the community. Which meant, of course, that no one else wanted the job, and she had been neatly maneuvered into a position where she had to make an honest effort to secure the post. Although she placed the lowest plausible bid that her finances would allow, there was no serious opposition and she had been confirmed with ease. It was a challenge, she had to confess, even without Scarab, and she had learned a great deal here that might not have been possible in the other quarters. But it had also been a source of endless frustration, anger, and bouts of deep depression.

Her mind still churning over recent events, she entered the small, enclosed garden which adjoined her home, attention elsewhere but not so far distant that she didn't notice sudden, apparently surreptitious movement to her left.

Marym did not ordinarily carry weaponry; her position was in administration rather than direct enforcement. She routinely kept a heavy duty stinger locked in her lifter, however, and she quietly retraced her steps, retrieved the weapon, and returned to the garden. Although she'd often envied the greater privacy available in Kishamkur, suddenly her comparatively isolated position seemed terribly remote. She could have made a distress call from her lifter, of course, but if the Prefect of Nashamata was forced to request personal assistance from the Moshamadur authorities, it would be a snide little joke among members of the administration for months, even if it didn't turn out to be a false alarm. There was even a chance that it would reflect on her chances when her certification was next evaluated, officially or by innuendo.

The sun was low in the sky and the enclosed area was shadowy and indistinct; the thought of what might be lurking there made her heart beat painfully within her chest.

The movement had stopped by the time she returned, and although she stood with her back to the woven wall surrounding the garden and peered into the darkness, trying to resolve the shadows into a shape, menacing or otherwise, she saw no evidence of an intruder.

"All right, come on out. I see you there." The words seemed pointlessly melodramatic, and the possibility that she might be addressing them to no more than a stray merecat or someone's pet frobster made her feel even more ludicrous. Fortunately, it was unlikely that she would be overheard by her neighbors.

There was a triple beat of silence, then a short, uncertain sound. An animal mumbling a warning, perhaps. She took a tentative step forward, then moved slightly to her right, edging around a tacaranda vine and slipping between a pair of flowering shrubs. A barb tore at the shoulder of her uniform, but she pushed past without pausing to free herself.

Just at the limit of her vision, a human arm and hand were suddenly visible, palm down on the ground. Marym tensed immediately, brought her weapon up. "You there, near the back wall.

Come out now, slowly, and put your hands where I can see them. I'm armed and I won't hesitate to fire." Her palm was sweaty where it wrapped around the cool butt of the stinger.

There was neither reply nor movement; the hand remained immobile. Marym pursed her lips, considered advancing, instead sidled further to her right, trying to gain a vantage point from which she could see more of the recumbent human. Visions from Tantra Brach's apartment flashed through her memory and for a second she imagined the arm was just that, a dismembered fragment from yet another victim, left here as a taunt by Scarab.

She took three quick steps to the right, then leaped forward over a small hedge and crouched, weapon up and ready.

An adult male lay crumpled on the ground, one arm outstretched, the other tucked under his body, face averted, half crushing some low ground cover she'd planted only a few weeks before. There was no sign of blood and, thankfully, it appeared that all of his limbs were still connected.

Still proceeding as carefully as possible, Marym approached to within arm's reach, watching the prone man with one eye, scanning the surrounding area with the other. Once she felt reasonably certain there were no other figures waiting to jump from obscurity, she rose to her full height, used one foot to roll the body over onto its back.

"Kruzer!"

She quickly ascertained that he was in fact alive, although he felt unnaturally cool to the touch, his skin covered with a sticky sheen of sweat that felt unhealthy. Although not trained to render medical assistance, Marym quickly checked for wounds, broken bones, any obvious trauma, all to no effect. While rearranging his limbs more comfortably, she thought she heard him say something, although his eyes remained closed. Peering closely, she saw his lips move, bent forward.

"Mmmmarrym . . . lights so strong and . . . sweet."

"Kruzer, this is Marym. Can you hear me, Kruzer? Try to talk. What's happened to you?"

The comatose man gave no indication that he had heard her; his lips continued to move, but soundlessly now. Marym scanned the area again, still wary, then rose, strode quickly to her front door, accessed the security system, and slipped inside. She called for medical assistance immediately, unnecessarily provided the address, even though the medicators would have identified the caller instantly, and described what she could about Kruzer's situation before signing off and returning to the garden.

There was no indication of any change in Kruzer's position or condition. She had brought out a pillow, which she now used to prop up his head. As she did so, Kruzer began to speak again, disjointed fragments of sentences, none meaningful, occasionally intermixed with nonsense syllables. He didn't recognize her presence at all, but was obviously addressing his remarks to someone he could see on the inside of his mind, someone whose name Marym didn't think she had ever heard before.

The name was "Slee."

* * * * *

Although Sandor had told Marym a partial truth about his intentions when he took leave of her at the Prefecture, he changed his instructions to the pilot not long after they were airborne and instead directed Izik to drop him in the city, not far from the building where Tantra Brach had been murdered. The inexplicable linkage of the last few murders was not as puzzling as Marym believed it to be; Sandor felt he had already determined Scarab's reasoning, at least in broad terms. The linkage itself was important, not the individual elements. Sandor believed Scarab had chosen Mikki Seurat as a common factor almost at random, although there might be some contributing factor for that choice that was not obvious.

"Would you prefer that I wait here or should I go back to the hostelry until you call?" Izik was clearly uneasy abandoning his charge without a companion.

"Why don't you take the day off, Izik? I've sat around enough for the past several weeks. I can find my way back with no difficulty and the walk will be good for me."

His pilot remained uncertain. "It's quite easy to get lost in this area, Ser Dyle. The streets are not well marked and there is no direct access to the main concourse unless you loop under the main trunk and come around from that side."

"I'll manage. I can always ask for directions if I have a problem." Which was unlikely. Sandor had studied the city schemata quite thoroughly. As chaotic as the web of traverseways, pedways, and concourses might appear, there had been an underlying system which the original city architects had used to lay out the district, and any system had a pattern. Sandor could assimilate patterns in a matter of seconds and recall them even years later.

"All right, then. But I will remain at the hostelry if you change your mind. Good luck, Ser Dyle."

Sandor waited until the lifter was out of sight before turning away.

He walked the streets of Nashamata for the better part of the afternoon, sometimes at random, sometimes seeking specific addresses which he had memorized earlier. A Prefecture lifter was parked unobtrusively not far from the Seurats' apartment complex, and an obviously bored subprefect lounged against the side of the vehicle watching the main entrance. He did not recognize Sandor when he passed, eyes tracking to the seventh floor, wondering which window might open into the Seurats' home. As it happened, they lived at the rear of the complex, and he was never actually within sight of their quarters.

Sandor then spent some little time sitting quietly in an underway station, bought a yuba fruit drink, and wisely refrained from descending to any of the lower levels. Refreshed by the break, he wandered through a small market place, crossed an esplanade upon which he paused to observe an ineptly played game of ultima, then made his way up a series of short stairways to an infrequently traveled pedway that led under the main trunk line to Moshamadur, descending just beyond to a slightly better maintained neighborhood.

Everywhere he went, he was the slowest pedestrian; Nashamatans seemed uniformly in a hurry to reach their destinations. Even the children played with a determined ferocity that he found quite daunting. Signs of a stagnant economy were visible as well; although there were crowds in the illicit market areas, few made purchases. Sandor saw evidence of temporary living arrangements in alcoves, on several lower tiered roofs, in corners of less well traveled thoroughfares. It surprised him that there were no beggars; perhaps the nearly universal credit hoarding on Tashista made such activity pointless. Two blocks further on, he was in sight of Tantra Brach's apartment building.

The cordon had been lifted by now and Sandor walked slowly past the front entrance, his eyes taking in the empty lobby. Without stopping, he continued to the end of the block, located a public datanet station, and punched in a local code he had memorized earlier. Satisfied that there was no answer, he broke the connection, then made his way along the side of the apartment building to the system supervisor's entrance. Using the passcard which he had surreptitiously removed from Marym's belt pouch while she was out of her office, Sandor opened the door and slipped inside, allowing it to close soundlessly behind him. He was prepared to bluff his way past anyone who might be present, posing as a municipal inspector of some sort, but there was no need to do so. The room was empty and so was the corridor into which he emerged a moment later.

His brief examination of the inner workings of the apartment door earlier in the day had been instructive. Security systems on Tashista, in this building at least, were painfully primitive. The locking code was electronically triggered by pulses emitted upon proper recognition of thumbprint, passcard, or manual release from within. The sequences had been recorded on the master panel inside the door, thankfully spared from the general destruction, and Sandor now used a small pulse generator drawn from a pocket to reproduce the code, pressing the device firmly against the appropriate location on the frame. He imagined the authorities possessed an equivalent device in order to gain entry in an emergency. The door slid open immediately. The interior was dark, the investigators having frugally shut down all non-essential functions when they closed the room and left.

Sandor was working on impulse as much as to a plan; if he was to outwit Scarab, he must also avoid establishing a predictable pattern. The only thing of which he felt certain was that he needed to introduce a factor into the equation that did not involve the Prefecture. Although he had grown fond of Marym Dunnis and believed her to be genuinely determined to bring Scarab's career to an end, he was also aware of the fact that the killer seemed to possess an extraordinary ability to circumvent official efforts to apprehend him. Even making allowances for the inadequate manpower and equipment, there should have been some progress in the case. Its absence and the sudden change in Scarab's methods contributed to Sandor's growing certainty that he was being personally challenged, that Scarab was aware of his involvement and was expressing his contempt by deliberately creating a pattern for

Sandor to discover. A false pattern. Clearly, Scarab was in a position to know a great deal more than the general public, either directly or through an intermediary, witting or unwitting.

The body had been removed, of course, and although some superficial effort had been made to clean up the mess left behind by the technicians, it was clear the apartment would need to be thoroughly rehabilitated before it could be allocated to a new resident. Nevertheless, at the moment it provided the privacy Sandor desired. Once again, he admired the woman's artistry and regretted a social structure that would not recognize such talent quickly. If he had needed an additional incentive to concentrate on solving the Scarab killings, this terrible loss to the creative world would have filled the bill.

Sandor didn't expect to discover anything overlooked by the technicians who had scoured the location earlier, nor did he. They had patched the outer door and restored its internal functions, but the inner panel was missing, and scorch marks were visible on those few internal components which remained. A rectangular section of carpet had been cut free, that containing the discharge from the tearspray. Someone had also removed the cushion upon which Brach's severed hands and feet had been found.

He walked through the adjoining rooms almost without seeing their contents, then returned and crossed to the datanet, powered it up, and signed on with Tantra Brach's code rather than his own. It would limit his access, but no one was likely to be able to discover the direction his investigation was taking, and it was extremely unlikely that anyone would be monitoring the activities of a dead woman.

* * * * *

Shayne Seurat had been unable to learn from the subprefect who questioned her just why they were looking for her brother. Mikki worked for the gangs from time to time, of course; nearly everyone in Nashamata dealt with them in some fashion, either as employee or client. It was an inevitable consequence of living in such close proximity to the underways where they laired. But he had always fastidiously avoided the really dangerous assignments that were periodically offered, even though they paid substantially more than he usually earned, simply because he was aware of her helplessness should she be left without his support. She could appeal to the Department of Charity, certainly, and they might feel obligated to render some assistance, but it would be inadequate to maintain her in a private domicile, and she wouldn't last long in a public shelter. Her infirmity notwithstanding, Shayne was an attractive young woman, and despite her relative isolation from the world, she knew her future would inevitably involve prostitution or worse if she had to fend for herself. The thought of ending her days in the back room of some flesh parlor in Cassio or sleeping in some dark corner of the underways was so repellent, she firmly believed she'd take her own life before surrendering to such hopelessness.

Once the subprefect left, she had returned painstakingly to her own room, where the videonet had been showing a serial drama she watched more through habit than interest. Now she switched to a public service program, wondering if there might be something in the news updates that would provide a clue about the Prefecture's sudden interest in her brother.

She was listening to an account of a multi-vehicle accident in Kishamkur when the screen suddenly blinked and went completely black. The ready light was similarly dull. It wasn't the first time this had happened; there'd been a major power failure twice that very year, and the datanet system itself had been shut down for nearly a full day once when an inattentive program monitor had inadvertently deactivated the administrative control program and caused a partial core wipe. Levering herself upright with her cane, she hobbled back into the front room, noted that the time display in the kitchen was still illuminated. Not a power failure then.

The door beeped at her.

It was not true that Shayne never had visitors. Some of the children in the neighborhood occasionally dropped by, often sent by parents who felt sorry about her isolation, but not sorry enough to take time off from their own personal quest for more credit. At other times, a rare adult might come by, usually declining the offer of a seat to facilitate their early departure. Tantra Brach had employed her as a model on more than one occasion, and old Stouffer used to drop by occasionally with a gift of handmade cookies, until he died of suratic cancer. The apartment had also been burglarized four times since they had moved in, twice while she was present. In neither case was she harmed, the thieves more interested in making off with whatever loose goods might be traded for hard credit.

"Yes, who's there?" She stood at the opposite end of the room, facing the door.

"Prefect Jedgar, Ser Seurat. I need to speak to you about your brother. May I come in for a moment?"

It was not the same man as before. Shayne moved painstakingly to the door, touched the viewing icon. The man standing in the corridor was reasonably nondescript, although his face struck her as vaguely familiar, someone she had seen on more than one occasion, but not recently. He wore the uniform of a subprefect. She frowned, trying to pin down the memory, isolate the context, but it hovered at the borders of her awareness, temporarily unattainable.

"I've already told the other officer, I don't know where Mikki is working today. He left early this morning and told me he might be late."

"I realize that, Ser Seurat. But we think you might be able to help us with some of our inquiries while we try to locate him."

"What do you want to know?"

"It's somewhat complicated. Could I come in for a few moments? I promise not to take up too much of your time, and if you can help, there would be a small credit award for your assistance."

Shayne frowned. The previous man had been willing to deal with her through the door. "I don't know. Mikki told me never to let anyone in that I didn't know personally."

"I'm from the Prefecture." He emphasized the last word. "There's no reason to be alarmed. If you'd feel better, you can call and confirm my identity. I have some holos I need you to examine." He lifted a large bag into view.

Shayne thought about the disabled datanet unit, frowned deeply. The two incidents were just a bit too coincidental. One did not survive long in Nashamata if one was too willing to dispense trust, even with an able older brother in the wings.

"I'm sorry but you'll have to come back when Mikki's home. Or you can hold them up to the viewer, I guess."

"You're making this unnecessarily difficult, Ser Seurat." But the man no longer sounded patient and helpful; in fact, his voice resonated with anger. Shayne had moved a step back from the door, but now she pressed forward, staring intently at her visitor. He had turned to the fibermesh bag hanging from his shoulder, and now his hand emerged holding something she recognized immediately. And as he turned in her direction, she realized as well where she had seen his face before.

Without a word, she turned and began to retreat toward her room. She was just crossing the threshold when the door slid open. Without a moment's hesitation, she used her free hand to retrieve a small, metallic item from its place on a shelf just inside the door.

"You could have made this a lot easier for both of us, Ser Seurat." The man's voice was positively ugly now, and he was already halfway across the room by the time Shayne turned, bringing up her hand. The small gasjet discharged as the intruder raised his own weapon, and under other circumstances, his startled reaction might have been comical. He jumped quickly to one side, stumbling, his hypogun firing wildly. A dart splattered harmlessly against the ceiling above Shayne's head. Her own shot shattered one of the two large bowls partly filled with bruised fruit that sat on their small dining table. She adjusted her aim as calmly as possible and fired a second time, just as her target ducked and ran around a partition into the adjoining room. The bag he carried trailed behind, slamming against the doorjamb just before disappearing from sight. The gasjet discharge had hit it dead center.

Scarab crouched inside Mikki Seurat's bedroom, staring into his bag, considering his options. The second pellet from the gasjet had struck his equipment with just enough force to shatter the spare capsules for the hypogun. He carried a stinger as well, but even if he could get into position for a shot, he might kill his quarry or do other serious damage which would make her unsuitable for his purposes. His face began to redden with an infusion of blood as the old, familiar fury surfaced. Never before had it come so soon; he had always been able to suppress the rage until after the sacrifice was complete. The ceremony of expulsion had always been performed with cold precision; he never allowed the pent up anger to express itself physically until he had done what was necessary. Never before had he felt his control slipping this soon. But then, never before had his intended victim interfered with his plans.

The memories boiled through his mind, images from the past, from the dank, dark underways. He saw those subterranean realms again now, felt the physical presence of the relentless heat, heard the laughter of the Sharith, the Ten, the ruling council bent on subordinating the entire underworld to their control. The scenario was one he had experienced in both dreaming and waking states again and again these past three years, their masked faces as they watched their victim struggling hopelessly to escape the iron post upon which they had impaled him. Hopelessly because they had already removed his hands and feet, cauterizing the wounds so that he wouldn't bleed to death too quickly.

In the second bedroom, Shayne Seurat struggled to control very different emotions. She was frightened, terrified in fact, but she knew that panic was her worst enemy. They had achieved a standoff of sorts. Her gasjet still held two charges, and her enemy would have no way of knowing that the remaining two cylinders were empty. Mikki had taken her to a deserted area months before, determined that she would learn to fire the weapon in safety before she had to learn suddenly in an emergency. He had meant to replace the two discharges but had just never gotten around to it. There was no way to alert the authorities with the datanet link severed, and the living units themselves were reasonably soundproofed, certainly sufficient to adequately muffle the sounds of the gasjet. She was trapped in her room, but her adversary was trapped as well; there was no exit except through the front door and he would have to cross her line of fire to reach it. There might be a long wait, but sooner or later, Mikki would come. Her heart began to race. What if Mikki came through the door unsuspectingly?

The tableau held for a subjective eternity, objectively long enough that Shayne's under-developed legs began to ache despite her conscious effort to throw most of her weight onto the support provided by her cane. She was beginning to sag against the door jamb when something dark came rushing out from behind the corner. She raised her arm and fired, then again before her self-control returned. The first hit the pillow Scarab had thrown, which exploded into scores of fragments of piloplast; the second hit the far wall, scarring the surface in a detonation that only seemed loud within the confines of the small room.

Gasjets had virtually no recoil, but Shayne had fired while startled, and now she tried desperately to move her cane to a supportive position. For a split second, she hovered on the edge of balance, then stumbled forward to one knee, no longer concealed. She recognized her danger immediately, but her treacherous limbs refused to cooperate. In desperation, she raised the useless gasjet as Scarab emerged, leaping across the old fashioned singleform recliner that separated them.

Even had it been armed, she probably would have been unable to discharge her weapon before he knocked her hand aside. Then his clenched fist struck the side of her head, and she didn't even see the floor coming up to meet her face.

Scarab stood over his unconscious victim, shoulders heaving with stress and fatigue; the brief exchange had left him feeling emotionally and physically exhausted. The overwhelming rage of a few moments before was simmering now, ready to burst forth at any moment, but for the time being it was under control.

Thoughtfully he examined his hypogun before packing it away in the bag; it appeared to be functional, but without an intact dart, it was of no present use to him.

"You've been some trouble to me this time," he told the unconscious woman in a deceptively calm voice. "But ultimately, it doesn't matter. We always end up the same way, and we always will, year after year, until you finally stop coming back."

He removed the metal spike and other tools from his bag and set them on the floor beside her, then rolled Shayne over onto her back, waiting for her to regain consciousness.

"You have to see everything, you know. Seeing is an important part of the process. It's all for nothing if you don't know what's going on. That's the way of Sharith, you remember? Rule through terror. And now you've just made things more difficult for yourself, because I don't have any more anesthetic."

He lifted the spike and held it ready. "So I guess we'll just have to do without."

* * * * *

Tamara Stoat sat in an interview cubicle at the Prefecture substation nearest her apartment, nervously rubbing one hand against the other. "He never came home at all last night. That just isn't like him." The bare walls and plain, functional furniture gave the room an antiseptic appearance that unnerved her.

The clearly bored subprefect seated across the table raised a skeptical eyebrow. "I appreciate your concern, Ser Stoat, believe me. But you just told me a moment ago that he's had trouble sleeping and has gone for early morning walks before this."

"But he always comes back before first light. He wouldn't let me go off to work not knowing what might have happened to him."

The uniformed woman tried unsuccessfully to suppress a sigh. "Sometimes when we live with someone for a long time, we think we know everything about them, how they think, how they'll react in new situations. That isn't always the case. Everyone is different, and unpredictable. Maybe he lost track of time, maybe he's back at your place right now, wondering where you are."

And maybe he's found himself another woman, she thought but did not say. Instead Tamara pressed her lips tightly together. "It's easy for you to take all of this casually. You don't know him. He . . . he hasn't been well lately. I'm afraid he's collapsed somewhere, or has been attacked."

"There are no unidentified patients at any medical facilities, no anonymous bodies. It was actually a pretty quiet night."

"So you're saying there's nothing you can do." Tamara rose to her feet, anger and concern making her voice crack with emotion.

"That's not at all what I said, but we are somewhat limited. I've posted an advisory; if anything does turn up you'll be notified immediately. I'd suggest you stay home today and wait for him, or if you have to go to work, make sure you leave a message so he knows how concerned you are."

She shook her head. "I've already netted in for the day off. They owe me one."

"Well then, go home and try to relax. He'll turn up sooner or later. Missing people almost always return within a day and a night. I wouldn't be surprised if he's there now."

But even as Tamara was leaving the substation, she was convinced by some preternatural certainty that she would never see Ramis Marchok again.

At least not while he was alive.

* * * * *

Sandor sat at the late Tantra Brach's terminal, attempting to gather his thoughts. Scarab had begun his killing spree three years ago, and except for the single incident where he was interrupted at his work, he had managed to kill over two dozen people without leaving a useful clue of any sort. Up until Sandor's arrival, neither pattern analysis nor more conventional methods had made any progress in solving the string of crimes. Scarab had managed to avoid even incidental observation by the admittedly inadequate automated surveillance system, varied his hunting areas widely enough to be effectively random. There was in fact a detectible structure to his activity—he struck outdoors, in good weather, during the hours of darkness, always made the same mutilations, immobilized his victims with hypodarts and nemesol, remained long enough after his victim expired to batter the corpses to near unrecognizability. At least, that had been his procedure until recently. None of this provided any really useful clue that might lead to his apprehension.

But the last two victims had been a different story. Tutellatis had been decapitated; Brach was attacked indoors with increased if not unacceptably great risk to Scarab. The gaps between attacks had contracted sharply. Both of his subjects were connected to the man who had discovered the body of the previous victim, possibly a coincidence, but Sandor distrusted coincidences. It was possible, though unlikely, that one or both of these crimes had been committed by a copycat killer, but he doubted that as well. Nor did he believe that Scarab would make such an obvious effort to randomize his activities, only to abandon that strategy and begin conforming to a pattern. Which meant it was a false pattern, a construct designed to mislead the Prefecture. No, not the Prefecture. It was designed to mislead Sandor Dyle.

And that meant that Scarab had a connection to the Prefecture, either directly or indirectly. Sandor's involvement in the case had not been made public, but references to his presence in the city existed, however circumspect. He had noted at least two news items mentioning his visit to Soshambe while perusing the current reportage of the latest atrocities.

Otherwise his investigations during the past two hours had been largely fruitless. He had been able to access a complete listing of Prefecture staff, both enforcement and administrative, under Brach's access code, but had finally been reduced to exiting and signing on again with his own clearance in order to view schedules, logs, performance reports, and the like. Thankfully, Soshambe's artificial intelligence system was flexible enough to assist him in what might otherwise have been a drawn out, boring series of cross-references. When he finally signed off for the last time and powered down, he was reasonably certain of one thing.

None of the registered staff and employees of the Nashamata Prefecture could be Scarab. Every one of them could have performed one or more of the murders; none of them could have performed them all. The reliability factor exceeded ninety-nine and six decimals. There was always the possibility of some combination of two or more, or a co-conspirator outside the Prefecture, both contingencies which Sandor hoped he would not have to consider more seriously. Multiple perpetrators left patterns just like single ones, but they were interlaced, intricate, and often hard to differentiate. He had also run a check on every individual who had serviced Prefecture equipment during the same period, with similar results. He had noted a surprisingly heavy data transfer traffic level between Marym Dunnis's home and her office, but credited that to her high degree of motivation and personal ambition.

Sandor had very much hoped that this line of investigation would prove fruitful. He suspected that Scarab would continue to strike with increased frequency, responding to whatever insane impulse had initiated the sequence of murders, until his quota for the year was complete. Scarab was clearly unbalanced; if he had been a thrill killer of some sort, he would hardly have refrained during the other nineteen secants of the local calendar. Thrill killers rarely displayed any willpower in such matters. Scarab was well named; his activities were, for some as yet unknown reason, specifically linked to this season of the year. His victims were essentially random despite the recent grouping, and the post-mortem mutilations pointed to irrational impulses even more than the dismemberments themselves.

At this point, he could only speculate about Scarab's motivation, although he thought he had evolved a fairly accurate model in gross terms. Despite the negative results of his afternoon's work, Sandor now believed that he had a viable plan by which to capture Scarab and bring the string of deaths to an end. He rose abruptly and started for the door. There was no time to waste. If he was right, Scarab would kill again, probably this very night. He would have to be stopped.

* * * * *

Marym Dunnis sat in a private office, awaiting the medicator's report on Kruzer. She had started for the public lounge, but one of the administrators had recognized her and insisted she use the small cubicle set aside for senior staff. Marym started to protest, but the woman seemed so genuinely sympathetic, and the privacy so appealing, that she ultimately acquiesced.

"Prefect Dunnis?"

She glanced up, saw a middle-aged man wearing the stark white gown of a medicator. "Yes. Is there any news?"

He hesitated, his eyes refusing to meet hers. "The patient," he glanced down at the screen of his datapad, "Nils Kruzer. He's a personal friend?"

"After a fashion," she admitted. "Please, Ser . . ." she glanced at his name tag, "Ser Larek, please be completely frank with me. I've seen neurostim overdoses before."

"Yes, well . . ." he walked across the room, ignoring an empty chair, stared sightlessly at the bulletins clipped to the adjacent wall. "This wasn't neurostim."

She blinked. "Then what was it? The lowered temperature, coma, dermal secretions . . ."

"Most of the overt symptomology is identical, at least in gross terms." He slowly turned to face her. "But the systemic effects are radically different. The patient has been using a synthetic drug, introduced directly into his cortex."

Marym winced; Tashista tolerated a wide variety of chemical and physical self-abuse because of its libertarian charter, but the use of neurocortical stimulants was banned on virtually every world within the human sphere of influence, including Tashista.

"One of the proscribed substances?"

He shook his head. "No, nothing I've seen before, as a matter of fact. It appears to be a new variant of one of the cytoplasmic inhibitors. Technically legal only because it's too new to have been proscribed."

"Addictive?"

"Absolutely, both physiologically and psychologically, I would imagine. I can't address the psychological component with any authority, but based on our examination, he's been involved with the drug over a period of nearly a year."

"All right," she straightened her shoulders. Much to her surprise, she was able to deal with this situation from a reasonably detached viewpoint. On anything other than a purely physical level, she and Kruzer had begun to drift apart over an extended period, and although she felt some personal loyalty to the man with whom she had shared her bed off and on for five years, it was more concern for a friend than empathy for a lover. "What's the prognosis?"

"He'll recover in due course." The man looked uncomfortable and turned away, no longer willing to meet her eyes. "At least, he'll be conscious of his surroundings and capable of functioning in some semblance of normality. Given a prolonged period of rehabilitation and assuming there are no further exposures to the stimulant, he might even recover close to his full functionality. At present, however, his sensual interpreters are blurred and dysfunctional. He tastes colors, for example, and sounds are sometimes interpreted somatically. I doubt he'll be able to live unsupervised for at least several secants."

She was prepared to feel a devastating sense of loss, was surprised and somewhat guilty to discover that her reaction was a mixture of relief and sadness. She got to her feet. "Thank you, I appreciate your candor. You will, of course, keep me informed of any change in his status."

"Of course."

And then she left.

Chapter Eleven

Mikki Seurat had never felt so strong a sense of relief as he did when he'd finally completed his latest contract with the Straka. Ordinarily, he would never have agreed to such a risky assignment, but the recent increase in his credit level had generated renewed hope that he might finally be able to make the jump to Moshamadur within a year or two. He already had the minimum for a softcredit account, a plateau that had seemed to hover perpetually just beyond his reach. It was still a long way to the absolute minimum required for social advancement, but as one barrier fell, the next seemed more tantalizingly achievable than ever. Paradoxically, the closer he approached to the realization of his ambitions, the more desperate he became to close the final gap. Despite his consistently optimistic attitude in Shayne's presence, he was well aware of the obstacles that still faced them, knew that even if he hoarded enough to finance the initial move out of Nashamata, the rest of his life would inevitably be spent trying to earn enough to pay the higher expenses of maintaining a larger apartment, with its higher taxes and heavier fees for city services. He knew people who had advanced only to fall back within a year or two, sometimes even more quickly, because they lacked the resources to meet their expenses when the economy fluctuated or they made an unwise decision.

In the past, Mikki had always turned down the relatively high-paying gang errands; he was willing to risk minor infractions of the law, but the more serious violations—trafficking in proscribed drugs, sabotage of maintenance systems in rival gang territories, intimidation of recalcitrants, physical violence of any sort—had always frightened him. The thought of Shayne having to survive alone had always been sufficiently terrifying enough to overcome the promise of higher fees.

Today he had broken one of his own personal rules. Every citizen of Tashista by right of birth was entitled to access the public datanet, at no charge if one was willing to travel to Data Center in Tashamir, for a nominal annual connection fee if one used a private terminal. Public units were available as well, scattered liberally through the city, even in Nashamata, but they were more expensive, requiring hard credit. Much of the database was restricted, however, requiring special codes, authorizations, or corneal recognition. Certain aspects of each citizen's personal files were closed to the public, for example, along with most Prefecture records and the majority of those for other sensitive city services, public and private security arrangements, maintenance access numbers, the majority of private business transactions, and so on. For a price, it was possible to secure copies of certain restricted files; gang members either bribed or coerced authorized individuals or even Data Central staff members to download the appropriate material to a disk or cube, which could then be read using a free-standing computer not tied into the planetary or municipal systems, thereby minimizing any chance of discovery. Data theft was a very serious crime on Tashista, as was true almost everywhere in human space.

The most common source of such requests was Moshamadur, mid-level merchants looking for some leverage to steal market share from their competitors: records of transfer of goods, warehousing contracts, customer lists, credit exchanges. Less frequently came requests from Kishamkur, where the more successful had already reached the pinnacle of the social system. Most Kisham lived on the income from their accumulated fortunes, unwilling to risk losing the minimum required to subsist comfortably in the most expensive quarter of Soshambe. Thus, those who were theoretically the most ingenious entrepreneurs were encouraged by the system to become conservative, depriving society of its greatest source of innovation and progress.

It was to one of the latter that Mikki had traveled today, delivering a pair of cubes whose possession could have resulted in an extensive prison sentence for himself and anyone else proven to be involved. He had hoped to be in and out of Kishamkur quickly; he looked and felt out of place in those luxurious neighborhoods, and although it was quite common for Nashamatans to be employed there as personal servants or in other menial capacities, he always felt that he was being watched suspiciously from the moment he crossed the line separating one district from the other. The surly woman to whom he had delivered the cubes had insisted that he remain for most of the afternoon while she ascertained that everything she had requested had in fact been provided. To ensure his compliance, she resolutely refused to hand over the significantly large amount of hard credit due until she was satisfied.

The shadows of late afternoon had already blurred the less open areas of the city when he returned to Nashamata. The sun had dropped even closer to the horizon by the time he finished the transaction in the waiting room of an underway station, receiving a contemptuous stare and derisive smile along with his fee for the day's activity.

"Told ya long time ago this was the way to go." Tord was one of Mikki's least favorite people, a sarcastic bully with a reputation for recklessness and a bad temper. If he'd known who the payoff man would be, he might have turned this job down despite its high value. Tord wore the lurid scars on his face and bare chest proudly, but Mikki found them repulsive and unnecessary. Simple cosmetic surgery could have made them virtually invisible, and the treatment would have been provided at little or no cost under the city charter since it didn't require a human medicator. But rather than submit to the automated medichines, Tord repeatedly reopened his wounds while they were healing, determined to sport as impressive a disfigurement as he could manage.

He shrugged. "Don't like dealing with the Kisham. Smug bastards with too much credit and too little sense." Kisham bashing was a good way to score points with Tord.

Tord smiled more broadly, revealing uneven, green-stained teeth. "Too bad Scarab don't walk their streets. Might make 'em think twice. You willin' to do this again sometimes now?"

Mikki thought about declining, remembered the haughty woman's rudeness and arrogant insistence that he subordinate his own time to her own. She hadn't condescended to offer refreshment even though she took some herself while scanning the data. "Might. We'll see. I keep pretty busy."

The gang member nodded. "Okay, we'll see. But don't play too hard to get. There's plenty willin' to work for that kinda credit. You'll never get to Moshamadur delivering messages and stuff."

"I make out all right."

"Sure, you do. That's why your boots got holes in 'em and your cloak's so old all the shine's gone."

The truth was, Mikki could easily have afforded a new wardrobe even before his recent windfall, but every credit spent unnecessarily now added days to the time that would pass before they could escape the trap that was Nashamata. "Who've I got to dress up for?"

Tord tucked the heavy cylinder of hard credit into his tote. "No one far's I can see. See you around."

Mikki made his way quickly to the surface, almost running up from the station into the open air. He wasn't really claustrophobic, but there was something about the underways that always got to him; he'd start sweating even before he reached the warmer levels, and couldn't sit or stand still. Sometimes he'd have trouble breathing, and once or twice he had felt so lightheaded that it had been necessary to sit down before he could continue. As a courier, he had to use the tubecars from time to time, but generally he chose surface transport or walked, even if it meant a longer journey.

An oversized public videoscreen was mounted just outside the entrance, and the face it was displaying caught his eye as he rushed past. He came to such a sudden halt and a matronly woman ran into him from behind; she immediately began to berate him for his lack of consideration, but Mikki paid no attention, probably didn't even hear her. His attention was riveted to the image of Tantra Brach, identified as the latest victim of Scarab.

The accompanying text was sparse; few of the details had been made public.

Even though he'd been on his feet most of the day, Mikki ran as he turned toward home. Shayne had admired the older woman, considered her as close to a real friend as she possessed. While posing for the artist, she had formed a strong attachment, and despite her busy schedule, Tantra did speak to her on the net regularly, even visited on very rare occasions. Mikki did not like to think of his sister learning of Brach's murder without having someone to talk to about it.

Concerned and preoccupied though he might be, caution came as second nature to Mikki Seurat. There was a Prefecture lifter parked near his building, and the sight of the official vehicle and the subprefect who stood just beyond it made him feel nervous and guilty. Misgivings over the trip to Kishamkur returned in a rush, and he slowed to a more sedate pace, his lungs working furiously as he feigned a casual walk. He watched the subprefect surreptitiously, noted that the man seemed bored but alert. Several unpleasant scenarios occurred to him. Perhaps the data cube had been inadequate after all and the Kisham had found some way to report him to the authorities without implicating herself. Or there might have been a raid on the Straka, who might have offered him as a scapegoat. Mikki adjusted his route to angle away from the door to his building, picking his way through the pedestrian traffic. Several food carts were moving along the traverseway, most apparently en route to the lower esplanade, and their presence suddenly seemed opportune.

He crossed between two of these, a fruit vendor and a portable bakeshop, then turned and walked parallel to the latter, pretending to be choosing among the overcooked loaves of doldren bread hung from hooks along its side, actually using the body of the cart to conceal himself from the subprefect's view. As they were passing the door to the apartment complex, he disappointed the hopeful vendor by turning and sprinting up the stairs, pressing for admission, and entering before the door had fully retracted, banging his shoulder in the process.

From within the poorly lit lobby, he could see the subprefect still standing across the way, leaning against the side of his lifter. Satisfied, Mikki turned to the turbo and ascended to his own floor.

He was almost calm when the door to his apartment slid back obligingly, but within two steps a pungent smell assaulted his senses, and almost immediately he saw what lay on the floor of the front room. It was quite a while later before he was able to accept that the body was in fact his sister, and that she would never be moving to Moshamadur after all.

* * * * *

Once again, Sandor had altered his plans. Despite his original intention to walk back to the hostelry, he called Izik from Tantra Brach's apartment. "My apologies, Izik, but time has become a factor. Could I prevail upon you to pick me up the public lifterpark near Denobia Park? I must return to the Prefecture immediately."

"No apologies are necessary, Ser Dyle. I'll leave immediately."

"Excellent. You may have to wait briefly, so don't be concerned if I'm not there when you arrive. There's a call I must make before I can leave here."

"Take as long as you desire, Ser Dyle."

Sandor nodded and broke the connection, then netted the Prefecture, where he learned that Marym Dunnis had departed for the day. Tani explained that she had apparently been feeling poorly and had left early, originally to go home, but "she called in and told the night officer she could be reached at the Moshamadur Medicatory. Do you want their code number?"

After waiting with more than his usual patience while efforts were made to locate Marym, Sandor learned she had left the facility some time previously. No, they couldn't discuss the reason for her visit and no, they had no idea where she had gone. Frustrated, he tried her apartment, was greeted by an icon indicating that the unit in question was engaged. He broke the connection angrily and rose.

* * * * *

"Another change of plans, I'm afraid. Take me to Moshamadur, Prefect Dunnis's home. Do you know the location?"

Izik nodded. "I've taken her there a few times." The pilot was clearly curious, but Sandor had no time for explanations even if it been judicious to provide one. He was still trying to detect any flaw in the chain of reasoning he'd followed to his present conclusions, and if he was correct, the last thing he wanted to do right now was reveal his plans to a member of the Prefecture.

"There's no reason for you to remain," he told Izik as he disembarked minutes later. "I expect to be occupied for most of the night."

In contrast to the spare, antiseptic setting of Savram Aras's apartment, this one was abutted on every side by foliage: a formal garden in the front, small stands of chiruga trees at staggered intervals along the adjacent wall, the roof decorated with a flowering liana vine, the oversized iridescent blossoms somewhat subdued in the failing light of late afternoon. It was the first really pleasant location he'd visited since landing on this backwater world.

There was such a long wait between the time when Sandor touched the call plate and the moment when Marym answered the door that he was concerned that she had gone off leaving the datanet engaged for some reason and wasn't present after all. When she did appear, she looked older, drained, dark lines under her eyes, face realigned in a distant, troubled expression.

"Sandor! Come in, please." There was surprise but no real enthusiasm in her voice.

He brushed past as she keyed the door open. "I'm sorry for this unannounced visit, Marym, but I needed to see you immediately." In the brighter illumination, she looked even more distraught. "Pardon my impertinence, but is something wrong? Not another murder?"

She shook her head. "No, nothing like that. Please, find yourself someplace to sit." Marym led the way into a good-sized living area, sparsely furnished and decorated by Sandor's standards, but each piece tasteful and, if he was any judge, of quite high quality. "I've had something in the way of a personal emergency today."

"Your office said you hadn't been feeling well."

"That was the least of it." She followed his example, seating herself in an overstuffed lounger. Sandor was pleased to note that she also had chosen inanimate furniture. "I came home to discover Kruzer—a very close friend of mine—comatose in the outer garden. An adverse reaction to a very illegal drug."

"I see. You have my deepest sympathies."

"Oh, it's not what you think. I mean, he was a friend and we had been intimate, but there wasn't . . . isn't any strong emotional attachment. I think we'd been drifting toward a break for almost a year, but I was too preoccupied to deal with the situation. I suppose I feel slightly guilty for not noticing that he was in trouble."

He nodded understandingly. "Will there be a scandal?"

"Inevitably. The drugs are only part of the story, though they're the root cause, I suppose. He'd apparently been dabbling in neurostimulants for some time; I just finished running through his financial transactions for the past three years." Her lips pursed angrily and she turned to look off to one side. "He's pretty well run through his discretionary credit, and the medical treatment will have to come out of his basic funding. When he recovers, if he does recover, he'll no longer be able to afford to remain in Moshamadur. He'll be lucky if he has enough to remain in Nashamata without finding employment."

"A tragic situation, but as I understand it, abuse of this sort is quite common. You'll undoubtedly have to keep a low profile for a while, but the furor will pass."

Marym shook her head. "I haven't told you the worst yet. Apparently, Kruzer had taken steps to supplement his income.

Somehow he learned my departmental access code. I don't know how; I don't have it written anywhere and I don't talk in my sleep, and I certainly didn't tell him. Probably he watched my fingers when I wasn't paying attention. The mechanics of the situation don't matter. He'd been coming to my apartment while I was at work and accessing Prefecture files from here, confidential files, in particular those which we have kept from the public eye in order to protect our citizens." She turned back, facing him directly. "Particularly prominent citizens, you understand. The ones with wayward children, or whose financial indiscretions were sufficiently trivial that we took no action in return for support at council hearings. That's how we fund marginal projects like flittercams and lifter upgrades; we trade discretion for political support." Her voice drifted off.

With a sigh, Sandor sat back in his seat. "Blackmail, I assume. Did he implicate you? Claim you as an accomplice?"

"He's in no state now to say anything. Who knows what'll happen when he regains his senses? What difference does it make? At the very least, I've been indiscreet, careless, unprofessional, and have probably earned myself some powerful and motivated enemies. I was preparing to net my resignation to the Kudara when you arrived."

"Which brings me to the point of this visit. Please accept my sincere condolences, Marym, but there is a more pressing issue which must be addressed immediately. It is nearly dark now, and I suspect Scarab will strike again this evening if we don't stop him."

"That's as may be, Sandor, but I'm afraid you'll have to continue this investigation with my successor. They'll probably make Tiko Acting Prefect until the bidding process is complete; he'll do as well as anyone, but he doesn't have the credit to bid for the position officially."

Sandor shook his head vigorously. "You haven't resigned yet; you are still Prefect. There's a life at stake here, Marym. This man may have damaged your career, I admit, but don't help the situation along by abrogating your responsibility in the matter. Besides, if I'm right, and I usually am, we have a very good chance of bringing Scarab's killing spree to an end tonight. I don't know if that will save your career, but it should certainly make your departure less devastating."

Despite her deep mood of depression, Marym felt a faint stirring of interest. But before Sandor could say another word, the datanet shrilled insistently from the other room.

* * * * *

Mikki Seurat was clearly in shock. A neighbor had discovered him sitting in his own doorway, legs crossed, head down, staring at the floor between his feet. Under ordinary circumstances, the woman would have continued about her own business, seeing no profit in involving herself in the affairs of her neighbors. She could not resist a curious look as she passed, however, and her eyes had trailed up just far enough to see what lay on the floor inside the apartment.

Two subprefects were present now, one trying fruitlessly to catch the young man's attention while the other struggled to suppress his rebellious stomach long enough to call in coherently to the Prefecture. Despite a firm resolution not to do so, he kept glancing toward the dead woman, whose missing feet were presently sitting in a fruit bowl on the floor beside her battered torso. The young woman's head was across the room, on a shelf at eye level, bracketed on either side by inexpensive holographs taken at the seacoast, resting balanced between her own cupped hands.

* * * * *

"Excuse me a moment," Marym rose to answer the call while Sandor fretted at yet another interruption, another delay. He glanced out the window, noticed that the exterior illumination had just been activated, showering a soft, gentle light across the adjacent pedways. There was still time, he knew; Scarab would not strike until full darkness, would not stir from hiding until he could move freely without being identified. That was one thing of which Sandor Dyle was certain.

But on this occasion, he was wrong.

He could not have imagined that anything would upset Marym even further, but when she returned, her face was pale and drawn. "Scarab has killed again; they've just found another body."

Sandor was so visibly disconcerted that, under other circumstances, it might have been comical. "No, that's not possible." He struggled for understanding. "Unless he's trying to confuse things even further, randomize even the false pattern. Why would he strike twice in the same evening?"

She shook her head. "This time he killed during the day, within the past few hours. Another woman struck down in her own apartment; Mikki Seurat's invalid sister. We should have realized, should have taken her into protective custody."

Shaking his head vigorously, Sandor rose to his feet. "Even if you'd placed guards on everyone Mikki Seurat ever knew, Scarab would simply have struck outside the pattern. The links are artificial, a twisted, insane game. But Scarab couldn't possibly strike during the daylight. He'd be seen; it would be far too great a risk."

"Nevertheless . . ."

"Perhaps this time it really is an imitator, someone else using his methods." But one fact after another clicked into place in his mind. Another connection to Mikki Seurat, another break from the old pattern. "Unless he's even bolder, or madder, than I thought." Marym opened her mouth to say something, but he cut her off abruptly. "May I use your datanet for a moment? I must learn something immediately."

"As you wish." She stepped back. "It's in the bedroom."

Sandor stood at the console, quickly established a connection with a unit whose designation he had memorized earlier that day. There was no reply, not proof in itself, but strong confirmation of what he believed to be true.

"No success?"

He glanced back over his shoulder. "On the contrary, I fear. Are you on good terms with the local Prefect?"

She made a face. "Hardly. He was the only one on the board of certification who opposed me. We rarely speak unless it's unavoidable, but he does take his duties seriously. He's out of the city at the moment, though; we rotate serving as representatives to the quarterly convocation in Samarka and it was his turn. I believe one of his assistants is Acting Prefect at the moment. Why?"

Sandor frowned. "We need someone with the power to move decisively and untraditionally, and we need action right now. Can we reach the Kudara?"

"Possibly, but the Prefecture is functionally independent of his office. He'd have to contact the Acting Prefect and request cooperation."

"Damn it, Marym, there's no time for protocol!"

"All right." She crossed to the terminal, punched in a new code. "We'll call Leskar. Officially he has no authority here, but unofficially, he can impose his wishes with relative impunity. As we all saw when he decided to bring you into this investigation."

The Prefect of Kishamkur answered the call himself. Even through the poor resolution of the viewscreen, Sandor noted the man's deterioration. The skin over his cheekbones sagged darkly and the eyes themselves glittered nervously. "What is it, Dunnis?" He caught sight of Sandor. "Ser Dyle," he acknowledged. "I don't suppose you're calling to tell me you've apprehended my son's killer."

"As a matter of fact, in a manner of speaking we have. Or we will anyway, if you could provide some assistance."

Leskar broke the connection a short time later to make the arrangements Sandor had outlined. Marym was staring at him in quite evident disbelief, having heard what he had requested.

"Why did you insist that no official channels be used?"

"Because he can and does monitor whatever passes through them. That's why you never picked him up on the surveillance equipment; he checked which areas were being covered and just avoided them. He could anticipate every precaution you took and circumvent them."

She shook her head. "No, it just doesn't work. Even if it were physically possible . . ."

Sandor raised a hand. "Rest assured, Marym. Scarab and Savram Aras are the same person. You yourself told me his paralysis had been diagnosed as largely psychosomatic, and the physical effects themselves are intermittent. I accessed his medical history this very day. The onset of these brief periods of confusion, disorientation, and physical malfunction is quite gradual; he would have ample warning to complete or abort an activity before he was rendered helpless. He risked being incapacitated before he could return to his home, but we don't know yet by what means he moved around the city. Certainly he took elaborate precautions. Even in the darkness, all it would take was a single person to recognize the popular previous Prefect and the charade was over."

"You've forgotten something. Savram and I witnessed one of Scarab's assaults. I saw the man we interrupted running off into the distance."

Sandor shook his head. "A quite unrelated murder, I assure you. The coincidental similarity worked to his advantage, obviously. Nor was it as close a correspondence,as you were led to believe."

She stared at him. "I don't understand . . ."

"Scarab only killed ten people that first year, just as he did the second and, I suspect, just as he intends to do this time around. The third incident attributed to him was unrelated. Other than the coincidence of timing, the only reason it was included as a Scarab killing was because of the presence of nemesol in the victim's body and the insistence of the then-Prefect, Savram Aras, that it was part of the same chain of events. How do you know there really was nemesol in this case?"

"The examination, the post-mortem."

He allowed himself a tight smile. "The original on-site post mortem report almost certainly revealed no such thing. Nemesol only showed up in a second autopsy performed after the body had remained overnight in the Prefecture morgue. We'll never know for certain because the first report appears to have been erased from the case file, along with all references to the identity of whichever contractor won that particular bid. I even tried a cross-reference to city credit transfer records, found the appropriate entry. It was to someone named Levkas Finn at a fictitious address and, needless to say, I can find no reference to anyone named Levkas Finn in the city register. The supposed second autopsy is a nearly word-for-word copy of the one filed for the first murder, and it's also attributed to a fictional contractor."

"But that can't happen. There are safeguards."

"Safeguards to prevent accidental erasure, or outside tampering. Is there anything to prevent the assigned investigating officer or the Prefect personally from overwriting this information? Particularly if the two are one and the same? You did say, did you not, that Aras took personal charge of the investigation beginning with the third death? And he maintained that authority throughout the first two years."

"But why? He has always been such a dedicated man, a good man."

"I can only speculate. It almost certainly has to do with the death of his wife and the disappearance of his son. His disease has been known to cause mental disorders of various kinds. Sometimes the deterioration manifests itself as anti-social violence in one form or another."

"But his mind is as sharp and clear as ever," she protested.

"His intelligence has not been affected, I grant you, but his judgment, his rationality, has been damaged irreparably. I only wish I'd been quicker to realize that I was being deliberately taunted."

"How so?"

"Aras is a pattern analyst, and a rather good one. He routinely reviewed the data you'd accumulated on the murders and examined them as objectively as possible. If there were any indications that he was settling into a predictable pattern outside of the obvious, intended one, he'd make adjustments during subsequent killings to distort the data. For all we know, he may have altered other factual aspects of the cases as well while he was still serving as Prefect, although now that he has a read-only clearance, I imagine the more recent data is safe."

"So you think he created a false pattern in order to mislead you."

"After a fashion. I believe the selection of victims from among Seurat's associates was an impulse, a method of implying a relationship that didn't exist. We could very easily have shifted our attention and other resources into a fruitless line of inquiry. The other variations from his old methods, the decapitation, the shorter intervals . . . I don't know. I think Aras realized discovery was inevitable, or perhaps his illness is progressing more quickly. Possibly he plans to complete the set of ten quickly and then lay low until after I've departed; he knows I have a limited amount of time on Tashista. Or perhaps he wants to be caught. Beneath the insanity, some trace of his former personality must be intact. I imagine he suffers under a great burden of guilt."

The door clamored for attention, and a moment later, Prefect Leskar had joined them. "I still find this all very difficult to accept, Ser Dyle." He ignored Marym's offer of a seat. "But I suppose it must be true. Savram Aras is missing from his rooms, but the prosthesis is there. He either walked away or someone carried him."

"The former, I assure you. Have my suggestions been implemented?"

"We're coordinating with the other Prefectures for a city-wide search. Please realize though, even with stepped up patrols and flittercam surveillance, he could easily elude us for some considerable time. We have trouble enough apprehending ordinary citizens; Savram is intimately familiar with our techniques and capabilities."

"You've remained off the Prefecture network, I trust."

"As you suggested, we're contacting everyone through alternate means and coordinating activities using the disaster emergency system. It's slower, not nearly as secure in the ordinary sense, and I'm quite certain Aras still remembers the access codes, but he's not likely to tap into it unless he suspects we're on to him. If Aras really is Scarab."

"That conclusion seems inescapable."

Leskar suddenly wilted, sank limply into the chair he had earlier spurned. "I hope you're right, Ser Dyle. This needs to end. I haven't been able to sleep since the day my son died. I wake up, driven to do something; I've prowled the city myself at night, watching people, hoping against hope that by chance or fate I'll see something that will tell me why my son died and at whose hands." He looked up toward the ceiling. "Do you know what my son was doing in Nashamata?"

Marym was looking distinctly uncomfortable, mumbled something about being thirsty, and walked off.

"He was something of a hedonist. Not a good looking boy, I fear, took a bit too much after his father." The statement was delivered flatly, without any sense of disparagement or humor. "He'd always had difficulty establishing any sort of sexual liaison, and I knew he was spending credit to purchase satisfaction in Nashamata. I suppose I could have stopped him, but there was no good reason for it, and it would only have made him less happy. It seemed better to keep the situation open and aboveboard. I even knew his favorite place, a flesh shop in the Cassio district. That's where he had gone . . . that night."

"You shouldn't blame yourself . . ."

Leskar laughed sharply. "Don't be foolish; it's nothing like that at all. I want compensation for my loss, revenge if you will. If I knew where Savram Aras was right now, and if I was completely convinced that you are right in your conclusions, I'd be on my way there rather than talking to you."

"If your people have been diligent, we should have him shortly."

Savram Aras was well inside Moshamadur, following a route he had selected long before. Just beneath the surface of the city, and just above the upper reaches of the underways, an intricate web of tunnels provided access to the urban infrastructure, power grids, water mains, huge channels through which sewage was drawn to holding tanks before being siphoned down into the subterranean waste treatment facilities. Almost all of these were equipped with walkways, rarely frequented by human beings unless there was a problem that eluded the diagnostic abilities of the maintenance equipment. On only a single occasion had he encountered another person within this labyrinth, and then from a distance. Like veins, the service system threaded out throughout all four quarters of Soshambe, an unseen world whose existence was largely forgotten.

There were limitations, naturally, but Aras could move from his home to almost any location in the city without ever exposing himself to view except for the few brief seconds it took to move from his building to the service tunnel hatchway on the opposite side of the pedway until he emerged near his destination. Under cover of darkness, it was an ideal means for moving about without being recognized. It was necessary to crawl on hands and knees for the first hundred meters or so, until he reached the junction with a larger feeder tunnel, but that wasn't too harsh a price to pay for virtual invisibility.

Aras had just turned into a cross tunnel not far from his home when the indicator strapped to his wrist beeped once, faintly. He paused, but it wasn't repeated. Thoughtfully he advanced and within a few seconds the sound repeated, more pronounced this time. Another few steps and it began to chirp regularly, like a heartbeat. He stopped where he was, bemused.

"So you've found me out, have you?" He smiled broadly. "And now you're waiting for me to walk into your trap. Well, you won't catch me that easily. You may have killed my son, but I'm another matter entirely. I've killed you once, I've killed you twice, I've killed you three times each. And I'll do it again, as many times as it takes to make you stay dead forever." He deactivated his wrist unit, which was linked to a small transmitter activated whenever the door to his quarters was opened.

"You thought you could elude me by taking on different appearances, masquerading as ordinary people, but I was too smart for you. My eyes see through the illusions to the underlying patterns. I found your hiding place when you were alive; do you think I'd be any less capable now that you're dead?" Aras felt his anger rising, fought to keep it under control. There was no point in going forward now; there was no haven for him here. "You can hide for a while, you can trick others into believing you're the innocents you appear, but you'll never stop me. The power to destroy you resides here," he clenched a fist, "and here," he raised the bag clutched in his other hand, "and the power to find you lies here." He raised the fist to his forehead. "I haven't found all of you yet, but I know where the next one is hiding."

Without a backward glance, he turned and began to retrace his steps, eventually turning into a different branch tunnel, one which he had never explored before but whose outlet he knew. He moved parallel to a major watercourse, which was contained entirely within an oversized pipeline initially, eventually decanting into a well maintained canal which made up part of the border between Nashamata and Moshamadur. He was caught up in his own thoughts, oblivious to his surroundings, never even noticed when he passed the broken body of Ramis Marchok, jammed against the buttress where the canal passed under a pedway, having floated downstream from the bridge where the despondent man had leaped to his death the previous evening.

The passageway turned toward the heart of Nashamata, but Aras had a different destination.

Chapter Twelve

Since the search for Savram Aras was being conducted on a city-wide basis, Leskar announced his attention of leaving immediately for the Kishamkur Prefecture to coordinate activities, inviting Sandor and Marym along almost as an afterthought. They traveled in his private lifter, a roomy luxury model fitted with a sophisticated communications link. They sped northwest through the darkness, watching the lights of Moshamadur disappear below, giving way to the far more sparsely settled Kishamkur neighborhoods. They turned from the residential area almost immediately, finally settling to the ground in a lifter park not far from the main entrance to the Kishamkur Prefecture building. The facility was at least three times the size of the one that housed Marym Dunnis's office, and it was of recent construction, or renovation.

The contrast with the corresponding organization in Nashamata was startling. Instead of a crumbling, multi-storied building, this was a gracefully sprawling complex whose architecture showed clear offworld influence, particularly in the use of programmed risers in the foyer and in some of the more purely cosmetic appointments. The front desk would have been more at home in a private industrial reception area than a law enforcement facility; there were plush chairs (multiform, of course), the man and woman who staffed the area wore no uniforms, just ceremonial sashes, and the terminals they worked with were, if not state of the art, certainly as close to it as one could find on Tashista.

There were other, less obvious, differences as well. Leskar was assisted by a much larger staff than Marym, despite the fact that her district contained many times the population of Kishamkur, and immeasurably more crime. There was a constant hustling of these individuals from one office to another, although Dyle suspected part of this was for dramatic purposes rather than because they served any real purpose. Discipline and equipment were observably more sophisticated but, Sandor suspected, largely for show; he doubted these bright young men and women had ever been seriously tested and began to have even deeper reservations about the likelihood of their capturing Aras quickly.

Leskar led them through a maze of corridors to a large room labeled "Emergency Operations Center." Inside, two women and one man were busily engaged with an impressive bank of communications equipment, pausing periodically to examine schematics on their monitors before relaying fresh instructions.

"They've been cautioned to be circumspect even on the emergency network, just in case Aras taps in. It won't fool him for long if he pays attention, but it might gain us a little time. We're sweeping every public area in the city with infrared scanners—parks, pedways, the market areas—checking everyone we find who fits his gross physical profile."

"He might be hiding indoors." Sandor did not add that if he was inside, it might mean he was already with his next victim.

"Or down in the underways," Marym added.

Leskar didn't look in her direction as he answered. "If he's in the underways at this time of night, there's a good chance he'll never come out. If he does, we'll find him eventually. We've already taken steps to ensure he can't leave the city." He gestured abruptly and gracelessly to a conference room. "If you'll excuse me for the time being, I'd like to review what progress has been made thus far." He pointedly did not invite either Sandor or Marym to accompany him, and he turned and walked off without waiting for an answer.

"I apologize for the tactlessness of the Prefect, Sandor."

"Tact is sometimes a luxury we have to forswear, Marym. I don't suppose I'd take the time for social niceties if I were about to capture my son's murderer." He indicated the proffered seating. "After you."

It was only once they had settled in that Marym responded. "Are you certain we're going to capture him this easily?"

"There's no absolute certainty, of course. I must confess, it wouldn't surprise me very much if he figured out what we were doing. We've had only a few hours to plan, and he may have been preparing for this eventuality over a course of years. Insanity and stupidity do not necessarily go hand in hand. I'm not happy with the fact that he hasn't returned to his home; either his mania is taking a decidedly new turn, or he is alert to what we're doing. I'd guess the latter."

"We can't hope to keep anything on this scale secret for very long. With every minute that passes, more people have been stopped on the street, more subprefects have been called back to duty. News will spread like a plains fire that something's up; Savram doesn't even have to know the details to suspect he's been identified."

Sandor nodded. "My guess is that he has a safehouse to hide in. Somewhere in the city is a place where he can conceal himself, possibly for a quite extended period of time. He was a Prefect himself; he knows the search techniques, the areas likely to escape attention. I can't imagine him lasting indefinitely, given his physical problems and Leskar's personal stake in the issue, but I fear that if he isn't captured quickly, we'll find ourselves in an even more complex and unpredictable manhunt by sunrise."

* * * * *

Sandor's bleaker scenario turned out to be accurate. Time passed slowly in the command center; the technicians read their displays and redirected the efforts of those actually performing the search. They rarely spoke; instructions were sent via the datanet and too much was happening to allow casual conversation among themselves. With nothing concrete to contribute, Sandor eventually found himself nodding off to sleep.

Marym touched his shoulder just before he toppled from the chair. "Why don't you go back to your room, Sandor? There's not much either of us can accomplish here, and while I suppose duty requires that I see this through, there's no reason to inconvenience you as well."

He yawned indecorously. "Regretfully, I suspect you're right. You will inform me, I trust, if anything happens?"

"Of course. Wait here a second and I'll see if I can arrange for someone to drop you off."

* * * * *

The lifter into which Sandor was bundled moments later was taking two subprefects out to supplement a group searching the warehouse district in Tashamir, but Sandor was able to squeeze his spindly form into the rear seat. It was cramped, but the ride back to the rooftop landing area at the Black Ark Hostelry was mercifully brief. It had been a quiet ride; the men and women called in from their off-duty time to participate in the sweep clearly lacked the motivation of their superior.

It was actively chilly on the unprotected roof, and Sandor quickly crossed to the tube and descended to his own floor. The chill blast had dissipated some of his sleepiness, and he was already thinking about signing onto the datanet to check a few permutations of the case he had previously neglected. There was still tight security on transmissions relating to the search, but Sandor was irrationally certain that Aras was now aware that he had been identified. That probably made him even more dangerous. If there was a particular agenda he was following, and Sandor was convinced that that was in fact the case, then he might rush through the final sequence of murders right now, rather than chance being captured before accomplishing whatever mission his diseased mind had set for him.

He slapped the recognition pad outside the door to his room and waited while it retracted softly into its frame. Within, the lights were off except for the blinking cursor on the datanet screen that indicated the system was ready for input. Sandor had taken a half step through the door before realizing something was wrong, and was off balance as he tried to stop, took a quick hop on the down foot and banged his shoulder against the door frame struggling to maintain his balance.

That probably saved his life.

A stinger bolt flashed past the side of his face, tugged briefly at the material of his shirt as it grazed his shoulder. The tiny projectile would have stunned him just as effectively as a hypodart if it had struck squarely, discharging its powerful energy cell into his system, overloading his nerves, and sending them into temporary shock. "Close!" he shouted, spinning away into the corridor.

Without waiting to see if the door would obey his command or whether it would be overridden from within, Sandor broke into a sprint for the end of the corridor. Although not the athletic type, his long limbs did make it possible to cover ground quickly, particularly with such a powerful incentive to overcome his normal disinclination toward physical exertion. He rounded the corner, risked one quick look back before starting for the tube at the end of the hall.

Savram Aras had already emerged from the room, stinger clutched in one hand, a large bag of some sort in the other.

The tube capsule was still in place; no one else had come or gone since Sandor had arrived in it seconds earlier. Now he punched for the ground floor, sank back thankfully against the rear wall as it started to descend.

It had almost reached the lobby when it came to a quiet stop. Sandor blinked, glanced at the monitor, noticed that a telltale light was blinking angrily. He couldn't decipher the labels on the panel—it appeared to be a holdover from the original Tashistan language—but he could guess what had happened. Aras possessed a device which enabled him to institute an emergency override, probably common issue within the Prefecture.

He tried the door without success, then studied the panel once more. For reasons of safety if nothing else, there should be some sort of manual override. The enigmatic labeling offered no clue. Cursing in three languages, none of them to be found on Tashista, Sandor felt around the edges of the panel, located the release, and popped it open, revealing a web of microcircuitry. Given time, he could probably have made a fairly good guess about the nature of the individual strands, but somehow he didn't believe Aras would be content to leave him imprisoned in a tube capsule indefinitely. From his pocket he removed the same device he had earlier used to gain entrance to Tantra Brach's apartment. In this case, he didn't need to know the sequence that was countermanding the tube's normal programming; all he had to do was interfere with it. He used random search mode, tried to remain patient while it began emitting pulses, unconsciously glancing at the ceiling of the capsule.

Instead of neutralizing Aras's signal, he activated the manual emergency mode. The interior lights began to flash in unison and the entranceway irised open. Sandor crouched and jumped down to the second floor corridor, then immediately ran toward the central stairwell.

He paused and listened for the sound of descending footsteps before starting his descent. Most likely Aras would use the tube at the opposite end of the building, although Sandor didn't see how he could know for certain on which floor his quarry was trapped. Still running, he descended to the lobby and sprinted out into the main reception area. The comparatively large, open space was deserted at this hour, and for a moment Sandor thought no one had been left on duty.

A sullen looking young man with heavy brows rose from where he'd been lying on one of the multi-form lounge chairs. "Yes, Ser Dyle. May I help you?"

Although the attendant sounded resentful at the interruption rather than genuinely interested, Sandor was in no position to be fussy. "Get the Prefecture . . . emergency. Tell them . . . where to come, where we are." His lungs were clamoring for more air and the effort to speak intelligibly tore at his chest. "Tell them Scarab . . . tell them Aras is in the building."

"Scarab?" Rising to his feet, the young man displayed a mixture of bewilderment and disbelief. "Scarab here? But this is Moshamadur."

"Just make the call. Now!" Sandor was not predisposed to argue the matter, and it was all academic a split second later. A stinger bolt struck the attendant in the left shoulder, fired from somewhere to Sandor's rear. The young man's eyes and mouth both opened wide as he toppled immobile to the floor.

Sandor threw himself down behind a waist-high retaining wall topped with flowering plants.

"That won't do you any good, Sharith."

Crouching, Sandor called back. "Savram Aras, this is Sandor Dyle. What is this all about?" His eyes moved frantically back and forth, searching for a weapon, a way out, even a good bluff. Except for a handful of plants, innocuous and tasteless furniture, and a small maintenance unit mindlessly cleaning the floor nearby, there was nothing at hand. The outside door loomed enticingly close, but he doubted that he could cross the intervening distance before Aras brought him down with the stinger.

"You might have been Sandor Dyle once, but not any longer. If I needed another reason to destroy you once more, the loss of such a talented man would be enough."

"But I am Sandor Dyle, Ser Aras. You know me; we talked only a day or two ago."

"You were Sandor Dyle then; now you are Sharith. Did you think I would just let you return to start your evil all over again? Oh, you've been clever, I admit. When I set off that concussion bomb down in that hell pit where you were all spawned, I thought that was the end of it. You made a mistake when you killed my son, you know. I realize you probably didn't even know who he was; Randil and I had grown apart since his mother's death, and we no longer understood one another. At first I thought he went among you in an effort to find the murderers, but later I came to realize he'd been seduced by the dark magic you people possess. He became one of you and eventually a rival for your power, didn't he? That's why you killed him!" His voice rose to a near scream toward the end.

Sandor waited until Aras was silent, trying to judge his location by the sound of his voice. The half wall extended most of the way across the lobby, and he began crawling on hands and knees, not having a plan, just trying to delay things until something external changed the situation. "I didn't even know your son, Savram. I've only been on your planet for five days."

"I was almost on time, wasn't I?" Aras seemed closer and Sandor moved as quickly as possible without making unnecessary noise of his own. "You hadn't quite finished with him when I tracked him to your lair. There was nothing I could do by then; I didn't even realize it was Randil until you all moved away from his body and I recognized his face. You stuck him up there on that pole with his hands and feet cut off and let him bleed to death, didn't you?" Now the voice was unnaturally and frighteningly calm.

This time Sandor chose not to answer at all. He scurried to the end of the wall, cautiously peered around the corner. Just beyond stood a small table and three chairs, then a wide open space leading to the front door. There was absolutely no cover and, if he could trust the evidence of his ears, Aras was on the opposite side of the partition only a few paces behind, almost certainly moving in the same direction.

"I had to leave him there. There was no way to get his body out, and there would have been questions . . . questions I would not have wanted to answer. It was only a shell by then in any case; Randil himself was gone, beyond pain, beyond your reach. I gathered his pain up and took it into myself, and I followed you, found out where your secret lair was. Yes, that's right. You may have fooled all those witless, puerile fools you preyed upon, but I outsmarted you all. I fired a homing dart into one of your cloaks that night and I came back with a seeker and with the concussion bomb. It led me to the substation you were using and I waited, sat for hours in a maintenance duct where I could see you coming and going all that day and most of the night. I kept counting, you see, wanted to make certain that all ten of you were there before I pressed the key that set off the bomb. And afterwards, I went in and found your bodies and before I threw them into the sewage intake, I cut each and every one of you just the way you cut Randil. And that should have been the end of it."

Sandor gathered his feet under him. The voice was coming closer and he would have to move now if ever. The door still seemed impossibly distant, but there was no other safe ground, no other hope of avoiding this madman's misdirected fury. He tried to think of a reason to hesitate, failed, and then jumped erect and forward, not even looking back to see where Savram Aras was standing.

The stinger dart took him in the meaty part of his right thigh. There was an explosion of pin pricks throughout his entire body and the lobby doors seemed to rotate to his left, up, out of sight, and then he was staring at the ceiling for a few seconds until he wasn't seeing anything at all.

* * * * *

Sensation came back slowly, almost before consciousness. He was aware of a tingling in the center of his chest and an oddly dissimilar resonance inside his head. Each nexus spread slowly, and almost half his body was experiencing threshold pain when he opened his eyes. Although he'd never been hit by a stinger before, he'd heard the experience described often enough to know what had happened. His stunned nerves were slowly recovering from the effects, and the touch of an invisible, flameless fire moved up and down his body. He gritted his teeth, eyes shut, and concentrated on the wave of discomfort, imagining it as a physical mass, willing it to compress, grow smaller, less significant, shrinking until it was something that could be ignored entirely. And when the wave had subsided to a lingering memory of discomfort, he opened his eyes.

"Back with me, are you, Sharith?"

Sandor was lying on his back on the floor, limbs spread wide; Savram Aras sat in a chair just to his right. When he tried to lift a hand to his forehead, Sandor discovered that his limbs had been fastened down.

"Pressure cuffs," explained Aras. "You needn't bother struggling. They're quite strong enough to hold you, standard Prefecture issue."

Sandor turned his head away, saw the attendant lying prone a few meters away.

"I had to stun him again, I'm afraid," explained Aras. "He's not one of you, so I regret the necessity, but it would have been a lot worse for him were it otherwise."

"I tell you again, Ser Aras, I am Sandor Dyle. I am not one of these Sharith. You've made a mistake."

The other man leaned over and pointed to his eyes. "You see these? I have a vision denied to other men; I can pierce these fleshy disguises you use to conceal yourselves. That first year you came back, I recognized you right away, knew that I had to act again, but not as I had before. Obviously my mistake was in removing your extremities after your bodies were dead rather than before. So I adjusted. I tracked each of you down separately this time and acted properly. First the impalement, then the amputations. It took weeks to find you all out, but I never even considered letting you survive. And when the last of you was gone, I felt a wonderful relief."

"Those were innocent people you butchered, not the Sharith. The Sharith are dead, Aras; you killed them and they can't come back. You've already had your revenge."

"That's what you'd like me to believe, isn't it? It's what I wanted to believe too, not only when I was throwing you into the sewage, but again and again as I tracked down your new bodies and destroyed you over and over again. It made sense the first time; I hadn't done it properly and had allowed you to return. But when you came back yet again, I nearly despaired."

He had turned away, staring off into some private world where dead murderers returned to possess the bodies of the living. Sandor tugged at the pressure cuffs, semi-circles of synthetic material which temporarily bonded themselves to the floor. Sometimes if the surface to which they were affixed wasn't clean enough, the bonding was disrupted and they could be shifted, even jerked free. Such did not seem to be the case in this instance.

"You can't do this any longer, Ser Aras. The Prefecture knows who you are. They'll monitor every escape route from the city. It's only a matter of time now until they catch up to you."

"Yes, I know that." Aras was busying himself with something out of Sandor's direct line of sight. "I've suspected for a while that some of you had infiltrated the Prefecture in this incarnation. There was something about Marym the last time I saw her that rang false. It makes sense; I'm rather surprised you didn't try it sooner. But then maybe you knew how closely I've been monitoring everything that happens there and were afraid of exposing yourselves to me."

Then Aras raised what he'd been holding into full view and Sandor knew with absolute certainty that he was going to die. In his right hand was a long metallic spike; in the other was a sort of adze, a chopping tool. He didn't need to be told to what use these were about to be put.

"You can beg me for mercy now, if you'd like. I don't imagine Randil did when you hoisted him up for his execution; he was a strong boy, never gave in to pain, physical pain anyway. It was the emotional kind that brought him down. I think I'd rather enjoy hearing you beg. Maybe that's what I've been doing wrong, anaesthetizing you so that you couldn't call out for help. Maybe this time you'll stay dead."

Sandor was desperately trying to find an argument that would pierce the cloud of illusion through which Aras was filtering his perceptions, but as the arm bearing the spike drew back for the thrust, an overwhelming sense of finality and defeat paralyzed his tongue.

And then someone called Savram Aras's name.

The spike fell across Sandor's thighs as Aras dove to one side, rolling out of sight behind the near end of the same wall where Sandor himself had hidden moments earlier. The voice had been that of a woman and he was almost certain it was Marym Dunnis who had interrupted them. What she was doing in the lobby of the Black Ark Hostelry at this hour was a mystery he would have to explore later. Right now, he was happy for the reprieve, no matter what the reason.

"He's got a stinger. Watch yourself!" He found it strangely difficult to shout while lying flat on his back. The warning was undoubtedly unnecessary; the soft whine of the stinger's discharge was audible immediately, followed by a sharp concussion as it struck something other than flesh. A miss then.

There was a crackle, accompanied by a flash and the smell of a laser burn. Helpless, he was unable to see either combatant from his present position, couldn't even tell if Marym, if it really was her, had come alone or with companions. He heard a rustle above and to his right, craned his head back, thought he saw something dark move just at the very limit of his vision. One of the chairs crashed to the floor and the laser discharged a second time.

Oddly enough, he struggled to suppress a laugh. The absurdity of his situation had finally penetrated his terror, aided by a touch of hysteria. "I don't suppose either of you would care to tell me what's happening? This isn't the best seat in the house."

No one answered, but he really hadn't expected a response. He tried to shift the cuff holding his right wrist, felt or imagined he felt, a slight give but only after he had bruised his wrist and strained the muscles in his shoulder and arm. There had been no other sound during his own quiet struggle.

"Savram?" This time there was no question; it was Marym's voice. "Savram, it's Marym. Marym Dunnis. I don't want to hurt you, but you have to drop your weapon and come out."

There was no reply.

"Savram, for the sake of our friendship, don't make me kill you."

"Marym was my friend, all right." Aras's voice was disturbingly close. He must still be right near the end of the half wall. "I should have known that you Sharith would take her body to use against me."

"I don't understand what you're talking about, Savram. The Sharith are gone, probably dead."

"Dead but not gone. You know it as well as I."

"He's insane, Marym; the Sharith killed his son years ago and he believes they come back in other bodies. That's why he's been killing people; he thinks they're possessed."

"Sandor, are you all right?"

"For the moment. I'm not particularly mobile, however, and I really don't care for my present accommodations. I don't suppose you've brought any neutralizing agent for pressure cuffs?"

"There's some in the lifter."

"Wonderful. Aras, would you mind holding your fire while Marym goes out to her lifter?" There was no answer. "Well, I really didn't think so. I don't suppose you brought anyone along, Marym?"

She didn't answer, and when Sandor thought about it, he understood why.

"Be very careful, Marym." But he whispered it.

The climax was initiated from a totally unexpected quarter. The attendant, twice stung, apparently had regained some semblance of consciousness. Outraged nerve endings were no longer simply hovering on the threshold of pain, not after two successive stingings; an unearthly shriek echoed throughout the lobby.

The attendant cried out just as Aras was about to race across from the low wall to the more adequate shelter of a column that split the center of the lobby, the first in a row that stretched back toward the rear of the building. He hesitated for a split second, apparently distracted, just long enough for Marym to fire from her position near the door. There was the acrid smell of burning flesh and a subdued groan, but Aras spun away, still on his feet, and reached his destination.

The attendant's screams were cut off suddenly as he fainted. The ensuing silence was broken only by an uncertain and intermittent series of small movements from the vicinity of the column. Sandor craned his head so far forward that his chin struck against his chest, trying to see what was happening. Just as he did so, Aras reappeared, staggering slightly, his left arm hanging loosely, seared flesh visible there and along his side where Marym's bolt had caught him glancingly. Blood dripped softly to the floor.

"At least I'll get one of you," he was advancing on Sandor, the stinger discarded. He stooped low and retrieved the metal spike from the floor.

"Savram, no!" Sandor turned at the sound of Marym's voice, saw her step into view from somewhere in the distance, the laser steady in her hand. His head moved back and forth from one to the other. The metal spike rose high into the air, the sharpened point aimed at the center of Sandor's chest.

The laser flashed one more time. Savram Aras hesitated, arm still upraised, then relaxed his fingers and allowed the spike to fall to the floor. It bounced on its point, fell with a clatter somewhere near Sandor's feet. The rage slowly bled from Aras's face and he blinked repeatedly, as though unable to recognize his surroundings. He glanced down at his intended victim and smiled uncertainly. "Maybe I'll find the way to come back as well, Sharith." And then he fell backward and Sandor couldn't see him any more.

Marym Dunnis walked over to Sandor then past, stood staring down at the body of the ex-Prefect of Nashamata. Her second shot had struck him in the middle of the chest.

"Is he dead?" Dyle found it very awkward to carry on a conversation from his present position, and it infuriated him not to know what was going on.

"Yes." She sounded profoundly sad.

"You had no choice, Marym, and he's probably better off this way. The suratic cancer was destroying his mind."

"It doesn't matter." Her words were lifeless, flat. "This wasn't Savram Aras. I think he must have died some time ago. This was just Scarab, and Soshambe will be better off for his passing." She gave an odd sort of shrug, as though discarding some unpleasant reality, then turned and looked down at Sandor. Slowly her mouth twisted into a mischievous grin. "Lying down on the job, I see. You certainly did get yourself into a mess."

"Spare me the humor. I trust you weren't kidding about the solvent?"

"No, I have some. I'll bring it in." She turned away, paused. "Don't go away."

* * * * *

The sun had risen, the body of Savram Aras had been removed from the lobby, the attendant had been lifted to a nearby medical facility. Sandor had been offered the same courtesy but he had declined, insisting that the only lingering effects were taut nerves that would be better allowed to mend themselves. Prefect Leskar himself had arrived to oversee the removal of the body and when it was gone, just before leaving himself, he had turned and met Sandor's gaze in a brief, wordless exchange. Sandor doubted very much that the other man had found any real peace even with the death of his son's killer, but there was no additional solace he could offer.

"What in the world brought you to my lobby at that hour?" He and Marym had walked three blocks to a local autoteria where they were sipping kaffy and letting their nerves settle.

"More luck than insight. Shortly after you left, I decided to go home for the night. Leskar wasn't about to let me take any of the credit for the operation, and I didn't relish sitting around as supercargo any more than you did. I found an open terminal and entered your number, intending to leave a message on your queue. When the connection was made, the telltale said your terminal was in use. Theoretically, you could have gotten back here and signed on that quickly, but it seemed unlikely."

"I was surprised but not alarmed and I left a message and borrowed one of the small lifters. About halfway home, it started to bother me, so I changed course to include a fly-by of your building. Then I tried netting you again, same response, so I used my override code to attract your attention. Still no reply."

"I think Aras was using my terminal shortly before I arrived. I saw the cursor blinking when I opened the door; that's what alerted me that there was an intruder."

"Anyway, I landed on your roof and called the tube. No response. That struck me as even more ominous, so I found a small park a block from here, landed again, and walked over. I still half expected some simple explanation, but I brought the laser along just in case. Fortunately."

"So you bagged Scarab after all, and personally. I imagine this will be a big boost for your career."

She shook her head, eyes downcast. "No, I'm resigning from the Prefecture. I haven't changed my mind since last night."

Sandor reached out and gripped her forearm tightly, so that she raised her head and met his eyes squarely. "There's no reason for you to throw away your career because of Savram Aras. The real Savram wouldn't want you to do that."

"You don't understand; it's not because of that. It's not even really because of Kruzer and the inevitable scandal either. I think I've just realized that I don't want to travel this particular path any longer. I have enough credit to remain in Moshamadur the rest of my life without working at all, so long as I'm careful. Why should I spend years struggling in a job I really don't like and for which I have limited aptitude just to move to a bigger house in another part of the city?"

"Why indeed?"

* * * * *

Thirteen local days passed before Sandor Dyle was finally able to leave Tashista. The *Spawn of Dagon*, a passenger vessel in regular service between Ventana and Alcibiades, had been rerouted unexpectedly when revolutionaries on the latter world instituted a strict but shortsighted isolationist policy. Sandor would have been willing to sleep in crew quarters and work in the galley in order to gain passage, but both turned out to be unnecessary. There were a number of empty staterooms aboard, and the liner was moderately well accoutered.

The *Spawn of Dagon* was a mid-range ship that carried as many as a thousand passengers, not a full-blown luxury vessel but certainly a cut above the crude colonial ships that were the cheapest form of interstellar transportation. There were several holochambers, a games room, swimming pool, temblar courts, two gymnasia—one with zero gee—and even an overpriced restaurant for those too haughty to dine in the autoterias. Ordinarily, Sandor spent most of his traveling time in staterooms, exploring the ship's library, or working on one of his papers, but the sojourn on Tashista had made him hungry for human companionship. Tashistans were far too interested in building credit to spend the time necessary to acquire friends.

He rose on the third morning, dined quickly, then walked over to the games room, hoping to find Darryl Eddis or Rosada Andras, two engaging travelers from Shim and Ventana respectively, whom he had met the previous day and who reportedly spent much of their time playing cards or nanodice. He scanned the room, comparatively crowded for such an early ship hour, but was unable to locate either of them. He did notice something that attracted his attention, however.

Two people, one male, one female, were sitting at a table toward the rear, intent upon an ultima set arranged between them. Curious, he made his way through the crowd, close enough to see the participants. The man was a complete stranger, swarthy, his forehead incised in the manner of the Negav Priesthood. The woman was Marym Dunnis.

"Marym! I didn't know you were aboard."

She glanced up, smiled warmly. "Hello, Sandor. I was going to look you up when I had a chance. This is Czarra Kroft, from Negav. Czarra, this is Sandor Dyle, from Hazard."

The two men shook hands, exchanged polite comments about the *Spawn of Dagon*'s facilities.

"Vacationing?"

"No," she shook her head. "Emigrating, in all probability."

"To anywhere in particular?"

"I'd thought about trying the Presidium worlds. I know they're only recently settled and conditions are pretty primitive, but I think I could learn to like living outside a city."

"No more lusting after luxury and ease, I take it."

"Well," she laughed, "I take my ease where I can get it, and luxury is relative."

Someone called Sandor's name and he glanced up to see Darryl Eddis beckoning from the opposite side of the room. He rose. "I'll be talking to you again before we reach port, no doubt. Perhaps I can convince you to visit Hazard for a while before you settle down for good." He turned to the Negav. "And a pleasure meeting you as well, sir."

As Sandor started across the room, he was suddenly struck by an absolute conviction that he had not seen the last of Marym Dunnis.

Her presence felt like a part of a greater pattern.